I0767818

DON'T *fight it*

Hazard Falls
Book 1

SAMANTHA COLE

Copyright ©2018 Samantha A. Cole
Published by: Suspenseful Seduction Publishing
All Rights Reserved.

Don't Fight It and its individual listings are a work of fiction. Names, characters, businesses, organizations, places, events, and incidents either are the product of the author's imagination or are used fictitiously. Any resemblance to actual persons, living or dead, events, or locales is entirely coincidental.

Cover Artist: Samantha Cole
Editing by Eve Arroyo–www.evearroyo.com

AI RESTRICTION: The author expressly prohibits any entity from using any part of this publication, including text and graphics, for purposes of training artificial intelligence (AI) technologies to generate text or graphics, including without limitation technologies that are capable of generating works in the same style or genre as this publication.
The author reserves all rights to license uses of this work for generative AI training and the development of machine learning language models.

All rights reserved. No part of this book may be reproduced or used in any manner without the express written permission of the publisher except for the use of brief quotations in a book review. This ebook is licensed for your personal enjoyment only. This book may not be re-sold or given away to other people. If you would like to share this ebook with another person, please purchase an additional copy for each recipient. If you're reading this book and did not purchase it, or it was not purchased for your use only, then please return to your favorite ebook retailer and purchase your own copy. Thank you for respecting the hard work of this author.

To the Sexy Six-Pack's Sirens

Chapter One

"What's up, cuz?" Shane Wilson asked as he leaned back in his office chair, his cell phone to his ear. He was grateful for the excuse to take a breather from reviewing the current week's accounting that sat on his desk. It was the one thing he hated about running the twenty-seven-hundred-acre cattle ranch he owned with his husband, Tucker. Shane would rather be outside, doing manual labor instead of crunching numbers. With Tuck's dyslexia, though, dealing with all the invoices was ten times more difficult for him, so Shane took care of the business end of things. But he only had to go through the stacks of paperwork on Monday and Thursday mornings. Thanks to their office staff, Shane labored alongside Tuck and the ranch hands for the rest of the week and loved every minute of it.

"Hey, Shane," his cousin, Quinn Alexander,

responded from somewhere in San Francisco. "Did you replace your housekeeper yet?"

That was just another thing on Shane's ever-growing "shit I gotta do" list. Hannah Gilman, the ranch's seventy-year-old housekeeper—actually, house manager was a better description—had begun to feel the effects of her advancing age. She'd reluctantly retired recently after two and a half years working in the three-thousand-square-foot main house on the Red River Ranch in Hazard Falls, Kansas. Rheumatoid arthritis had started making routine tasks difficult for her, and she'd finally agreed to move in with her daughter's family in Oklahoma. While Tuck and Shane were definitely missing the older woman, the one who seemed to be suffering the most was the men's six-year-old daughter, Arianna. The little girl was still reeling from the death of her mother a little over twenty-six months ago, and now, she'd lost the woman who'd been like a grandmother to her. At least Hannah could call Arianna several times a week to chat.

As odd as it was to some, Tuck, Shane, and Arianna's mother, Sarah, had been in love with each other—as in a three-way relationship. Shane and Tuck had both fallen for the beautiful blonde who'd captured their hearts, but they'd also fallen for each other. Hazard Falls was a small town, and there'd been some obnoxious gossipers who'd ridiculed their unconventional marriage at first, but over time that had lessened as people had gotten used to the idea. There were others, though, who still referred to them as "those perverts," among other things, however, Shane, Tuck, and Sarah had learned to ignore them. While the three hadn't been able to make their ménage union legal, they'd found a way around the laws. Shane and Sarah had gotten married before the local magistrate. Then they had a separate ceremony, which included exchanging vows with Tuck. Both Sarah Edelman and Tucker Jones had willingly taken Shane's last name. After that, they had a lawyer draw up their wills, powers of attorney, and other paperwork to make sure if something happened to one of them, the other two would be taken care of financially and have a full say in any medical decisions. Unfortunately, a time had come when the latter had been necessary.

The threesome had six years of marital bliss—and one adorable child—before Sarah was diagnosed with Stage 4 pancreatic cancer. It'd been so advanced and aggressive that by the time it was discovered, Sarah succumbed to the disease only eleven weeks later, leaving behind two devastated widowers and an almost five-year-old little girl.

Propping his feet up on the corner of the desk, Shane answered Quinn. "No, we didn't. We've had a couple of inquiries and even hired one for a few days, but they weren't right for the job for one reason or another. Not many women have the experience to help run a ranch with fifteen workers to feed two or three times a day, plus keep the house clean, and watch Arianna when she's not in school. A few had been more interested in getting into mine and Tuck's bed, and that's not gonna happen. Why?"

"Well, I've got a client looking to make a fresh start where no one knows her."

Shane's brow furrowed. Quinn was a US Marshal with the Witness Security Program—or, as most people called it, the Witness Protection Program. He relocated people who had to start their lives over after testifying in court or helping law enforcement investigate someone they knew—someone who probably wanted them dead. Quinn found them new places to live and gave them new identities. "I'd love to help, cuz, but I can't have a woman hiding out here and possibly have someone show up looking to kill her—not with Arianna here."

"I would never put your daughter in danger, Shane —I'm not a thoughtless ass." He could almost hear Quinn's eye roll through the phone. "Paige no longer has anyone after her other than the fucking press. Her husband was found guilty of running a multi-million-dollar Ponzi scheme and sentenced to twenty-five years last week. He committed suicide the next day by hanging himself in his cell. All their assets have been frozen while the courts determine the awards to his victims. Paige knew nothing about what he was up to. When she did find out, she went straight to the feds. Without her, it might've been a few years and dozens more victims before he got caught. She filed for divorce after his arrest and wants all his victims to be reimbursed before she sees a cent of what might be left over—which won't be much at all. Anyway, she wants to get out of San Francisco and start over in a place where no one knows her and isn't looking at her like she's to blame for what the rat-bastard did. As I said, the only people who might try to track her down are a few jackass reporters, and even they'll forget about her after the next big scandal hits."

Staring at the ceiling, Shane let out a sigh. "I don't want to sound like . . . I don't know . . . a reverse snob, I guess, but it seems like you want to send us a high-society, city chick who's used to having her own maids and chefs, Quinn. We need a cook, housekeeper, and part-time babysitter, not someone who'll want to call in a delivery order for every meal, need to ask how to use a vacuum, and pull her hair out when Arianna starts playing twenty questions."

A horn blasting made Shane realize Quinn was driving somewhere. "I wouldn't have called if I didn't think you all would be a good fit. She's from a small town in Nebraska, so she knows what it's like to drive an hour to the closest Walmart. She went to college on a full scholarship. Otherwise, she and her parents would never have been able to afford it. That's where she met her husband. She's got a bachelor's degree in business and had her own interior design company. Unfortunately, her husband's name was on the paperwork since he'd fronted the startup money, so that was seized too. I'm telling you, Shane, she's a nice woman. Her folks are dead, and she doesn't want to return to her hometown in disgrace. Paige just wants to find someplace where she's not front-page news anymore so she can figure out where to go from here. You can set it up on a trial basis. If it doesn't work out, I'll help her move on."

Again, Shane's eyes narrowed. "This isn't on the clock, is it?" As far as he knew, Quinn wasn't taking on any new cases. After fourteen years with the US Marshals, he was going into the private sector, where there would be far less stress. It hadn't been a decision made lightly since he'd needed six more years to get his full pension, but he feared the job would kill him before that rolled around.

"Not anymore. I had her in protective custody until she testified against him. The FBI was worried he'd try to put a hit out on her. After he was found guilty and then killed himself, she no longer needed to be in the program. I'm just trying to help her out, and after our conversation the other day, I thought if I sent her to you, it would solve everyone's problems."

Shane mulled it over for a few moments. His trust in his cousin was what finally swayed him. "All right—on a trial basis, though. I'll tell Tuck about her later. How soon can she be here?"

"Is tomorrow afternoon too soon?"

He snorted. "You bastard—you knew I was going to say yes, didn't you?"

A hearty chuckle came over the line. "I wasn't a hundred percent certain, but pretty damn close, yeah."

Dropping his feet to the floor again, Shane sat up.

"What's her last name? I'm gonna Google her and find out what you're getting Tuck and me into."

"Merritt—two Rs and two Ts. First name is P-A-I-G-E. She's thirty-five. And don't hold her husband's crimes against her. Like I said, she knew nothing about what he was into and turned him in as soon as she did."

He jotted down the name and age as he heard the front door open and slam shut. Seconds later, a blonde-haired, dark-eyed tornado came racing into his office. "Daddy! Look what I drew in art class," Arianna exclaimed, holding up a piece of white paper with a multi-colored drawing on it.

Seconds later, Tuck's sister, Lila, stuck her head around the door jamb, saw Shane, and mouthed, "I have to run."

He nodded, and she disappeared again. Holding up a finger, he smiled at his daughter. "Hang on, sweetie. I'm talking to Uncle Quinn."

"Hi, Uncle Quinn," the little pipsqueak shouted, causing both men to chuckle.

"I gotta go," Shane said into the phone. "As you obviously heard, Arianna just got home from school. Tell Carson we said hi." Carson Matthews was Quinn's fiancé.

"I will. I'll also talk to Paige and let you know what time to expect her—I'll get her on a flight tomorrow, and one of you can pick her up at the airport. Once you all are sure she's staying, she'll send for the rest of her stuff. Say hi to Tucker and give Arianna a hug for me. And, Shane . . . thanks."

"You owe me."

Disconnecting the call, Shane pushed his chair back from the desk and pulled Arianna into his lap as she began to chat about her day. She was the spitting image of her mother, and he was so grateful to have her in their lives. She was Sarah's legacy. They didn't know if her paternal DNA had come from Shane or Tuck, and neither man felt the need to find out. As far as they were concerned, she belonged to both of them, just as they belonged to each other.

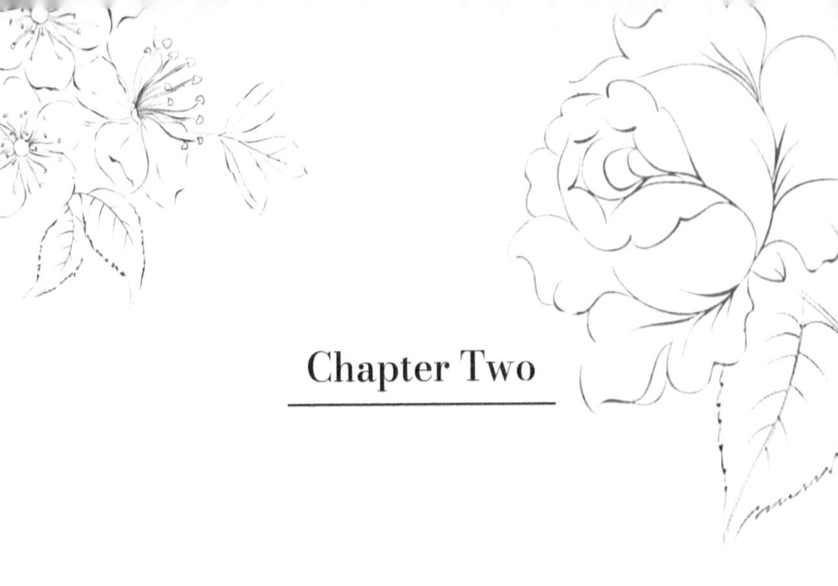

Chapter Two

Paige Merritt finished packing the two suitcases she was taking to Kansas and set them on the floor by the door. *Kansas.* In one way, it was weird heading back to small-town life after living in San Francisco for the past seventeen years ever since she'd left Nebraska for college and never looked back. On the other hand, though, she was kind of looking forward to it. Anything to get away from the press dogging her every move, trying to get an exclusive, and the dirty looks she got practically everywhere she went. Some were from those who thought she'd known what her husband had been doing and had been turning a blind eye to his crimes, while others looked upon her like she'd been a rat for turning her husband in to the feds.

All Paige wanted to do now was go where no one knew her or what her husband had done. It was one of the reasons she'd taken back her maiden name. It didn't stand out as much as Winthrope did—as in California Governor Kyle Winthrope, Myles's uncle, although the older man had managed to distance himself from his brother's family years ago. Kyle and Peyton, Myles's father, had had a falling out in their twenties and had rarely spoken since. Even though Myles loved to exploit the fact he was a blood relative of the governor, Kyle had barely acknowledged the relationship, especially after his nephew's arrest.

With her parents gone, and no siblings or children, Paige didn't have any familial ties left—Myles's family hated her for turning him in—so she had nothing keeping her in San Francisco. Nor did she have any reason to go back to Nebraska. The "friends" she'd thought she had in California had turned their backs on her, except for Marcella Hartford, who'd worked for Paige for years.

Paige had felt awful when the FBI had seized her interior design business, along with all the other assets she'd shared with Myles, because her twelve dedicated employees had suddenly been without jobs. Thankfully her name had still carried some weight before the whole sordid story about the Ponzi scheme had hit the papers, and she'd been able to help most of them find jobs within the same field. Marcella had been with Paige from the day she'd opened the doors of Zen Spaces, and the two had become fast friends. She'd been Paige's moral support throughout the whole trial, having been worried sick while Paige had been incommunicado during her time in protective custody. At least she had one friend who'd stuck by her. Two, if she counted Quinn Alexander, the US Marshal who'd been in charge of her protective detail.

Talk about sin on two legs. Too bad Quinn was gay and in a long-term relationship with his boyfriend—not that Paige had been interested in getting involved with another man after what she'd gone through with Myles. Nope. Celibacy was in her immediate future until she found somewhere to settle down and get past the insane zoo that had become her life over the past eighteen months. Even though Paige was no longer in the Witness Security Program, Quinn had helped her out once again, going above and beyond the call of duty. After stopping by Marcella's condo, where Paige had been staying while trying to figure out the next stage of her life, to check on her yesterday morning, he'd called her several hours later with a job offer. His cousin's cattle ranch in Kansas needed a house manager/cook/nanny. Shane Wilson and his husband, Tucker, were the parents of a six-year-old girl, and the woman who'd helped take care of them had resigned for health issues, and they hadn't been able to find someone to replace her yet. Paige would look after the little girl during the day when she wasn't in school while the men tended to their ranching duties. The job gave Paige the weekends off, although she wasn't sure what she'd do with herself in the small town of Hazard Falls, population 3821, according to the latest census reports she'd found online. It was actually bigger than the town she'd grown up in. Johnsonville, Nebraska, currently had about fifteen-hundred people living there. Paige had been surprised the Wilsons wanted her to start tomorrow, but there wasn't anything holding her back from getting on a plane in the morning. Since she didn't have many options and couldn't afford to live in San Francisco much longer, she'd jumped at the offer, although she and her new employers had never even met or much less spoken over the phone.

A knock on the spare bedroom door had Paige looking up to see Marcella. "All packed, I see." When Paige nodded, the other woman continued. "Are you sure you want to do this? You know you can stay here as long as you like."

Standing, Paige closed the distance between them and hugged her friend tightly. "I know. But I think it's best for me to leave California . . . at least, for a little while. Maybe when the press stops knocking on your door, I'll come back, but for now, I need to get out of here." Somehow, several reporters had figured out where she was staying, and they'd been hounding her for an interview following Myles's conviction and suicide. She was still in shock he'd hanged himself in his prison cell using some pieces of a shirt he'd ripped and tied together. But she also wasn't surprised. Despite all the evidence to the contrary, Myles had thought he'd be found innocent or, at the most, receive a slap on the wrist—parole with time served during the trial. Mentally, he never would have survived a twenty-five-year sentence, even in the cushy federal prison he'd been sent to.

Leaning back far enough to look Paige in the face, Marcella smiled. "Well, then, since it's our last night together for who knows how long, let's break out a few bottles of merlot and French kiss the pillows."

Paige threw her head back and laughed. "You're on. It's the most action these lips will see for a long time."

Arm in arm, the two women walked out to the living room to toast their friendship, and Paige couldn't help but wonder if it was the last time they'd ever do so.

Chapter Three

"Night, Papa." Arianna kissed Tuck's cheek after he'd squatted down for her.

He hugged her tightly before releasing her. "Night, pumpkin. Don't forget to brush your teeth."

"I won't."

Tuck watched her skip out of the extra-large kitchen and head for the stairs before returning to the dirty dishes piled up in the sink and on the counter. It was his night to clean them while Shane read Arianna a few bedtime stories, and Tuck would rather be doing anything else *but* the dishes. The two men had been swapping the cooking and cleaning chores since Hannah had left for Oklahoma two weeks ago, and Tuck hoped his husband found someone to replace her soon. For the past fifteen days, breakfasts on the ranch had consisted of cold cereal, followed by fried bologna or peanut butter and jelly sandwiches for lunch, and steak or chicken and baked potatoes on the grill for dinner. That was the extent of the culinary talents of any of the men who lived and worked on the Red River Ranch. The one woman they'd hired to replace their elderly housekeeper had lied about her cooking skills, which they'd discovered during the first meal she'd attempted to prepare. Tuck had thought the fried pork chops she'd made couldn't get any worse than looking like burnt hockey pucks until everyone tasted them. Apparently, she'd mistaken a bag of powdered sugar for flour. That, topped off with raw potatoes, which she'd forgotten to turn the oven on for, had been the dinner from hell. Needless to say, she was fired, but not before she'd come on to both Tuck and Shane.

Rolling up the sleeves of the long-sleeved T-shirt he'd donned with sweatpants after a shower before dinner, he turned on the faucet, grabbed a sponge and the bottle of dish soap, and began scrubbing. As he worked his way through the dirty dishes, utensils, and glasses, he thought back to when Sarah had been alive and doing the dishes hadn't felt like a boring chore. Every night, after Arianna had gone to bed, Sarah had washed the dishes while Shane and Tuck had dried and put them all away. They'd chat about how their day had gone, what was new in the small-town rumor mill, and any other topics that came up. More often than not, the work had turned into play. Sometimes Sarah flicked water and suds at her husbands, or one of them snapped a towel at someone's ass or any other silliness, and it wasn't long before they moved the fun into their huge primary bedroom.

Damn, he missed Sarah. Two years felt like two months to Tuck. He didn't think he'd ever get over the loss. If it hadn't been for Shane and Arianna, he doubted he would've gotten out of bed those first few months, and then he probably would have drunk himself to death, as his grandfather had done years ago.

After forcing the depressing thoughts from his mind, Tuck was scrubbing the last of the forks and knives when strong, masculine arms wrapped around his waist, and he felt a hard, sculpted chest against his back. Goosebumps pebbled over his skin as his husband kissed and nibbled on his neck. Tuck's arms went slack, his hands dropping below the waterline in the sink, as he tilted his head to the side, giving Shane better access. Moaning, he shifted his hips, rubbing his ass on Shane's stiff erection and wishing there weren't two layers of clothing between them. The two men were the same height and general weight, but that's where the similarities between them ended. Tuck's longer, dark-brown hair and hazel eyes were courtesy of his British and Canadian heritage, while Shane's dark Irish and Greek DNA gave him his black hair and chestnut eyes.

Grasping the hem of Tuck's shirt, Shane whispered, "Lift your arms." When he followed the directive, Shane pulled the shirt up and over his head, then tossed it onto the counter next to the sink. Arianna must have fallen asleep during story time—she was a deep sleeper—because Shane pushed Tuck's sweatpants and briefs down to his knees. Letting his husband take the lead as he preferred, Tuck stood there. As expected, Shane knelt behind him and kneaded his ass cheeks before separating them. Tuck's eyes fluttered shut, his hands gripping the edge of the sink for support, when Shane's tongue rimmed his asshole. A hand snaked around Tuck's hips and grabbed his stiff cock, pumping it in time to the wet, thrusting tongue.

Shane had been bisexual since his teens but was the only same-sex lover Tuck had ever had. It'd come as a shock to Tuck the night he'd realized he wanted his new ménage partner as much as he'd wanted the woman they'd been sharing. His attraction to the other man was something he'd fought for several weeks before finally giving in to Shane's seduction. The resulting full-ménage relationship was far better than anything Tuck could have imagined. He'd realized much later that Shane's reasoning for suggesting they join forces in pursuing the woman they'd both wanted was because he'd also been lusting after his foreman. The successful ranch had been in Shane's family for five generations. Tuck had been the foreman for two years before Sarah had moved into town to take a teaching position at the local elementary school. His sister also taught there and had invited the newcomer to the traditional barbecue that was held every fall at the Red River Ranch, where Sarah had caught the eye of several men from Hazard Falls. Thankfully, the ones she'd fallen in love with had been Tuck and Shane.

Pain shot through Tuck when his husband bit his ass cheek. "Where'd you go, Tuck? Because it wasn't here with me." Shane stood, dragging his calloused hands up Tuck's sides. "Hmm?"

Tuck knew better than to lie—Shane had a way of seeing right through him, and it would only cause an argument. "Just missing Sarah."

An uneasy silence filled the air. Tuck felt tension build up in his lover's hands and knew he'd just ruined the intimate moment. When Shane removed his hands from Tuck's skin, he pulled his sweatpants back up and turned around to face him. The pain he saw in his husband's eyes almost did him in.

"Am I not enough for you?"

Tuck's eyes widened at the surprising question. "What?"

Taking another step back, Shane ran a hand through his hair as an exasperated expression stole over his face. "I mean, I miss Sarah too—there's not a day that goes by I don't think of her—but damn it, Tuck, I'm still here, and I need you. I need you to be my husband in every sense of the word. I've tried to give you time . . . but . . . shit, enough is enough. I'm sick of you just going through the motions where I'm concerned. It's been over two fucking years, and I get the feeling you'd rather be up in that cemetery with her than here with me and Arianna." Somehow, he'd kept the volume of his voice low enough so as to not wake their daughter, but there was still plenty of anger behind his words.

Shit. Tuck hadn't realized his inability to stop grieving for Sarah had negatively affected Shane and their relationship. Part of him understood where his husband was coming from, but the other part was pissed Shane had been able to move past their shared loss. Tuck grabbed his T-shirt and pulled it back on. "What do you want me to do? Forget about her?"

Quickly closing the distance between them, Shane cupped Tuck's jaw with his hands. "No, I don't want that at all. Neither one of us will ever be able to forget about Sarah. But we both have so much more living to do before we join her, and I want to enjoy that time while we have it. Do you remember the last night we had with her?"

Tuck bit his bottom lip and shut his eyes to keep back the tears he felt forming. Shane wasn't asking about the night before Sarah had died. Instead, it was the night before that. They'd brought hospice in a few weeks earlier to help manage her pain. A hospital bed had been set up in one of the spare bedrooms, so the nurses and aides could tend to Sarah's needs at any hour. Meanwhile, Shane and Tuck caught what sleep they could in the primary suite, in between work and caring for Arianna. Sarah had been so thin and weak toward the end, and it'd been painful for her loved ones to see her like that. The night before she'd slipped into a coma, she'd asked her husbands to carry her into their bed for a little while so that she could lie with them on either side of her. She must have known it would be the last time. Shane had carefully picked her up, carried her into their room, and placed her in the middle of the extra-large king-sized bed they'd all shared while Tuck closed the door behind them. It'd been difficult for Sarah to speak for long periods of time, but somehow, she managed.

"Promise me something?" Sarah's voice was low and raspy with fatigue and the effects of the morphine.

Climbing onto the bed, Tuck stretched out as close to her as he could without hurting her. The pain medication had helped, but she was still suffering. Her pale skin was almost translucent, and she bruised easily now that the cancer had ravaged her body. Her hair had been gone for the past few weeks, and she wasn't wearing one of the scarves she used to keep from frightening Arianna.

Tuck barely got his words past the lump in his throat. "Anything, baby."

"What, sweetheart?" Shane asked as he laid down on the other side of her and stroked her cheek, his eyes filled with the same despair Tuck felt. They didn't have much time left with her, and it was ripping both men to shreds.

She licked her dry lips, barely wetting them. "Promise me you'll stay together. Don't miss me so much that you lose sight of each other. Someday, if you find someone who makes you both happy and is good to Arianna, don't be afraid to let them in." Tuck opened his mouth to say that would never happen, but she lifted a weak hand to stop him. "It won't mean you loved me any less—I know that. You both have so much love to give each other, and if that spills over to someone else, I'll understand. In fact, maybe I'll send you someone someday. I want your promise you won't let your grief stop you from living your lives to the fullest."

Through his watery eyes, Tuck saw tears rolling down Shane's cheeks, and he couldn't help the ragged sob that was torn from his own chest. Sarah reached up and cupped Tuck's jaw, then did the same to Shane. "Please don't cry," she begged them, despite her own tears. "I love you both so much. If I knew back then how this would end, I still wouldn't have changed a thing. Now, promise me . . . please?"

THEY'D BOTH MADE THE VOW—THEY WOULD'VE GIVEN her the universe if they could—however, Tuck couldn't imagine anyone else ever taking his beloved Sarah's place. But that didn't mean his heart was empty. Opening his eyes again, he found Shane staring at him, waiting for an answer. Tuck nodded. "Yeah, I remember—I'll never forget it. I'm sorry if you think I want to be with her more than with you." Grabbing Shane's hips, he pulled him closer and leaned forward to brush their lips together. "Please, don't ever think I loved Sarah more than you—Arianna, Sarah, and you each own a third of my heart. I love you so much. If you weren't here, I don't know how I ever would've made it this far after losing her." He sniffled and blinked away a few unashamed tears. It wasn't the first time he'd cried in front of his loving husband. "Please, don't give up on me, Shane. I'll try . . . I swear, I'll try to get my head out of my ass." Tuck kissed him again.

Parting his lips, Shane licked Tuck's mouth, silently demanding entry. Things heated up quickly again, reminding Tuck how explosive it'd always been between the two of them. Making love to Sarah had been mind-blowing, but her husbands had always been gentler with her. With each other, though, there tended to be a battle for dominance—sometimes Shane won, other times Tuck did. This time, though, the latter knew what Shane needed and let him take the lead.

Tuck's sweatpants were shoved down his legs again, but this time, when Shane went onto his knees, his mouth had another target. Tuck grabbed the counter behind him to keep himself upright as his cock disappeared between his lover's lips. Wet, scorching heat surrounded him, and he almost came from that alone. Add in the suction when Shane took him deep, and he knew this would be fast and furious. Fingers dug into his hips, pinning him to the counter. Shane wanted complete control, and Tuck gave it to him. He thrust his hand into Shane's hair without altering the pace of his bobbing head.

Slamming his eyes shut, Tuck gave into the sensations bombarding him. Shane's hand pushed Tuck's shirt up, and knowing what the silent demand meant, he grabbed the back of it and shed it once more. Shane would make Tuck come on his abdomen. He was so close and wasn't too proud to beg. "Please . . . oh, God, Shane . . . suck me harder. Shit! I'm gonna blow!"

He tightened his grip on the edge of the counter as his balls drew up closer to his body. Shane's mouth was replaced by his hand, squeezing and pumping hard. Tuck's breathing and heart rate were out of control. The orgasm hit him with such intensity it was surprising he managed to stay on his feet as cum shot out onto his abs and chest. When Tuck had nothing more to give, Shane took a swipe of the semen in his hand before spinning his husband around to face the counter. Tuck's lungs were still heaving for air when wet fingers lubricated his hole, almost viciously, moments before they were replaced by Shane's cock. Groaning, Tuck leaned over and pushed back against the invasion. It wasn't long before Shane was buried deep inside and began to fuck him as if their lives depended on it.

"Shit . . . so fucking tight. I love this ass . . . it's mine." Shane growled—a beast claiming his mate—as he pounded into him. A hand slapped across Tuck's ass cheek. "Fucking mine!"

With each thrust, the distance between Tuck and the counter diminished until he was up against it, his hands now flat against the tiled wall above the sink. He would have bruises on his hipbones in the morning but didn't care. He needed this . . . they both did.

Shane rammed into him, paused, then withdrew and did it again. The third time, he stayed deep and bit Tuck's shoulder to keep from roaring with his release.

Still trying to catch his breath, Tuck took Shane's weight as the man collapsed on top of him, chest to back, gasping. Closing his eyes and reveling in the afterglow, Tuck hoped to make good on his oath to get his head and heart back into their marriage. He didn't know what he'd do if he lost Shane too.

Chapter Four

Pacing the hallway near the security checkpoint of the small airport, Shane waited for Paige Merritt's puddle-jumper to arrive. It was four hours west to the Denver International Airport, the closest major hub to Red River Ranch, so Quinn had booked her on a ten-seater plane to Garden City, which was just under an hour's drive to the south. That was the thing about Hazard Falls, it took forever to get anywhere from there. Hell, the closest Walmart and McDonald's were about thirty-five minutes away.

His mind flittered back to breakfast a few hours ago. After what'd happened in the kitchen last night, Shane had never gotten around to telling Tuck about their new house manager. So right before the ranch hands started strolling into the huge dining room with its twenty-seat, honey-stained, oak table, Shane had mentioned it as he poured milk into Arianna's bowl of Cheerios.

. . .

"BY THE WAY, WE HAVE A NEW HOUSEKEEPER STARTING today."

Tuck's gaze shot to Shane's before he set down the two orange juice cartons he'd retrieved from the refrigerator. "Yeah? Who? I didn't know you found anyone else to interview."

"Does she know how to make pancakes?" Arianna asked, her face lighting up at the prospect.

Shane chuckled at his daughter. "I don't know, but I'll ask for you, pipsqueak. Now hurry up and eat. I'll drop you off at school on the way to Walmart and then the airport."

Standing on the other side of the table, Tuck raised an eyebrow at his husband. "Airport?"

"Yup. To pick up the housekeeper. Quinn called yesterday and had someone interested in relocating. Thought she'd be perfect for us." While he'd been talking, his gaze went every-where but to Tuck's face. He knew without looking the man was scowling at him.

"One of his clients?"

That growled question said that the first thought Tuck had was the same one Shane had had while on the phone with Quinn. Finally, his gaze met Tuck's. "Former. She's no longer with the program, and no one is looking for her." That's all he'd say about how Paige knew Quinn in front of Arianna. "I trust him, and I checked her out on the internet. She's just trying to put a failed marriage behind her and start over. She's got small-town experience and can cook and run a house. What more do we need to know?"

His stare dared Tuck to argue with him. Ever the pessimist, it wasn't often Tuck agreed with Shane on large issues without having all the facts and weighing the pros and cons for several hours first before making a decision. But they were out of local options for filling the position. "I told Quinn it would be on a trial basis. If she doesn't work out after a week, we'll start looking for someone else. Okay?"

Relenting but obviously not happy about it, Tuck nodded as the backdoor to the kitchen swung open, and their employees started rolling in. After breakfast, Tuck would be taking some of the men out to the northern pastures, where the fencing needed to be repaired before the cattle could be rotated there for the fresher grass. Later in the week, they'd be busy as all hell as they rounded up the young steers and heifers that hadn't been branded yet. It would be a two-day job to put the Red River Ranch's symbol on all of them for identification purposes. They used two back-to-back combined Rs, seared into the cattle's thick hides, as their brand and "notched" the animals' right ears. The two distinct markings would help identify them if they were ever stolen.

"Daddy?"

Taking his usual seat at the head of the table, Shane turned his attention to his daughter. "What, sweetheart?"

"Is the new housekeeper pretty?"

Shane's eyebrows shot up as he wondered where the question had come from and what difference it made to his daughter. Then he thought of the pictures he'd found of Paige Merritt, formerly Winthrope, online. Pretty wasn't the word he would use to describe her . . . downright gorgeous was more like it. Her honey-brown hair had been longer in older photos, but more recently, she'd cut it so it just reached the top of her shoulders. Her blue eyes, which once sparkled while she stood next to her asshole husband during some elite social event, had dulled when she'd been photographed coming out of the Los Angeles Federal Courthouse several weeks ago. But she'd carried herself regally in all the pictures he found online. Once again, Shane worried it wouldn't take long before the woman found them all beneath her and demanded a ride back to the airport and the more high-class civilization she'd become accustomed to in San Francisco.

"Yes, I saw her picture. She's very pretty, Arianna. Why?"

"No, I mean, is she pretty on the inside? Don't you and Papa always say being pretty on the inside means more than being pretty on the outside?"

Ruffling his daughter's hair, Shane grinned. Any doubts he had that he and Tuck were raising her right disappeared. They might go through some rough times in the years ahead, but they'd go through them together.

THE SOUNDS OF PEOPLE ENTERING THROUGH THE DOOR from the tarmac brought Shane back to the airport. He eyed them as they walked past the TSA agents on their way to the baggage claim or parking lot. First was a tired-looking couple, each carrying a sleeping, toddler-sized twin, followed by three men in jeans, flannel shirts, shit-kickers, and cowboy hats. The last person was the one he was waiting for. Standing about five feet six, Paige Merritt was slender with generous curves in all the right places. Her hair was not as elegantly styled as it'd been in the society page photos he'd seen from two years ago, but it still had him itching to see if it was as soft as it looked. He didn't know why he was surprised to see she was dressed in comfortable jeans, a long-sleeved T-shirt, and well-worn cowgirl boots—and not the fashion-forward kind that would never come close to a pile of cow manure. Her sapphire blue eyes searched the people moving around the terminal before settling on him. An unexpected burst of electricity shot through him as she smiled tentatively and stepped toward him.

"Hi. Are you Shane or Tucker Wilson?"

Shaking off the instant attraction he felt toward her, he reminded himself she was his employee now. Nothing more. Holding out his hand, he said, "Yes, hi. I'm Shane."

"I'm Paige Merritt. It's nice to meet you."

She shook his hand, and he tried to ignore how soft hers was. "It's nice to meet you too. Let me take your bag for you. I assume you have more luggage than this."

After giving him her small carry-on bag, she hiked her purse higher on her shoulder. "Thank you. And, yes, I have two more."

"The baggage claim is this way." Unlike the huge airports, it wasn't a far walk from one end of the main terminal to the other.

They waited in uncomfortable silence for her bags to come out, and for the first time in a very long time, Shane found himself unsure what to say to a woman.

Hoping to break the ice, he asked, "So . . . um . . . how were your flights?"

"Uh, a little bit of turbulence in and out of Denver, but other than that, they were fine."

Again, neither of them spoke for a few minutes, and Shane was grateful when the luggage appeared. Handing back her carry-on, Shane grabbed the two large suitcases she pointed out to him. It didn't escape his notice they appeared to be expensive. Hazard Falls might be in the middle of nowhere, but that didn't mean a few of the town's wealthier women didn't like to flaunt the designer brands they'd gotten while traveling or ordering over the internet.

Paige followed him to his pickup truck, with the Red River Ranch logo on the doors, where he secured her bags in the small back seat since the covered bed was filled with his purchases from Walmart. By the time he shut the door, she'd already climbed into the front passenger seat and put on her seat belt. Shane made sure none of her body parts or anything else would get caught before he closed her door and walked around the front of the truck. Minutes later, they were on the highway, heading north. Once they were cruising along, Paige turned slightly in her seat to face him. "So, tell me about the ranch and what my duties will include. I feel like we're doing this backward. I got the job, and now comes the knee-shaking interview part where I try to impress you without throwing up."

Chapter Five

Shane threw his head back and belly-laughed. The last thing he'd expected from her was a sense of humor. The awkwardness between them seemed to melt as he smiled at her. "Please, don't do that in my truck—the throwing up, not the trying to impress me part. Well, actually, you don't have to do that either—relax and be yourself." After changing lanes to get around a slow-moving vehicle, he glanced over at her before returning his gaze to the road, happy to see she appeared more at ease. "The Red River Ranch is on twenty-seven hundred acres and has been in my family for five generations. We've got over fifteen hundred head of cattle, seventy sheep, twenty-five horses, twenty-three chickens, four goats, three barn cats, and two dogs."

"What, no partridge in a pear tree to finish it off?"

Chuckling, he shook his head. "Nope, and do me a favor, don't suggest that around Arianna, otherwise, she'll be begging for one. Apparently, all those animals aren't enough for her."

"No partridge, no problem."

"Thanks. Now, let's see. What else do you need to know?" Shane drummed his fingers on the steering wheel for a few seconds while trying to gather his thoughts again. "We have eight ranch hands who will join us for breakfast since we usually use that time to go over everything that needs to be done during the day and any problems that need to be addressed. We have another fourteen hands who live off-ranch and usually show up after breakfast. At lunchtime, one of the two diners in town comes out to the ranch with a food wagon filled with hot and cold sandwiches, salads, fruit, and anything else the hands want. They've been doing that for the past two years, and a few of the ranches and construction sites signed on for the service. It gave our old housekeeper a break from having to feed everyone two or three times a day, and we'll stick with that. At dinner, the hands are usually on their own. They'll either cook in the bunk-house kitchen or head into town to eat. The only exception is Sundays. They'll join us at the main house for that. Otherwise, you'll just cook dinner for Tucker, Arianna, me, and yourself. You're off Saturdays and Sundays, too, and can do as you please, but you're welcome to join us for breakfast and dinner. Tuck and I take turns cooking—usually, cold cereal in the morning, which isn't exactly 'cooking,' and barbecue for dinner."

"Okay. That's not bad at all—completely doable. I've

always enjoyed cooking and used to throw dinner parties once a month for my hus—"

When Paige cut herself off, probably embarrassed about bringing up her criminal husband, Shane glanced over. He wasn't sure if she was aware he knew of her past but figured it was best to throw it out there and let her know he wasn't holding it against her. "Hey, Quinn told me most of what happened, and I also read some of the news articles. You were screwed over just as much, if not more, as the investors by your husband. You're a victim, just like the people he swindled. No one here is going to blame you for his actions. That said, you obviously loved him at some point since you married him. Don't *not* bring him up because you're embarrassed about what happened. The Red River Ranch is a no-judgment zone. Okay?"

A sweet smile spread across her face. "Thank you. That means a lot."

Shane tried to ignore how good her expression and words made him feel. She was his employee now, so she should be off-limits. Yeah, well, that excuse didn't do him any good. Tuck had been his employee for a while before they'd gotten involved with Sarah and then each other.

Shane had to get the conversation back to a more impersonal level again. "Good. All right. Let's see . . . what else? You'll have your own wing in the main house."

"Wing?"

He snorted. "Um, yeah. It's a big house with a 'nanny's quarters.' I think that's what the architect called it when he designed it for us a few years ago."

"How old is your daughter, again? I think Quinn said she was six."

"Mm-hmm. Arianna will be seven in a few months. She's in school from seven-thirty to two-thirty. The bus picks her up at ten to seven and drops her off at ten to three at the end of the driveway. You can walk or take one of the vehicles—it's a long driveway. My sister-in-law has been dropping her off after school for the past few weeks, but now that you're here, Arianna can come home on the bus again. Part of your duties will include watching her from the time she gets home until four-thirty, when either Tuck or I come back to the house—usually me. I'm in charge of the business portion of the ranch, and he's the foreman in charge of everything else."

He paused. "You're okay working for a gay couple?" Well, technically, they were a bisexual couple, but that wasn't something he was willing to throw into the conversation with a woman he'd only met twenty minutes ago. A very attractive woman, at that.

"Absolutely. I've had several gay friends, male and female, over the years. It doesn't bother me at all. In fact, I give you credit for being openly gay and raising a child in a small town where things usually get ugly when people don't follow the herd."

"Quinn mentioned you were from a small town too."

"Johnsonville,   Nebraska—population   thirteen-eighty-one when I lived there, but I think it's closer to fifteen hundred now."

"When was the last time you were there?" he asked.

"Eight years ago, when I had to bury my dad. My mom passed away the year before that, and I think my dad died of a broken heart. They were madly in love, and he was never the same after he lost her."

Shane swallowed hard and glanced in his side-view mirror to change lanes. He knew all too well how the death of someone who held your heart in their hands could shatter you. If it hadn't been for Tuck and Arianna, it was possible Shane would have died a broken man not long after losing Sarah.

Not wanting to wallow in sorrow, he pushed his loss from his mind and continued telling Paige about the ranch, the surrounding town, and what her job entailed for the rest of the ride to Hazard Falls.

Noticing the time on the dashboard clock as he drove through town, Shane decided to swing by the school and pick up his daughter. She'd be getting out in a few minutes, and it would save Tuck's sister the trip out to the ranch. Swinging into the parking lot, he stopped by the curb and left the engine running. "I'll be out in a minute."

"No problem."

Climbing out of the truck, he strode toward the front entrance of the school, passing several moms waiting for their kids to come out. Lila parked behind the school, so Shane had to catch her before the release bell sounded. Otherwise, he'd miss her and Arianna.

"Hi, Shane. What a pleasant surprise to see you today."

Inwardly, he rolled his eyes as a woman stepped into his path ten feet from the door, stopping him in his tracks. He kept his response polite but cool. "Hello, Bridget."

The twice-divorced blonde had been blatantly coming on to both Shane and Tuck since Sarah had become sick, clearly wanting to take her place, as if that would ever happen. And it looked like Bridget would take another stab at it again today. Closing the distance separating them, she ran a single finger down his forearm. "When are you and Tucker going to invite me to dinner? You both really need to get out and have a good time every now and then, you know."

He let out an impatient sigh. Bridget came from one of the few "old money" families that lived in Hazard Falls. Her father was the mayor, and her mother ran the local women's club, which Shane usually referred to as the snob's club. It seemed like the membership committee only accepted women who could live off their husband's or family's money. Work was beneath those women unless it was for some charity, which boosted their standings in the community. Another requirement appeared to be they had to belittle anyone they deemed beneath them. He often wondered why Bridget was hitting on him and Tuck because being in a ménage relationship would most likely make her an outcast of the club. Regardless, it was time to stop pussyfooting around the subject with the woman since it clearly wasn't sinking into her brain that they would never ask her out or into their bed. "Bridget, when are you going to give it a rest? Tucker and I have repeatedly told you we aren't interested in dating anyone, and even if we were, with the ranch and Arianna, there's not a lot of time. Now, I'm sorry, but I'm in a rush."

Sidestepping her, he hurried inside, not the least bit sorry, despite having said so. Entering the school lobby, he made a left toward Lila's fourth-grade classroom. While Arianna was only in the first grade, she came to Lila's room after classes let out, so her aunt could drive her home. Shane peeked through the narrow window next to the door and waved a few times before he got her attention. Holding a finger up to her class, she opened the door, stepped out, and closed it again. "Hi, Shane. Everything okay?"

"If you don't count getting hit on by Bridget again, yeah."

He got the expected eye roll. "Oh, jeez. Doesn't she get it?"

"Apparently not," Shane responded with a shrug. "Anyway, I was passing through town and figured I'd pick up Arianna and save you the trip."

"Great. I'll send her out after the bell."

"Thanks. By the way, we hired a new house manager on a trial basis. If she works out, you won't have to bring Arianna home every day."

Lila's eyebrows shot up. "Oh? Anyone I know?"

"Nope, she's from out of town. A friend of my

cousin's." A half-truth, but it was up to Paige if she wanted to give anyone the details of how she'd ended up in Hazard Falls.

"That's great. Hope she works out—not that I minded giving Arianna a lift." Laughter sounded from behind her classroom door. "Let me go. I have to assign them homework before the bell rings. I'll talk to you later."

Heading back to the front entrance, Shane prayed Bridget wasn't waiting to ambush him again.

Chapter Six

Watching Shane stride up the walkway to the doors to the school, Paige couldn't help but admire the way the man's ass and muscular thighs looked in his Wrangler jeans. Not surprisingly, she wasn't the only one. Several women's gazes dropped to his fine derrière after he'd passed them. The rest of him wasn't bad either, with those broad shoulders and narrow waist. Too bad he was gay. Then again, the last thing she wanted was to get involved with a man right then—especially one she was now working for.

Just before Shane reached the door, a bleached blonde, in tight jeans and an even tighter V-neck tee, stepped into his path. Even from the truck, Paige could see the lust in the woman's eyes. Paige snorted and spoke aloud since no one could hear her. "What? Does she think she can convince him to take a walk on the wild side and try some pussy for a change? It doesn't work that way, honey."

Somehow, Shane managed to get past the woman, who stared after him as he entered the school. A thought crossed Paige's mind. She wondered if Shane and Tucker had adopted their daughter or if they'd used a surrogate. Not that it mattered. She'd heard the affection in Shane's voice whenever he'd talked about Arianna. The little girl was clearly loved.

A sharp rap on the passenger window startled Paige, causing her to yelp. Her hand went to her chest as she saw a dark-haired woman with her hand over her mouth and her eyes wide. Paige hit the button to roll down the window.

"Oh, my God!" the woman squeaked. "I'm so sorry. I didn't mean to scare you."

Paige willed her heart and respiration rates to settle back down. "That's okay. I just wasn't expecting anyone to knock. It didn't help I was daydreaming."

"I'm sorry. I just wanted to introduce myself. I'm Nicole Mathers. You must be the Red River Ranch's new house manager."

It was Paige's turn to gape. "Um . . . I am . . . but how did you—" She rolled her eyes. "Never mind. I used to live in a small town. News travels fast."

Nicole giggled. "Yeah, it does. But in my case, my husband, Hank, and I both work at the ranch. I help out in the office part-time from eight to one, dealing with customers and orders. I saw Hank at lunch, and he said Shane had gone to the airport to pick you up.

When I saw you sitting here in the Red River truck, I figured I'd introduce myself."

Opening the passenger door, Paige hopped out and extended her hand. "Now that the butterflies have settled in my stomach again, it's nice to meet you, Nicole. I'm Paige Merritt."

The shorter woman shook her hand. "Nice to meet you, too, Paige. My daughter, Joey, short for Joan Marie, is in Arianna's class. They're actually best friends. Anytime you have any questions, and Shane and Tucker are busy, feel free to call me if I'm not at the ranch. The guys have a class phone list on the refrigerator."

"Thanks. I appreciate that. I'm sure I'll have a lot of questions—especially about the town and where everything is." Movement out of the corner of Paige's eye had her turning her head. Shane was on his way back, and this time, he managed to get by the blonde bimbo without being stopped. But Paige didn't miss the dirty look the scorned woman gave his back.

"That's Bridget Kline," Nicole murmured conspiratorially. "Her nose is so high in the air she could drown in a rainstorm. She's had her beady little eyes on Shane and Tucker for a while now, but they want no part of her."

"I wouldn't think so, considering they're gay."

Nicole opened her mouth to respond to Paige's statement but let the subject drop as Shane approached them.

"Hey, Nic."

"Hi, Shane. Just introduced myself to Paige. I told her to call me if she had any questions when you and Tucker weren't around."

"Thanks. I'll make sure she knows where the class list is. How're the rodeo plans coming along?"

"Fantastic! We're expecting another great turnout." Nicole's gaze shifted to Paige. "Hazard's big Rodeo Bonanza is coming up in about six weeks. It's an annual event that draws participants and fans from all over. I've been on the organizational committee for the past five years. If you've got any spare time, we could always use some help that day. No pressure, of course."

Paige chuckled at the huge grin on Shane's face. He winked at her, and she was surprised at the warm, fuzzy feeling it gave her in her stomach and even further below. "Subtle, isn't she?"

"Very. Well, since I haven't even seen the ranch yet, and I'm still learning what I'll be doing there, I'll have to get back to you on that, Nicole. But if I can help, I will."

The woman grinned. "Great!"

A loud bell signaled the end of the school day, and Shane crossed his arms and leaned against the front quarter panel of the truck, his gaze on the front door of the building, watching for his daughter to emerge. It wasn't long until two little girls came running down the walkway toward them, each with a knapsack on their back. One was blonde, and the other brunette, and they both had their hair up in pigtails.

The darker-haired girl ran to Nicole, who said

goodbye to Paige and Shane before leading her daughter toward her vehicle. Meanwhile, the towheaded girl leaped into Shane's outstretched arms when he squatted down. "Daddy!"

"Hey, pipsqueak." Shane gave her a tight squeeze before letting go and standing again. "How was school?"

"Good. I got a hundred percent on my spelling test and a gold sticker next to my name on the board."

"Fantastic. C'mere. There's someone I want you to meet." Setting his hands on the little girl's shoulders, he turned her to face Paige. "This is Paige, our new house manager. Paige, this is my daughter, Arianna."

Extending her hand to her new charge, Paige smiled. "It's nice to meet you, Arianna."

A shy grin spread across the little girl's face as she shook the proffered hand. "It's nice to meet you too. I like your name—it's pretty."

"Well, we have something in common, then. I like your name and think it's pretty too."

"Thank you." A curious expression spread across her face. "Do you know how to make pancakes?"

"I certainly do. I can make them plain or with blueberries, chocolate chips, or butterscotch chips."

Arianna's eyes lit up in delight. "Butterscotch? I love butterscotch! Hannah used to make me butterscotch pudding all the time, but I've never had it in my pancakes. That sounds yummy!"

Her smile widened, and Paige gave her two thumbs up. "Butterscotch-chip pancakes are my favorite. As soon as I can get some, I'll make them for you and your dads. Okay?"

"Okay!" She tilted her head back until her gaze met Shane's. "I like her, Daddy."

He chuckled and gently tugged on one of her pigtails. "Glad to hear it, pipsqueak. What do you say we get out of here and show Paige the ranch?"

"Okay. You're gonna love it, Paige. We have lots of animals."

They loaded up into the pickup, with Arianna buckled into the back seat behind Shane, then drove toward the Red River Ranch. The little girl showed off her bubbly personality, telling Paige all about the menagerie of animals at the ranch and what she'd done in school that day. As she rambled on, Shane shook his head and whispered in Paige's direction, "She does stop to inhale every once in a while—you just have to wait for it."

Paige chuckled. "No worries. She's sweet."

"Thanks."

When they turned off the main road onto a long dirt drive, Paige took in the surroundings. A large, overhead, wrought-iron sign they passed under had a logo with back-to-back Rs inside a circle. The Red River Ranch was huge. Fenced-in pastures sat on either side of the driveway, and while one was empty, about half a dozen horses grazed to Paige's right. The main house was about a half mile from the road, and beyond that, several bunkhouses, barns, and a silo could be seen. It was a typical ranch like those she'd grown up near. Although her family had lived in a house in what was considered "town," she'd had many friends who'd lived on nearby ranches. Paige might not have wanted to return to her own hometown, but with each moment that passed, she remembered how much more relaxing small-town life had been. The fresh air alone brought back welcome memories of a simpler time in her life. No, it hadn't always been perfect, but what was?

Shane parked the truck under a carport attached to the house and killed the engine. Arianna was out of her seatbelt and opening her door in the blink of an eye. "Come on, Paige! I'll show you my room!"

Climbing out of the driver's seat, Shane chuckled. "Easy, sweetheart—there's no rush. Paige will get to see the whole house, including your room. Right now, though, you have homework to do at the kitchen table, so hop to it."

An exasperated pout appeared on the little girl's face, but she didn't argue, taking her knapsack into the house. Shane retrieved Paige's carry-on from the back seat, then called out to a ranch hand who pulled up in a pickup truck behind them. "Hey, Seth, do me a favor and bring in the two suitcases from the back. I'll be out to help with the rest of the stuff in a bit."

The man was in his late twenties, with short, light-brown hair under his cowboy hat, wicked blue eyes, and an easy grin that lit up his face. "Sure thing, Shane. Howdy, ma'am," he added, with a tug on the brim of his hat.

Shane grimaced. "Sorry about that. I should have done the introductions first. Seth Parker, this is our new house manager, Paige Merritt."

The cowboy held out his hand and winked. "Pleasure to meet you, Paige. Welcome to Red River. I maintain the property around the main house and bunkhouses—fixing whatever needs fixing—and running errands into town as needed. I'm kind of a jack-of-all-trades, so just let me know if you need anything."

"Thanks, Seth," Paige said with a smile as she shook his hand. "And it's a pleasure to meet you too."

Paige didn't miss how Seth held onto her hand a little longer than necessary, his gaze roaming down her body in appreciation. Apparently, neither did Shane because he growled. "I doubt your latest girlfriend would like to know you were hitting on another woman, Seth."

The younger man barked out a laugh as he let Paige's hand drop. "Yeah, well, as of last night, I'm a single guy again—thank God."

Shane smirked. "Let me guess, she said the M-word?"

"Something like that."

Taking Paige's elbow, Shane turned her toward the front entrance of the house. "Seth's allergic to the word marriage. C'mon, I'll show you around inside while he gets back to work."

The interior of the large home was tastefully decorated, and Paige wondered if the gay couple had done it themselves or had hired an interior designer. Each room had been done in earth tones, giving them a rich yet comfortable feel. A small living room appeared not to be used much, as nothing was out of place in it. Between the country kitchen and the dining room was a large table that could seat twenty people. A family room that ran from the front to the back of the house seemed to be the most used. There were comfortable couches and chairs in front of an entertainment center with a sixty-inch wide-screen TV. An area had been sectioned off for Arianna's toys, and from the look of things, she favored Barbie and anything to do with horses. Off to one side was a crafting area complete with a sewing machine. Paige figured it had been for the former home manager—Shane had said she was an older woman. Well, Paige could cook, clean, and do a lot of different crafting projects, but sewing, beyond a simple button, wasn't on the list of things she was good at.

Shane gave her a tour of the house and showed her where Arianna's bedroom was on the second floor as the little girl trailed behind, pointing out things she thought Paige should know about or see before her father instructed her to return to her homework. A guest bedroom wasn't in use, and the primary bedroom suite was huge with a sitting area, an attached bath, and the biggest bed Paige had ever seen.

"Sorry about the mess," Shane said with a frown as he grabbed some discarded clothes from the floor and tossed them into a nearby hamper, then pulled the covers up to the pillows on the bed, trying to straighten them. "I'm a little tidier than Tuck."

Paige smiled. "It's okay. My husband wasn't the neatest man in the world either."

Crossing to the other side of the house, Shane showed Paige where she'd be staying. She was surprised to see it was almost a duplicate of the primary bedroom. She had a sitting area with her own television, a king-size bed, and an en-suite bathroom. Although she was used to a grand bedroom from the mansion she'd lived in for several years before her life had turned upside down, she hadn't expected it on a ranch in a small town.

Seth had already been there and gone, leaving her bags on the bed for her. Shane set her carry-on next to the two suitcases. "The mattress, box spring, sheets, and pillows are all brand new. So are the towels and things in the bathroom. If you need anything we missed, just let me know, and I'll have Seth grab it for you the next time he goes shopping in Garden City."

After glancing into the large bathroom, which included a walk-in shower and spa tub, Paige turned to her new boss. "I don't think I'll need anything else, but I'll let you know."

Shane shoved his hands into the front pockets of his jeans. "Um . . . why don't you unpack, and we'll head into town for dinner later? I don't want you to have to cook your first night here. Once in a while, Tuck, Arianna, and I go to Bar None for dinner. It's a combination restaurant, bar, and dance hall. Best food in town."

"That sounds nice. Thank you. What time should I be ready?"

He checked the watch on his left wrist. "It's three-thirty now, but we won't be ready to go until six. If you're hungry, there's plenty of food in the fridge and pantry."

"I'm good," Paige answered with a shake of her head. "I'll unpack, then take another walk around the house and outside. Get the lay of the land."

"Great. I'll be out in the main barn for a bit. When Arianna's done with her homework, you'll need to check it. After that, she can play for a while or watch TV. I'll give her a snack on my way out, so don't let her convince you she's *starving*." Shane rolled his eyes. "I swear that little girl can out-eat most of our ranch hands some days."

Paige smiled. "No pigging out. Check."

Glancing around, Shane looked like he wanted to say something else but then decided against it. Instead, he strode to the door. "I'll get out of your way. If you need anything, Seth is fixing the banister on the back porch. I noticed it was loose last night."

"Okay." Paige paused, then added, "And Shane?"

He stopped in the doorway and looked back at her. "Yeah?"

"Thanks for taking a chance on me. It was very nice of you."

The corners of his mouth tilted upward. "You're welcome, Paige. See you at six o'clock."

Chapter Seven

After closing the top drawer of the dresser that now held her underwear and bras, Paige slid the two empty suitcases under the bed. The ruffled, ivory bed skirt hid them from view. Pivoting around, she took in her surroundings once more. The walk-in closet could hold a lot more clothes than she'd brought with her. If things worked out, she'd have Marcella ship the rest of her stuff.

Suddenly thirsty, Paige wandered out to the kitchen, where Arianna had her school books spread out on the table. Next to her elbow was a glass with only a mouthful of milk left in it and a plate with a few slices of an apple on it. Arianna was nibbling on a piece of the fruit while frowning at the open book in front of her.

Paige stopped beside her. "What's wrong, Arianna?"

The little girl sighed like the world's weight was on her shoulders. "It's my math homework. We have to add up the pennies, dimes, and nickels, and I don't know if I got them right or not."

"Would you like me to take a look at it, or do you want to try to do it again?"

Arianna shrugged and turned the book so Paige could see it better. "You can take a look, but don't tell me the answers. Mrs. Dwyer says we're supposed to figure it out on our own. Just tell me if I got them right or wrong."

"Okay." She scanned the eight math problems and the penciled-in answers on the page. "Hmm. Well, you did very well on the first six, but you have to try the last two again, and then I'll check them."

"Okay."

While her new charge went back to work, Paige opened the commercial-sized refrigerator and the pantry beside it to find that there was plenty of food and drinks to choose from. With the number of people she'd be cooking breakfast and the occasional dinner for, she was glad to have a fully stocked fridge and pantry. The stove and oven were also larger than usual for a residential kitchen, and she looked forward to cooking for a big group again. She and Myles had often invited their friends over, and she'd cooked for them instead of having the meals catered. While she'd never be a renowned chef, she did enjoy experimenting and creating new culinary masterpieces.

Choosing an apple, she closed the door to the fridge and leaned against the counter while she took a few bites. Like the rest of the house, the kitchen had been decorated in warm and cozy colors. A backdoor led to the porch that wrapped around the east side and front of the house. Paige imagined herself sitting in one of the several rocking chairs she could see, relaxing and watching an evening sunset. That was one of the things she'd miss the most about California—the sun setting into the Pacific Ocean, painting the sky red, orange, yellow, and every shade in between. The multi-million-dollar Torrance Beach home she and Myles had lived in had been within walking distance of the ocean, and she loved to sit and behold the view as day became night.

"I'm done, Paige. I think I got them right this time."

She stepped over to the table and scanned the page again. "Yup, you did. Very good. Do you have more homework to do?"

"Uh-uh. Here's my social studies and science homework for you to look at. I finished everything except for my reading, and I do that at night with Daddy before I go to bed."

Once Paige approved the rest of the homework, which was simple enough for a first-grader to process, Arianna put her books and papers back into her knapsack. "Can I watch TV now? My favorite show is on."

"Your daddy said you could, so yes." From Arianna's chattering earlier in the car, Paige had figured out that Shane was "Daddy" and the as-yet-unseen Tucker was "Papa." "Which show is your favorite?"

With Paige following, the little girl skipped into the family room. "The man with the happy little trees."

Her brow furrowed. She had no idea what was on nowadays for six-year-olds, so she was clueless about a show with "happy little trees," especially since she rarely watched TV herself. Paige preferred to read and had three Kindles loaded with books she'd read or planned to. "What man?"

Arianna picked up the remote from the couch and pointed it toward the TV. "Mr. Bob. I like him. He's nice."

When the show came on, Paige had to chuckle. She'd forgotten all about Bob Ross and his gentle voice as he showed millions of watchers how to create beautiful paintings with "happy little trees" during a half-hour show. Her father had loved watching Ross's *The Joy of Painting*, even though he never attempted to paint anything himself. "Do you paint, Arianna?"

"Nope. I just like watching."

Paige glanced around, getting a better look at the room she'd passed through earlier. The sitting area for the entertainment center consisted of an L-shaped couch, two recliners, an ottoman, a coffee table, and several small side tables. From the books, newspapers, and other items scattered about, it was clear the family spent a lot of time there. On the wall behind one part of the couch were four floor-to-ceiling bookcases filled to the brim with books in various genres, a few tchotchkes, an assortment of framed photographs, and a thin layer of dust. Spotting a pad and pen on one of the tables, Paige snatched them up and made a list of things she would need to do on a regular basis around the house, separating them into days of the week, and other things that would need to be done occasionally. She made notes to ask her two new employers about certain things, such as if they wanted her to do their laundry or just Arianna's. Some people, Paige included, felt weird about others cleaning their unmentionables. Her bras and underwear were the only things that had been off limits to her own housekeeper, whom Myles had insisted on hiring.

How things have changed. Not that she thought being a housekeeper was beneath her, but Paige wondered what her so-called friends, who'd dropped her the moment her husband had been arrested, would think about her new job. Well, it didn't matter what they thought. She'd only been in Hazard Falls for a few hours but already felt comfortable there. It made her reflect on whether she'd ever actually fit in with the elite crowd she'd rubbed elbows with over the eight years she'd been married. Although she'd loved having her own business and not having to worry about a budget when it came to most purchases, there had always been a . . . stiffness, of sorts, to the people and environment she'd been immersed in.

Pondering what she was missing from her growing list, Paige eyed some photographs on the shelves beside her. There were pictures of Arianna, Shane, and another man who had to be his husband, Tucker. But in some of them, a woman was in the photos when the little girl was much younger. That was probably the surrogate they'd used to have a child, Paige thought, because Arianna was the spitting image of her. The woman clearly knew the men well since her arms were around both in several photos. Maybe a relative or close friend? And where was she now?

"That's my mommy."

Paige smiled at Arianna, who'd wandered over. "She's very pretty. You look just like her."

"Thank you. A lot of people say that. I miss her, though. She's in heaven with my cat, Shadow."

Squatting down, Paige brushed the little girl's hair back from her face. "I'm sorry to hear that. My mom and dad are in heaven too. I miss them very much. But you know what?" She pointed to the left side of her chest. "They're always here in my heart where I can love them forever."

"That's what Daddy says when we watch the videos Mommy made before she went to heaven. She reads stories to me in them and talks about things we did so I don't forget them or her. Papa doesn't like watching the videos, though—they make him sad."

The surrogate was probably a relative on Tucker's side then. "Well, everyone grieves in their own way. And he has you and your daddy to love and make him happy, right?"

"Right," Arianna said with a firm nod.

A deep rumble sounded from behind Paige. "Ahem."

She almost yelped in surprise as she stood and spun around, not having heard anyone else enter the house.

Holy hell, the man was gorgeous. This had to be Tucker Wilson. She recognized him from the photos, which hadn't done him justice. Where his husband was tall, dark, and handsome, this man was a brown-haired god—although a broody one, if his scowl was any indication. He could have been a Viking if his several-inch-long hair was blonde and they lived more than ten centuries ago.

Paige realized she was gaping when he raised an eyebrow at her, and she gave herself a mental shake, reminding herself the man was married and gay.

"Hi, Papa!" Arianna launched herself toward her father, who managed to open his arms in time to catch her.

"Hi, sweetheart."

"This is Paige. She knows how to make butterscotch pancakes!"

"Really?" He shifted her onto his left hip, holding her in place with one arm.

"Uh-huh. Paige, Papa likes butterscotch as much as I do. Daddy likes chocolate better, though."

Paige smiled. "Well, I'll have to remember to get both kinds of chips so everyone can have what they like. Hi, you're obviously Tucker. It's nice to meet you."

She stepped forward and held out her hand. Tucker hesitated, his gaze scanning her face. What he was searching for was beyond her. Paige almost dropped her hand before he reached out and shook it, then released it so he could set his daughter back onto the floor. "It's nice to meet you, too, Paige." His tone was flat, and she got the impression he wasn't thrilled about her being there despite his words. He glanced toward the kitchen. "Did Shane mention dinner?"

"Um . . . yes. He said something about going to . . . um . . . sorry, I forgot the name of the restaurant."

"Daddy said we were going to Bar None for dinner, Papa." Arianna twirled around in several circles as she spoke.

A slight frown appeared on Tucker's face again, and Paige quickly said, "If that's a problem, there's plenty of food in the refrigerator and pantry. I can whip up something for dinner so we don't have to go out."

Before Tucker could respond, Arianna stopped spinning and glared up at him. "But I want to go out, Papa. Daddy promised."

His gaze fell to his daughter, and after a moment, he tugged on one of her pigtails. "We'll go out, sweetheart. Daddy was right to suggest it. It would be rude to ask Paige to cook on her first night here."

"Yay!" She bounced up and down on the balls of her feet. "Will you dance with me if our song comes on?"

"Of course. Don't I always?"

"Yup."

Tucker glanced at the clock on the satellite dish box in the entertainment center and then back at Paige. "I'm sure Shane said we'd leave for dinner at six o'clock, so I have time to finish some more work." He stroked his daughter's head. "I'll be back in a little bit, sweetheart. Turn off the TV and read or play 'til it's time to go."

"Okay, Papa."

His mouth was flat as he nodded at Paige before turning around without another word, leaving her standing there. She heard the backdoor slam shut a little harder than necessary. She didn't know what Tucker's problem with her was—she got the impression he didn't want her there—and Paige hoped she wouldn't cause a rift between the two men. Not only did she need the job with all but one of her bank and investment accounts still frozen, but she had nowhere else to go. She couldn't go back to California, not with the press and people who blamed her for her husband's crimes hounding her, nor did she want to return to her hometown. There was nobody left there for her anymore. She'd been an only child and had lost touch with friends from her youth after moving to the West Coast.

"Come on, Paige. I'll show you our chickens."

The corners of her mouth ticked upward as she let the little girl take her hand and lead her to the backdoor. It was time to start over again. Hopefully, she could convince her new bosses they needed her as much as she needed them.

Chapter Eight

Tuck's teeth grinded together to the point his jaw hurt as he sat in the front passenger seat of Shane's extended-cab pickup. Behind him sat their new house manager, who listened as Arianna told her all about Bar None. Despite it being a place where the local cowboys went to tie one on occasionally, during dinnertime, there was a family atmosphere about the place. The dining room, with its dance floor and small stage, was separated from the bar area by swinging doors. It wasn't uncommon to have a bunch of rug rats running around, enjoying themselves, as long as they didn't wander into the adults-only bar. Shane and Tuck visited the establishment several times a month, with or without Arianna. When Hannah had been living with them, the two men had been able to have the occasional adult night out, although it was far less often than when Sarah had been alive and healthy. The trio would get a babysitter most Saturday nights and head into town for a date night. It allowed Sarah to unwind after chasing after their young daughter all week.

Arianna always looked forward to going to Bar None to eat and dance. She had her two favorite country songs that she'd dance to with her fathers. With Shane, it was "Daddy's Hands" by Holly Dunn, and with Tuck, it was "In My Daughter's Eyes" by Martina McBride. She still hadn't figured out that one of them would always slip over to the jukebox on the pretense of using the restroom or talking to someone and make sure the songs came on before they had to leave. Some of the regulars would probably grow sick of the songs someday, but he didn't care. Tuck was sure she'd figure it out soon, just like it would only be another year or two before she found out Santa Claus and the Easter Bunny were both myths.

The parking lot was about three-quarters full when they pulled in and found a spot. Tuck climbed out, and before he realized what he was doing, he opened Paige's door and extended his hand to help her out. The act, so innocent and polite to most, caused his gut to clench. It reminded him of all the times he'd helped Sarah out of the truck that had been too tall for her. He'd loved picking her up to help her in, not letting her use the running board.

Paige smiled as she placed her hand in his, then stepped down. "Thank you."

All he could do was nod, let go of her hand, and shut the door. Shane and Arianna skirted around the back of the truck, and Tuck followed the three of them inside. As usual, they were greeted by many and got the evil eye from a few. As long as any hatred or gossip didn't affect Arianna, the two men ignored it. If people had a problem with their unconventional marriage and bisexuality, that was just it—*their* problem. Yeah, it had taken Tuck a while to come out of the closet he begged Shane to let him stay in until he was more at ease with it, but when the time had come, it'd been easier than he'd thought it would be. His parents and sister, although a little shocked, had seen how good Sarah and Shane were for him, and they'd wholeheartedly accepted the relationship. And when Arianna had been born, well . . . they'd been over the moon at having a granddaughter and niece. They still were. His folks were now snowbirds, spending the warmer months of the year in Kansas and the colder months in a retirement community in Arizona. In fact, they'd be heading east in another seven or eight weeks for the summer.

It wasn't long before the three adults and one precocious child sat in a booth, the men on one side, the ladies on the other, perusing the menus. Well, at least Shane, Tuck, and Paige were. Arianna always got the same thing—mac and cheese with ketchup and mustard. Tuck liked the condiments as much as the next person, but he had no idea where his daughter had come up with the mixture. At least she ate it all.

"Hey, Shane, Tuck. Hi, pumpkin. How y'all doing tonight?" Betty Lou Davidson, the owner of Bar None, smiled as she stopped at their table. She'd gone to school with Shane and had taken over the business after her father had fallen ill. After a quadruple bypass, Rory Davidson turned over a few new leaves, one of them being retirement. While Betty Lou had several waitresses, busboys, and bartenders who worked for her, she had no trouble pitching in when needed. With a pad and pen in her hands and a black apron around her narrow waist, it appeared she was helping out on the tables tonight as she slid a children's placemat with games on it and crayons in front of Arianna.

"Hi, Betty Lou!" Their daughter jumped up and hugged the pretty, dark-haired woman around her hips before pointing at Paige. "This is Paige. She knows how to make butterscotch pancakes!"

Their new employee chuckled as she nodded hello. "Apparently, that's my claim to fame around here."

"Things could be worse," the other woman said with a small snort. "You could be famous for getting caught skinny dipping in the lake with JoBeth Harrington by her father—Pastor Harrington." She jutted her chin toward Shane.

The man had no shame when he shrugged and grinned at Paige. "I was seventeen and haven't been allowed back in his church since. But I'd be happy to share my skinny-dipping title with you."

Tuck realized their new employee thought he and Shane were simply a gay couple and didn't know about their ménage marriage when a flash of confusion passed over her face as she laughed. "I'll stay famous for my pancakes, thanks."

Gesturing between the two women, Shane introduced them. "Betty Lou—or just Lou—owns this fine establishment, and Paige is our new house manager."

The bar owner's eyebrows shot up. "So, you finally found someone to take the job. Great. Although, I think Marla will have a fit since she ordered a few extra cases of cold cereal for y'all."

Shane grinned and eyed Paige. "Marla Oberman owns the Stop & Go Grocery store up the street. It's not big, but it saves us from driving thirty or forty minutes to Walmart when we run out of a few of the basics."

While the others talked, laughed, and went through their food orders, Tuck's mood continued to sour. He wasn't sure what had put him in such a funk, but whatever it was, it had to do with Paige. Maybe it was because of how sweetly she'd been talking to Arianna about heaven earlier when he'd gone searching for Shane. He'd imagined Sarah having the same heartfelt discussion with their daughter. She should still be there for Arianna. It wasn't fair that the little girl wouldn't have her mother by her side as she made her first communion next year or went through all the changes in her body as she grew. Sarah would never see Arianna go on her first date, dress up for the prom, graduate high school, and walk down the aisle one day. It wasn't fucking fair at all. And here was Paige—a woman he didn't even know, giving his daughter words of wisdom. Granted, she'd done a better job than he could have managed—he heard everything she said—but it still grated on him.

Under the table, Shane pinched Tuck's leg, causing him to startle. He quickly glanced at his husband, then at Paige and Arianna, and finally at the woman standing next to him, trying to figure out what he'd just missed. "Huh?"

Betty Lou smacked his shoulder with the small pad. "I'm waiting on your order, stud. You just drifted somewhere. Go to la-la land *after* you tell me what you want to eat."

"Um . . . the bacon-ranch chicken sandwich with curly fries is fine. And a root beer, please."

"You got it." After adding his order to the list, she gathered their menus. "I'll have your drinks in a few."

As the other woman walked away, Arianna pushed her paper placemat toward Paige. "Will you do the puzzles and games with me, Paige?"

"Sure, sweetie. I used to love doing these when I was your age." She picked up a crayon and put an X in a corner square of a Tic-Tac-Toe game.

Tuck couldn't watch them anymore. With the elderly Hannah, it'd been easy not to imagine Sarah in her place, interacting with Arianna, but this much younger woman reminded him of all they'd lost. He glanced around at the patrons, searching for an excuse to leave the table. When he found one, he stood and looked down at two of the three curious faces. "Greer's over there. I need to talk to him about next week's feed delivery. I'll be right back."

Shane's frown silently called him on his bullshit. Tuck's husband knew he'd spoken to Greer Phillips, who owned the local feedlot, yesterday, but with a small, annoyed shake of his head, Shane let him go.

Tuck had managed to come up with something else to talk to Greer about, so he didn't sound like he'd forgotten their conversation yesterday. Then he moved on to a group of Red River ranch hands who'd come into town for their dinner too. When he found out they were planning to stay for a while, having a few more beers at the bar, he asked if he could get a ride home with them later on. Shane would be pissed, but he wouldn't start an argument here. Tuck just needed a few hours alone. He'd promised Shane he'd get his head out of his ass and work on their marriage, but he couldn't start tonight. After drowning his sorrows for a bit, he'd try to look toward the future starting tomorrow.

"Papa, dinner's ready." Arianna had skipped across the dance floor toward him, dodging several couples doing a two-step to Toby Keith.

"All right, pipsqueak. I'll be there in a minute."

"Okay." She went back the way she'd come.

Tuck pulled out a dollar and handed it to Seth Parker. "You know what songs to play."

The man grinned. "I think it's become a job requirement to know what songs to play. That little girl doesn't just have you wrapped around her fingers—she's got everyone at the ranch at her beck and call."

And wasn't that the truth? Not a single one of their

employees would allow harm to come to Arianna, and they'd give her the world if she asked for it. She had that bright, sunny personality that drew people in. Just like her mother. *Damn it.* Would that ache he felt deep in his heart every time he thought of Sarah ever ease?

Taking his seat again, Tuck ensured his mouth was full as much as possible so he didn't have to contribute to any of the conversations between Shane, Paige, Arianna, and anyone who stopped by their table to say hi. If he could get away with a grunted response, he did. If not, his answers were short and definitely not sweet. Shane was getting more pissed off at him, his muscles getting tenser as the minutes ticked by, but Tuck didn't care. What bothered him was the way Shane flirted with Paige. It had been a long time since he'd seen the man turn on his charm that drew in the ladies and men who swung that way, and it grated on Tuck's nerves.

After finishing her mac and cheese, Arianna asked permission to visit a few of her friends and their families at nearby tables.

"Just stay where we can see you, pipsqueak," Shane reminded her as he and Tuck always did. While there were plenty of adults around who would never let anything happen to her, Tuck and Shane were consistent about the rules concerning their daughter no matter where they went.

When Arianna ran off, Paige glanced over her shoulder, then slid toward the end of the bench. "If you'll excuse me, I'm going to the restroom."

As soon as she was out of earshot, Shane let out a low growl at Tuck. "What the fuck is wrong with you? You're being a rude asshole. In case you forgot, Paige is our employee now and lives in our home. The least you can do is be civil to her."

"Humph. Is that what you call what you're doing? Being civil? Because I call it flirting, and I don't fucking like it. Trust me. I know she's just an employee, but you seem to have other ideas."

Shane rolled his eyes. "I'm not flirting with her. I'm being friendly. She doesn't know a soul in town, and I'm trying to make her feel comfortable. That's all."

The word "bullshit" was on Tuck's tongue, but he caught it in time when Arianna appeared at his elbow. "C'mon, Papa. It's our song." She grabbed his hand and tugged. "We have to dance."

He hadn't even realized it had come on. Most of the anger boiling through him ebbed as he gazed into his daughter's pleading eyes. Seth had been right—she would have Tuck wrapped around her little finger until his dying day. Tossing his napkin on the last of his unfinished dinner, he stood. "Yup, we do. Lead the way, little lady."

Chapter Nine

Shane couldn't remember the last time he wanted to deck his husband. The only three things that stopped him were he'd been at a disadvantage on the inside of the booth, Arianna interrupted their argument, and he noticed Paige on her way back to the table. Using his hands to push himself up, he stood as well as he could between the bench and table when she slid in across from him. A worried expression on her face bothered him as he sat again. "Are you okay, Paige? Something wrong?"

"I . . . um . . . was just going to ask you the same thing. Did I do or say something inappropriate? Tucker doesn't seem to be happy I'm here." She twisted her napkin in her hands. "I really need this job, Shane, but not at the expense of coming between the two of you. If it's a problem, I'll stay until you find someone else."

"Hey . . . no. It's got nothing to do with you, Paige," he lied, reaching over and stilling her hands with his own. He waited for her to look at him. When she did, the despair he saw in her eyes almost did him in. "I'm sorry. It's . . ." He took a deep breath and let it out. He had to tell her the truth. She'd probably hear it by tomorrow anyway. In fact, he was a little surprised they'd gotten through the whole day without him having to explain about their unconventional three-way marriage. But here and now was not the time or place. "You're not going anywhere. I promised you a week's trial, and you'll get it. But I'll tell you right now, I doubt you'll give me any reason not to keep you on after that. Arianna likes you. I-I like you. And Tuck . . ." His mouth flattened as he tilted his head from side to side, trying to think of the right words. "Well, Tuck will come around. I promise. There's stuff I have to explain to you—stuff that'll make you understand a little better—but not here. After Arianna's tucked into bed, we'll sit and talk, okay?"

She'd nibbled on her bottom lip while he talked, and it took everything in him not to reach up and rescue the plump, abused flesh. He was relieved when she nodded. "Okay."

Releasing her hand and relaxing back in his seat, Shane caught Betty Lou's eye and signaled for her to put the check on his account. He then tossed money for a tip onto the table, knowing full well the owner would give it to the busboy who was working his ass off. Sliding out of the booth, he glanced around the large room before looking back at Paige. "Give me a minute to round up Arianna and Tuck, and then we'll be on our way."

Five minutes later, Shane realized his words had been easier said than done as he escorted Paige and Arianna to the door, leaving Tuck behind. The bastard had decided to stay with their ranch hands for another hour or so, drinking. The night could only go one way from there—downhill. Tuck usually didn't drink anything besides the occasional beer, but he knocked back his second shot of whiskey in front of Shane and then ordered a third. Any other time, Shane would have dragged Tuck's ass out of there and taken their daughter and argument home, but with Paige there, he figured it would do more harm than good. Seth promised he'd get Tuck home in one piece, albeit a little drunk, and Shane had taken him at his word. He'd deal with his husband later. For now, he had to get Arianna home to bed and explain a few things to Paige.

Shane didn't know where Tuck's jealousy was coming from. Yeah, Paige was pretty—very pretty—but he hadn't been hitting on her. He'd told Tuck the truth —he'd just been trying to put her at ease in her new environment. Arianna was already comfortable with Paige, and Shane didn't know where the hell they'd find another house manager if this one didn't work out. The last thing he wanted was for Tuck's folks to cut their time in Arizona short and return to Kansas weeks before they were scheduled to for the summer, as they'd offered. Shane loved his in-laws—they were great people—but they were retired now. They didn't need to be running after a six-year-old and everything else that went into taking care of the huge house. As much as the older couple loved their children, son-in-law, and granddaughter, they also enjoyed their time in Arizona with plenty to do and people their own age.

After tucking Arianna into bed and reading her a story, Shane closed her bedroom door and went to find Paige. She was sitting on the couch in the family room with an e-reader in her hand, but her gaze was focused on the TV's blank screen. She lifted her chin when she heard him enter the room.

Striding over to the bookcases, he reached up and found the key that was hidden from Arianna. Unlocking the built-in bar, he opened the drop-down door. "Would you like a little something to drink?"

"Um . . ."

He glanced over his shoulder and held up an empty, lowball glass. "It's not a big deal to have an off-duty drink, Paige. I'm going to have one. You're more than welcome to join me."

"Thank you. If you have something light, please."

There wasn't much in terms of "light," but he pulled out a bottle from the back. "I've got Bailey's. Is that okay?"

"Yes, that's fine."

After pouring a glass of the creamy liqueur, he put two ounces of his favorite scotch in a glass. Taking both, he handed Paige hers over the back of the couch, then grabbed a small, framed photo from a shelf. Skirting around the couch, he sat in the recliner closest to her. A sigh escaped him as he studied the photograph before showing it to Paige. "You might have noticed there are a lot of pictures of Arianna's mother, Sarah."

"I did. Arianna told me she passed away."

"Yeah, she did—two years ago." He inhaled deeply, then let it out slowly, his gaze not meeting hers. "She wasn't just Arianna's mother, Paige. She was my wife." He paused for a heartbeat or two. "She was also Tucker's wife. We had a ménage marriage."

Silence filled the room, and a few moments passed before he finally risked looking at her. Her eyes were wide, her mouth in an "O," but there was no condemnation there, just surprise. Well, at least she hadn't run from the room screaming. He took a sip of scotch and then forged ahead. "I've known since I was a teenager that I liked both men and women. When Tuck and I fell for Sarah after she moved here to teach at the elementary school, we fell for each other too. It may go against the norms of society, but for us, it felt right. I know I'm throwing a heap of personal stuff at you here, but you have a right to know—especially since the whole town knows already. Some people ridiculed us—still do—but many were supportive after they got over the shock. Hannah had no problems working for us, but I'm sure some curious people will want to know if we're having a relationship with our new house manager, who's closer to our age. How you handle that is up to you, as long as Arianna isn't swept into it. We'll do our best to discourage any false rumors. If it's too much for you, and you don't want to work for us, I'll understand, but I just ask that you give me some warning so I can work on getting a replacement."

Shane didn't know what he'd expected, but it wasn't the loud snort that came from her, followed by a grin and an eye roll. "Please—if I can handle the press and all my former friends and neighbors pointing fingers at me in California, I can handle small-town gossip. Been there, done that, got the T-shirt."

"You're not put off by the ménage?"

She shrugged her shoulders. "Why should I be? There are a lot of kinky things people are into out on the West Coast—a ménage marriage with all three people in love with each other is on the tamer side. So, to answer your question, no, I'm not put off by it. Have I ever known anyone in a ménage relationship before? No. Do I think there's anything wrong with it between consenting adults? Again, no. In fact, I give your Sarah a lot of credit. She bucked the norms of society and followed her heart. Many women don't have the guts to do that, even in this day and age."

Sagging back into his chair, Shane breathed a sigh of relief. "Thank God. I was afraid you'd be freaked out by it, and I'd have to find another house manager."

"Not at all. But now the skinny-dipping title makes a lot more sense." Shane chuckled along with her, then Paige tilted her head. "I do have a question, though."

He raised an eyebrow at her.

"What does Tucker have against me?"

That was the question of the hour. Shane grimaced.

"For some reason, he misinterpreted me being nice to you as me flirting with you. I've never given him or Sarah a reason to think I'd cheat on them, so I'm not sure where it's coming from. I will say that Tuck doesn't do well with any change in the status quo—at least, not right away. It takes him a little while to come to terms with it. Will you give him some time?"

"Absolutely. But, please, tell me if I'm causing any problems between you, and I'll let him know, in no uncertain terms, that I'm not interested in either of you."

His smile almost faltered, but Shane managed to keep it in place. Now, why were her words so disappointing? He'd only known her a few hours. "I don't think it'll come to that, but I'll keep you in the loop."

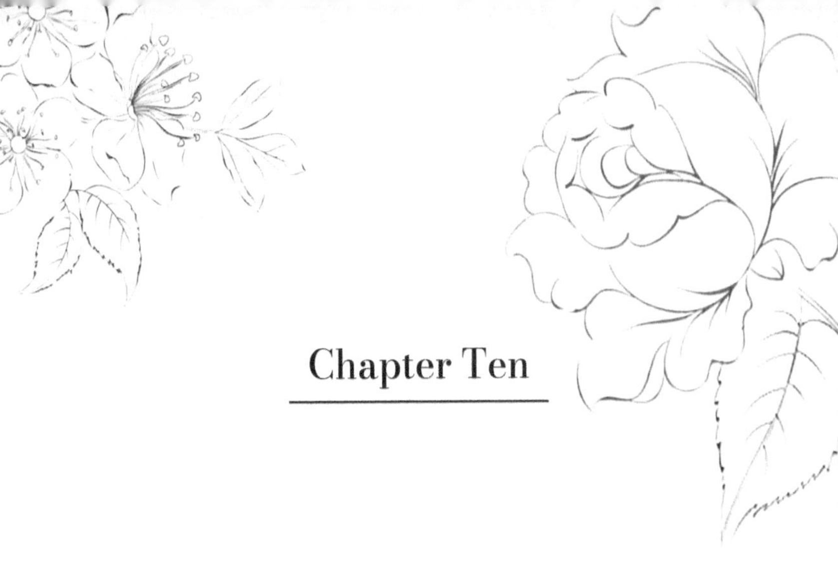

Chapter Ten

Tuck was convinced his head exploding wouldn't hurt as much as it did now. It throbbed relentlessly, reminding him why he didn't get drunk often.

"If you think I'm covering for you because you just *had* to tie one on last night, think again."

Tuck groaned as each of Shane's words stabbed him in the temples. Not answering, he pulled his pillow over his head and tried to remember how many shots he'd had. Vague recollections of the ranch hands dragging his sorry ass to Seth's truck and then the ride home flashed through his head. Hadn't they stopped at least once so he could puke on the side of the road?

Shit. He'd broken a rule Shane's dad had told him to keep when he was first hired as the ranch foreman—never let your employees see you out of control. It was a good way to lose their respect. And if they didn't respect you, they wouldn't respect their jobs. Shit just went downhill from there. Yeah, there were times when Tuck had gone out drinking with his workers before, but he always made sure to switch over to cola or sweet tea before he got too wasted. Even after Sarah died, he'd somehow stayed in control—Shane and Arianna probably had been the cause of that. He was a father, husband, and boss, and always had to remember that.

Sleep was pulling him under again, and he was just about to succumb when a loud clanging filled the room. It vibrated through the pillow and into his skull. "Shut it off," he mumbled when it registered that the racket came from Sarah's old-fashioned-styled alarm clock with its two bells and clapper—unfortunately, it wouldn't stop on its own for a full minute.

"Shut it off yourself."

Agony ripped through him when he pulled his head out from under the pillow and opened his eyes into mere slits. Shane strode out of the room and closed the door behind him, leaving the offensive clock sitting on the dresser—well out of reach. He'd also left on every lamp since their room didn't get the morning sun. *Bastard.*

Kicking off the covers, Tuck sat up too fast and immediately regretted it as the room spun viciously. "Uuuuuggghhh."

His eyes slammed shut as his stomach threatened to revolt, and he dropped his head into his hands. When he thought he could stand without the floor coming out from under his feet, he trudged over to the alarm and silenced it, but the noise still echoed through his brain. Using pieces of furniture and the door jamb to steady himself, he made it into the bathroom. After relieving himself, he turned on the faucet, washed his hands, and then cupped them. Gulping water, he tried to saturate his parched tongue and throat but had to slow down when it almost came back up.

He didn't even recognize himself when he caught his reflection in the mirror. His eyes were bloodshot, his hair in disarray, and his skin paler than he ever remembered it being. Death warmed over was an understatement. As much as he wanted to crawl back into bed for the rest of the day, he couldn't. If any of the ranch hands called in sick due to overindulgence, he'd give them a ton of shit, so he had to practice what he preached.

Returning to the bedroom, he checked the time on the alarm clock. If he skipped breakfast—which wouldn't be a hardship with how his stomach felt—he could go back to sleep for an hour before heading out to work. Not even bothering to shut off the lamps, Tuck tumbled back into bed and buried his head under his pillow again.

Almost an hour later, he reached into the shower and turned on the water, happy in the knowledge that they had a backup water heater. Shane couldn't have let it go cold on purpose. It would have taken him running a shower or faucet for well over thirty minutes to do so, and that would have also left Paige without hot water.

Once he was finally dressed, Tuck strode into the kitchen, much cleaner but in no less pain. Shane spared him a brief, annoyed glance before sipping his coffee and returning his attention to yesterday's local newspaper. Since it wasn't delivered until after they started their workday, he was often a day behind.

The smell of the coffee had Tuck's stomach roiling again, and he turned away from the half-full carafe on the counter. His gaze caught sight of several bottles lined up on the table—acetaminophen, water, and Gatorade. Next to them sat several individually wrapped hard candies.

"Paige left them for you," Shane said, not bothering to look at him. "If it were up to me, I would've hidden it all. The candies apparently have ginger in them—she said they'll help your stomach."

Tuck reached for the painkillers and water. "You told her I was hungover?"

"Nope. She figured it out for herself after you woke her up with your lousy singing while trying to open the bar with your car key. By the way, you get to tell Drake why the beautiful cabinets and shelves he spent weeks making by hand have deep scratches in them."

"Shit." He dumped three pills into his hand, then threw them into his mouth, washing them down with the water. He'd been singing? His aching brain scrambled to remember, but the last thing he could recall was puking on the side of the road. Yeah, now that *that* image filtered back into his mind, he remembered Seth had pulled over just in time. *Wonderful.*

"Uh-huh. He's going to be pissed, to put it mildly, and I'm throwing your fine ass under the bus for this one." Drake Hadley was one of Shane's oldest and best friends ever since they'd met in the first grade. He was an incredible artist when it came to turning plain planks of wood into masterpieces. "Just be grateful our daughter sleeps like the dead—she didn't hear the commotion you made." Shane stood and dumped the last of his coffee into the sink. Grabbing his straw cowboy hat from the coat rack by the backdoor, he set it on his head, then walked out of the house without a backward glance. Yup, he still had a burr in his saddle.

Tuck's empty stomach growled. Hopefully, some toast would stay down. He opened the bag of bread that was sitting on the counter and popped two pieces into the toaster. It was then he noticed a paper towel-covered plate. Lifting the edge of the towel, he thanked the gods above. *Bacon. Greasy, delicious bacon.* One of the best cures for a hangover, second only to a little hair of the dog, in his opinion. There was no way there'd been bacon left over if it'd been on the dining room table for the ranch hands—there was rarely any food left after they finished—so Paige must have set some aside for him. Shane definitely wouldn't have done it, as angry as he was.

Stuffing a full strip of bacon into his mouth, Tuck stepped over to the refrigerator and found the butter. Within minutes, he had a bacon and butter sandwich on toast, with two more pieces of bread being browned for another.

The front door opened, and Paige strolled into the room seconds later. Dressed in a comfortable red T-shirt, jeans, and well-worn boots, she looked like she'd fit right in with the rest of the residents of Hazard Falls. Hadn't Shane said she was from a rich area of California? She sure didn't dress like some high-society gal. If she was pissed he'd woken her up last night, it didn't show.

She smiled when she saw him. "Hi. Glad you found the bacon—one of the best things for a hangover. Can I get you anything else?"

"Um, no. Thanks. Did Arianna get on the bus okay?" Their daughter always took the bus to school, but for the past few weeks, since Hannah had left, Tuck's sister dropped her off in the afternoon, making sure at least one of the two dads was home. Sometimes, they got sidetracked, and emergencies popped up, and they didn't want Arianna to get off the bus and not have someone waiting. Now, with Paige there, she could ride home with her friends again.

Turning on the faucet, she started washing the dishes piled in the sink. "Yes, she did. I'll be there when the bus drops her off at ten to three."

"Good." After putting together his second sandwich, he tossed the butter back into the fridge. Grabbing the rest of his breakfast, including the bottle of Gatorade she'd left out for him, he took his hat from the hook by the door. "Thanks for leaving out all the hangover remedies. I'm . . . uh . . . sorry I woke you up last night."

She gifted him a brilliant smile as she rinsed a large

ceramic bowl. "No worries—I hope it all helps. And I wasn't really asleep when you got home—I was into a good book and was still reading."

"Still, I apologize. I'm not normally like that. I'm sure it was a shock on your first night here."

Her shoulders went up in a quick shrug. "Stuff happens. Again, no worries. Just remember to drink lots of water and Gatorade today."

Tuck nodded. "I will." When she didn't respond further, and he couldn't think of anything else to say, he opened the door and walked out onto the porch, squinting when the morning sun hit him in the eyes. Muttering a curse, he gently dragged a hand through the long strands of his hair, placed the hat on his head, and then got ready to start the work day.

Chapter Eleven

Paige had just finished drying her hands when there was a knock at the backdoor. Through the window, she saw Nicole Mathers standing on the porch, waving at her. Smiling, Paige opened the door. "Hi, Nicole."

"Hi, Paige. I usually just walk in, but I didn't want to scare the hell out of you again." She held up a thermos. "Just came to fill up. I hope the boys left me some coffee."

"Shane said you might be in, so I checked the urn—there's enough left."

There was a large electric percolator on a sideboard in the dining room, and Nicole stepped into the room to fill her container. She raised her voice, so she could still be heard. "Are you all settled in?"

Paige leaned against the door jamb. "Yeah, I didn't bring much with me since I'm here on a trial basis. If

I'm still here next week, I'll have the rest of my stuff shipped."

"My husband said you were from California. If you don't mind me asking, what made you leave there to come hang out in Hazard Falls, Kansas?"

Well, she did, but Nicole was probably just being small-town inquisitive. It came with the territory. From their brief conversation yesterday, though, Paige thought she might have found an ally and possibly a friend in the woman. Time would tell. For now, she'd keep things simple and vague.

"I'm starting over after a failed marriage. I grew up in a small town in Nebraska, but there's nothing left for me there. A friend of mine is Shane's cousin and recommended me for the job, so here I am. Did you grow up in Hazard Falls?" she asked, switching the focus of the conversation away from herself.

"Yup. I was three years younger than Shane in school. My dad and older brother are the local veterinarians, and my mom owns the hair salon in town. I took two years of business school before getting pregnant by my high-school sweetheart." She shrugged and then recapped the thermos. "Hank and I are still together, though, and love each other more than we did back then."

"Oh, so you have more kids than Joey?"

"Mm-hmm. She's our baby. We have three—Cody's the oldest, then there's Kyle and Joey—the first and last were total surprises. I'd gotten my tubes tied after we had Kyle. My GYN said she'd done hundreds of them, and mine was the first to fail. Go figure. Anyway, Joey's our miracle girl, and she's got her dad and brothers wrapped around her little finger."

Paige grinned. "Sounds like Arianna."

"Oh, yeah, she's another one. Those two are going to be hell-raisers someday. God help us all." Nicole gestured toward the kitchen behind Paige. "C'mon— Shane asked me to show you around a bit more since you haven't had the grand tour yet. He's out with the hands fixing the fence in the west pasture before the herd has to be moved there. We'll start with the office in the small cottage next to the horse barn."

A half-hour later, after Paige had been introduced to the other two office staff members, Clark Gibson and MaryEllen Stokes, she'd gotten a tour of some of the buildings surrounding the compound. As she and Nicole strolled back toward the main house, Paige blurted out the question she'd been trying to get up the nerve to ask. "Did you know Shane and Tucker's wife well?"

"*Phew.*" Exaggeratingly, Nicole wiped her brow. "I wasn't sure if they'd dropped that little bomb on you yet after you said they were a gay couple yesterday."

"Shane told me last night. He figured I'd hear about it sooner rather than later. I was a little surprised Quinn hadn't told me since it doesn't seem like it's a big secret or anything."

"Well, it's not exactly something you come across every day . . ." She gave Paige a lopsided smile. ". . . unless you read ménage romance like I do."

Paige chuckled. "Actually, I do. I'll read practically anything in the romance genre."

"Oh, good! Another bookie to compare notes with. MaryEllen and I are in a book club on Tuesday nights if you want to join us. There are currently eight of us. We just get together with some wine and munchies and chat about our favorites. Last week, we read Kristen Anders's new book, and this week, we're reading Avery Gale's new ménage. Have you read any of hers yet?"

"Love her! And Kristen Anders! I'd love to join your book club. I was in one in California." She didn't add that she'd dropped out after her husband's arrest—three of the women in the group had been among his victims.

"Great. Everyone will love having new input. Getting back to Sarah, though, she was one of my best friends. She was a sweetheart and a strong woman to boot. She had to be with Shane and Tuck. They can be overprotective at times. When they first went public with their relationship, you can imagine the talk. Mind you, I'm not telling you anything that's not common knowledge. The older folks did the traditional eyebrow raising and the sign of the cross . . ." She acted out her words. ". . . that go with everything they disapprove of. As for the rest, I think most of the gossiping women were more jealous than appalled, and the men . . . well, some jerks thought since she was involved with two men, she was a slut and easy. Then they either got their asses kicked by Shane or Tuck, or they got their balls kicked by Sarah—she didn't take crap from anyone. In fact, I think she was surprised more than most when she ended up in a ménage relationship.

"When they first got involved, Shane and Tuck weren't . . . um, together together, if you get my drift. While everyone knew Shane didn't discriminate when it came to sex—either gender was fine with him—Tuck had been straight 'til then." She shrugged. "Somewhere along the line, though, their relationship changed, but I think it was kept under wraps for a while until Tuck was more comfortable with it. He took Sarah's death harder than anyone. He's the quieter one, while Shane rarely lets anything get him down. Don't get me wrong —Shane was heartbroken, but he bounces back from whatever life throws at him better than Tuck does. If it weren't for Shane and Arianna, I think Tuck would be a hermit by now. They're the only reason he really smiles anymore."

Paige knew all about not wanting to smile anymore. While she hated what Myles had become—a swindler —he'd always been good to her, and she mourned not only his death but the end of their marriage.

"Well, here we are." Nicole stopped at the bottom of the stairs leading to the main house's back porch. "I've got to get back to work. The lunch wagon usually arrives at eleven-forty-five and lets us get our food before heading out to wherever the hands are. Come over and eat with us. Hannah used to do it all the time."

Shane had told Paige that since many of her duties would occur during the early morning, late afternoon, and evening when Arianna was home, she could take some time to herself during the day. Her pay was based on eight-hour days, so as long as she didn't lounge around all morning, she was free to make her own schedule. "That sounds great. I'll see you then."

With a wave to Nicole, Paige turned to go inside. As she climbed the stairs to the back porch, the kitchen door opened. Seth stepped out, and his eyes lit up when he saw her. "Just the person I was looking for. I'm heading into town for a few things and wanted to see if you needed anything."

"Actually, I made a grocery list last night after going through the pantry and fridge. I was going to drive into town myself—Shane gave me the keys to the SUV."

"I'll drive you if you want. I can show you where everything is for next time."

Considering she could barely remember how to get to the small town from the ranch—she planned to use the GPS on her phone—this was probably a better idea. She'd only seen the route from the school and the restaurant, which had been on the edge of town closest to the ranch. "That sounds great, as long as it's not too much trouble."

He held the door open for her. "No trouble at all. I can drop you off at the grocery store, run my errands, then pick you up again."

"Great." She entered the kitchen with him on her heels. "Let me just grab my purse."

"I'll meet you out front."

After pointing out several shops and businesses he thought she'd be interested in, Seth dropped Paige off at the bank across the street from the Stop & Go store. They didn't have a branch of the bank she'd used in California, so she needed to open an account here and deposit a $100 check for now so she had it for her first paycheck. If she stayed on after her trial run, she'd transfer the rest of her meager account over to the new one. Thankfully, the courts had let her keep the small inheritance she received after her father passed away while they'd frozen everything else.

"Hello, may I help you?"

Paige smiled at the older man who'd approached her after she'd walked into the bank. "Yes, hi. I need to open up a checking account."

"Well, then, you've come to the right place." He held out his hand. "I'm Willard Knutt. You must be new in town."

She shook his hand, then moved to the chair he indicated in front of a nearby desk. "Yes. I'm Paige Merritt. I just started working at the Red River Ranch.

"Oh."

Paige wasn't sure how that one word, or the fact he'd raised his eyebrows, should be taken. Her eyes narrowed. "Is there a problem?"

The man shook his head and pasted on a forced smile. "Uh . . . no, not at all." He opened a drawer and pulled out a piece of paper. "Just fill out this form. Then I'll need some ID and a deposit, and we'll get you all set up."

"Thank you." Paige coolly took the paper from him. She got the feeling this was one of the people who thought the owners of Red River were perverts. "Do you have a pen, please?"

"Oh, yes." He plucked one from a pen holder on his desk and handed it to her. "Sorry."

Paige began to fill out the form but realized she didn't know the address to Red River. Instead of asking the man in front of her, who suddenly appeared to want to be anywhere but where he was, she pulled out her phone and opened the internet browser. A quick Google search gave her the information she needed. After filling out all the boxes on the form, she handed it back, along with her license and a check.

Knutt swiveled his seat around to face the desk computer. A few minutes of silence passed as he entered her information. Paige glanced around. It didn't appear the bank had been updated, decor-wise, since the 1980s—typical of small towns. Many residents could be averse to change. In the big cities, though, if you didn't keep up with the times, your business would almost certainly go down the tubes.

"You're all set, Ms. Merritt. Here are some starter checks. And here are the designs you can choose from for us to order for you."

Paige picked out ones with hummingbirds on them, then opted for the script font for her name and address. Once done, she stood and put her license and new checks in her purse. "Thank you, Mr. Knutt."

She sighed when the sunshine hit her face after exiting the bank. It seemed she'd traded one stigma for another. One was the wife of a criminal who'd swindled their friends, and the other was working for a bisexual couple who'd been in a ménage marriage that only ended after their wife died. A sudden thought occurred to her. Had Willard Knutt assumed she was in a sexual relationship with Shane and Tucker? While the thought didn't disgust her, in fact, it intrigued her, she wasn't ready for a new relationship, especially not with her two new bosses, no matter how good-looking they both were. Nope. She was here to do a job, which meant she had shopping to do. Pushing aside all her wayward thoughts, she headed for the Stop & Go.

Chapter Twelve

After Tuck and the hands left to start their workday, Shane strode into the kitchen and dumped his coffee into the sink. Paige was wiping down the small dinette table that was rarely used for anything other than Arianna's homework and some food preparation. Her back was to him, and he couldn't stop his gaze from finding her ass as she bent over to reach the other side of the table. Damn, she filled out those jeans to perfection. He'd always been an ass man—men or women—and Paige had a mighty fine one.

When she straightened again, he'd barely had the chance to lift his eyes before she turned around. "Hi. Everything okay?"

"Yeah. Everything's fine—in fact, it's been great." A full week had passed, and there hadn't been one hiccup with her working for them. Well, there had been, but as far as he knew, she wasn't aware of it yet. A few of the ranch hands had told him the rumors of Shane and Tuck's new house manager sharing their bed had already started making the rounds. He wouldn't mind if the rumors were true—she was an attractive and nice woman—but it certainly hadn't happened. He hoped she wouldn't be too upset or offended when she got wind of them. "Tuck and I talked it over last night, and we'd like you to stay on with us if you want." Actually, he'd talked, and Tuck had grunted his non-committal response.

Paige's eyes widened a little, and he wondered if she thought they would let her go. Hell, no. It hadn't taken her long to whip the house back into shape, Arianna loved her, and well, Shane liked her—really liked her. The problem was that he couldn't do anything about his attraction to her unless Tuck was on board. He never cheated on anyone he'd been in a relationship with since he was a teen. His father had had numerous affairs during his marriage to Shane's mother—that was public knowledge—and his only son never wanted to follow in his footsteps. Shane had seen the light leave his mother's eyes every time she discovered another one of her husband's indiscretions, and he never wanted to do something that would result in someone he loved losing that light too. So, unless Tuck got his head out of his ass, seducing Paige was out of the question for Shane. That didn't mean he couldn't help things along at some point after Paige had settled in more and Tuck began to relax around her.

"Really? Um, yes, I'd love to stay on. Thank you."

He wouldn't tell her that the smile on her face right now was all the thanks he needed. "Great. Do you need any help arranging for your things to be shipped here?"

"Thanks, but no, I don't. Quinn said he'd take care of it once I knew if I was staying. His friend's trucking company has routes that run not far from here, and he'll arrange to get the boxes to me. There's not a lot of them."

Snorting, Shane grinned. "My cousin has more contacts than anyone else I know. If he doesn't know someone who can get something done, then I'm convinced no one does."

"I guess it comes in handy when helping people start their lives over."

The sadness that came over her face caused his gut to clench. Aside from their conversation on the day he picked her up at the airport, they hadn't spoken about her past again. "I'm sorry you had to go through that. It must've been hard."

Paige shrugged, stepped around him, and then turned on the faucet to start washing the dishes. Without thinking, he snatched a towel from the oven handle and began to dry for her. "I think what hurt the most, besides the betrayal I felt from Myles, was realizing all the so-called friends I thought I had turned their backs on me as if I was the one who'd done something wrong. Only a few stood by me. The money wasn't a big thing to me—I'd grown up in a simple family where extras had to be saved up for. After the government seized most of our assets, I realized that all those *things* I'd gotten used to hadn't been the reason for my happiness. Owning my interior design business and having a husband who loved me were the things that made me happy. Everything else had just been window dressing. Then, the only two things that meant anything to me were gone, and I realized all those people who dropped me like a hot potato had only liked me because of the money. I'd rather be poor and be with people who like me for me, not what they can get from me, than to be rich with false friendships."

"You're amazing." Shit, had he really said that out loud? When she lifted her confused gaze to his, he knew he had. "I mean, a lot of people would have let all that beat them down or would have screamed they were a victim too, trying to garner sympathy. Hell, many people would have turned a blind eye in the first place and prayed their moneymaker didn't get caught."

"I couldn't do that." She shook her head. "When I accidentally saw the books Myles had left on his desk one night when he ran out to meet someone, I knew exactly what I was looking at. They weren't the dummy ones he'd apparently been showing the IRS. At first, I was in shock and couldn't believe my husband was bilking people—our friends—out of millions of dollars. I talked to him the next day, trying to ask him questions about the investments without raising his suspicions, but his answers just made me realize it wasn't something that had simply gotten out of hand. I'd never noticed how greedy he'd gotten—nothing else mattered beyond how to look better than the Joneses.

It took me a few days to realize I had no choice but to turn him in, even if it meant my life as I'd known it—my marriage—was over. As much as I loved Myles, I couldn't be a party to his crimes. Now, I have to start fresh."

"Well, I'm glad you'll be doing that here. Arianna has fallen in love with you."

Paige grinned as she handed him a glass, and he tried to ignore the stirring in his groin. "The feeling is mutual."

When she pulled the plug at the bottom of the sink, he realized the dishes had all been cleaned. Time had flown while talking to her. After helping her put away the dishes, utensils, and glasses, he glanced around and failed to see anything that could keep him there. He really did need to get to work. Plucking his hat from the rack by the door, an idea came to him. "You know, Paige, if your interior decorator eye sees anything that could be done to spruce the place up a bit, feel free to change a few things."

"I wouldn't want to change anything Sarah did."

He set the hat on his head. "Sometimes change can be good. Nothing's been updated in over two years. If you're afraid to do things you don't think we'll like, make a list. We'll go over it and see what we agree on, okay?"

Her smile told him she did have a few ideas for the house. "Um, okay. Yeah, that'd be great. I'll look around later and see what I can come up with."

"Great. Welcome to the Red River family, Paige."

Chapter Thirteen

Not able to sleep, Paige pulled on a pair of sweatpants and a matching hoodie, before sticking her feet into her slip-on sneakers. During the last three weeks working at the Red River Ranch, she'd had numerous nights where slumber just wouldn't come easily. Tonight, it was due to her phone conversation with Quinn earlier. He hadn't wanted her to hear it from anyone else, but someone had vandalized the house she and Myles had lived in—windows had been smashed and vile words had been spray-painted on the front door, vinyl siding, and driveway. Since the security company her husband had contracted was no longer monitoring the property, the surveillance cameras had been off, and there were no known suspects at the time. Since the house would be sold, along with everything in it that Paige hadn't been allowed to take—she'd been able to keep her clothes and other personal items—the only way she was affected was emotionally. Knowing that the home she'd meticulously decorated, inside and out, had been desecrated hurt her, but there was nothing she could do about it. Hell, she didn't even own it anymore.

It was just after nine-thirty p.m., and she hadn't heard Shane get home yet. He'd left for a town commerce meeting after dinner, while Tucker had disappeared into the primary bedroom suite after tucking Arianna into bed. Grabbing her phone and Kindle, Paige shuffled her way to the backdoor and went outside. It was a beautiful evening—cool and crisp—and the moon was out. Instead of sitting on one of the rockers as she'd done on a few nights when she hadn't been able to sleep, she took the steps down and walked around for a bit, trying to clear her mind. Minutes later, she found herself outside the horse barn and took a deep breath. The scent of fresh hay and the musky equines drew her in. It reminded her of summer days hanging out with her high-school girlfriends at the ranches a few of them had grown up on. There had been many happy times spent lounging around in the loft of one barn or another, talking about boys, gossiping, and confessing their dreams.

Opening the pedestrian door, Paige inhaled deeply again. A few horses shifted in their stalls at the sound of someone entering their home. Some nickered, others snorted. Dim, overhead fluorescent lamps gave her enough light to see by, without flooding the expanse. She walked up and down the row of stalls, saying hello to the animals and scratching a few noses.

A gray cat ran past her, giving her a wide berth, and Paige wondered if it had a name. She knew cats were used in barns to keep the mice away. The ranch also had two Australian shepherd/border collie mixes, Waylon and Willie, which slept in one of the two bunk houses—they were working dogs, not pets, that helped to move and keep an eye on the herds.

Paige stopped at the bottom of a ladder that led to the loft. After sticking her phone in her pocket and her Kindle in the back of her waistband, she climbed up the rungs. Yup. Just like the barns of her youth, there were dozens of hay bales up there. A loading door that faced the house was wide open, letting in the comfortable night air. Several bales made a chaise lounge of sorts, and she laid down, pulling out her e-reader. From that position, she could only see the roof of the house and the sky filled with stars above. Within seconds, she was lost in one of her favorite authors' latest release—ironically, it was another ménage. Who would've thought she'd end up working for people who'd actually lived like the characters in the books she liked to read?

After she'd read a few pages, the pedestrian door opened below, and Shane's voice floated up to her. "C'mon, babe. It's been a while since we made love in here."

Paige froze.

"Shane . . ."

"What, Tuck? I want you somewhere other than our bedroom tonight. With Paige here now, screwing in the kitchen or family room, after Ari goes to bed, is off limits again."

Paige's eyes widened. *Holy shit!* Should she make her presence known? They'd know she'd overheard them and would probably be embarrassed. They couldn't have known she was there. In fact, she hadn't heard Shane's truck arrive and park on the other side of the house. Maybe if she was quiet, they'd never figure out she was above them. After they were gone, she'd sneak back into the house and pretend like nothing had happened.

Something was happening, though. Definitely happening. She tried to ignore the moans and soft murmurs coming from below. The shuffling of boots on the wood floor. The whisper of clothes being removed. The sounds of the two men kissing . . . the two drop-dead gorgeous men kissing. It was impossible—there was no way she could ignore any of it.

Biting her lip, Paige rolled to her side as quietly as she could. She set her Kindle on the hay, then turned the volume off on her phone before putting it down as well. It was doubtful anyone would be calling her at this hour, but she did have the notification settings on for several apps.

Just a peek. She wouldn't watch them. She'd just take a quick peek. It wasn't as if she'd never seen two men kiss before—she'd lived in California after all, and people were very comfortable with their public displays of affection there, gay or straight—but she'd never seen *these* two men kiss.

Easing up onto her knees, she stayed close to the hay bale that was hiding her from view and peeked around it and down. Shane's back was to her. He had Tucker pinned to the door of a closed stall, their hands clasped together above Tucker's head as they made out. Both men's shirts were off and tossed onto a nearby barrel.

Releasing his husband's hands, Shane took a small step backward. He made quick work of his belt and fly before pushing his jeans down just enough to give Paige a gander at his glorious ass. With his jeans around his mid-thighs, he switched places with Tucker, giving her a second stunning view. The man was hung. "Get on your knees and blow me."

Paige's panties dampened at the throaty command as she watched Tucker drop to his knees and take the thick cock into his mouth without hesitation. Shane's eyes slammed shut, and he leaned back against the door. "Fuck, yeah. Take it all." His hand delved into his husband's long, brown hair and guided him to the pace he wanted. One of Tucker's hands gripped Shane's hip, while the other toyed with the heavy balls hanging below the cock he was enjoying.

"God, babe, I'll never get tired of your mouth. Yeah . . . shit, yeah, do that again. Suck harder. I could fuck your mouth all night."

Clearly, Shane was very vocal during sex. He grabbed the hand at his hip and brought it to his mouth, spitting on the fingers. "Fuck my ass. Let me feel what it's going to be like having your cock balls-deep inside me."

Holy shit! Holy shit! Holy shit! This was the hottest thing Paige had ever seen in her life. She knew she should sit back down behind the bale and let them have their private moment, but she couldn't tear her eyes away. Her heart pounded as her nipples hardened. Her clit throbbed as Tucker's hand disappeared between Shane's legs. Letting her own hand drop, she rubbed herself through her sweatpants. She bit her bottom lip, trying not to gasp, moan, or pant.

"Oh, yeah. More . . . fuck me, Tuck. Fuck me hard. Make me come. I want you to swallow every drop I give you."

Tucker's head bobbed up and down while his hands and mouth gave his husband pleasure.

"Oh, shit! Yeah, that's it! Shiiiiiiii—" Shane's body went rigid as the orgasm hit him. As instructed, Tucker swallowed it all. His head slowed as Shane's fell forward. Holding out his hand, Shane helped the other man stand, then clutching his jeans to keep them from falling past his knees, he took a few steps before bending over two stacked bales of hay. Positioning himself behind Shane, Tucker shoved his sweatpants down to his knees. He spit on his fingers and then worked them into Shane's ass again.

"I don't want your fingers. Give me your cock. Fuck me like you mean it, babe."

For the first time since he'd spoken Shane's name after they'd first come into the barn, Tucker growled and then said, "I always fuck you like I mean it. I love you."

"Love you too. Now show me. Fuck me with that beautiful cock I love having up my ass."

Pulling his fingers back, Tucker lined his shaft up with Shane's asshole and eased forward, as he used more spit for lubrication. Shane reached for the other side of the bale and stabilized himself as Tucker fucked him. Paige's gaze was glued to where the two men were joined. It was mesmerizing watching Tucker's cock plunge in and out. Unable to help herself, Paige shoved her hand down her sweatpants, where she was soaking wet. Running her fingers over her labia, she curved them inward.

"Yeah, babe. Harder. Fuck me harder. Damn!"

The sound of flesh slapping against flesh filled the air, combining with the two men's moans and gasps.

"So tight. Fuck, Shane!"

"That's right. Only for you to fuck. Tight only for you. Give it to me, babe. I want your thick cock. I want it all."

Tucker's hips rocked faster, and Paige's fingers set the same pace as she finger fucked herself. She felt an orgasm building. Her gaze never left the scene below her.

"Oh, shit! Shane, I'm—"

"Come in my ass! Now!"

Tucker roared as he plunged in deeply, then held himself there. Paige silently slapped her hand over her mouth to keep her own climax to herself. Her release coated her fingers as her legs shook. She forced her lungs to draw in air through her nose. Her brain fogged over. Slowly and as quietly as she could, she lay down in her hiding spot, reveling in the afterglow. Below, Shane and Tucker both recovered, gulping for air and murmuring to each other. Moments later, she listened as they got dressed, then shuffled across the floor to the door. It opened, then closed again. Silence returned to the barn, interrupted only by soft noises coming from the horses.

Paige took several deep, cleansing breaths for the first time since the two men had walked in. "Damn, that was hot," she whispered to herself.

Picking up her e-reader and phone, she rolled to a sitting position and froze. The door below opened again, and someone took two boot-covered steps inside and then stopped. Paige's heart thumped in her chest. Who was down there now?

Shane's voice was loud and clear. "Have a good night, Paige."

Two footsteps, and then the door clicked shut.

Holy shit!

Chapter Fourteen

Instead of signing the payroll, Shane leaned back in his office chair and twirled a pen through his fingers. His mind replayed last night in the barn. After arriving home from the commerce meeting, he'd gone into the kitchen to see if any cookies were left. Paige and Arianna had baked them after school. He'd just taken one bite when movement out back caught his eye. Paige had stopped next to the horse barn, and even with the distance between them, he could see her take a deep breath. In her hand had been her e-reader. He'd watched as she disappeared into the barn and then waited for her to come back out. Moments passed before he saw a flash of light through the open loading door to the loft and realized it was from her e-reader. She'd made herself comfortable up there to read.

Behind him, Tuck had shuffled into the kitchen. "Hey."

Shane had glanced over his shoulder and saw his

husband frowning at the plate of cookies. Wearing a T-shirt and sweatpants, the man was as hot in those as he was shirtless in tight jeans. Shane had figured out what was going through Tuck's mind lately—having a pretty woman their own age living with them reminded him of all the little things Sarah had done to make their house a home—like baking fresh cookies. Paige was slowly making a few changes to freshen up the place—new throw pillows, scatter rugs, and placemats had appeared without warning after Shane had approved her list of things she wanted to update. She'd also reorganized most of the rooms, so they were back to being as neat as when Sarah had been alive. Without a doubt, Shane missed their wife—a lot—but he'd made her a promise to live his life to the fullest, and he wasn't going to let her down. He just had to figure out a way to help Tuck move on too, and, damn it, Shane wanted Paige to be the one to help him do it.

An idea had suddenly come to him. He'd overheard Paige and Nicole talking one day about a new book that'd come out. A ménage romance. His longtime employee and Sarah used to joke about the books, with Nicole wanting Sarah to compare real life to the fictional ones they read about. Shane should have known Paige had read some ménage romance books because while she'd been a little stunned when he'd explained about his marriage, it hadn't looked like a new concept to her.

"Hey, put your boots on and come with me," he'd ordered.

Tuck's frown had increased. "Where?"

"Just put your damn boots on and c'mon."

Following a few seconds of hesitation, Tuck had finally stepped over to where his boots sat by the back-door and slid his sock-covered feet in. After closing the door softly behind them, Shane had led him across the dirt expanse to the horse barn in silence, his cock lengthening in his jeans, anticipating what he'd been about to do—what he'd been about to instigate. Knowing Paige was listening, perhaps even watching, had made the whole thing hotter than hell. Shane's orgasm had been more explosive than he could remember it being as of late, and that was saying a lot because fucking his husband's mouth was second only to fucking his ass.

Tuck would be pissed if *he* knew *Shane* knew Paige had been in the loft above them, but if Shane's plan went well, the man wouldn't find out. Once he got Tuck on board with seducing Paige, maybe then he'd tell him, but for now, his mind fast-forwarded to this morning. He wasn't sure if anyone else had been aware Paige couldn't look either of her employers in the eye or had seen the blush that stained her cheeks. Not wanting to push her, Shane had resisted teasing her in a manner only she would have understood.

"Jamie to base. Shane, you there?"

Standing, he stepped over to the bookshelf where the ranch's base radio unit sat. Several cellular dead spots were scattered about the ranch, so they had this as a backup. Shane picked up the transmitter. "What's up, Jamie?"

"Need you to head out here with the truck. Tuck's horse spooked at a rattler and tossed him, then came down on his ankle. It's gonna need to be X-rayed, and he's in too much pain to ride back."

Shane could hear his husband cursing in the background. Tuck had a high pain tolerance, working through it more often than not. If he couldn't ride, it had to be bad. *Shit.* "I'm on my way. Give him a fucking bullet to bite on."

Jamie had already been laughing when he hit the transmit button again. "Yeah, you just got not one but two middle fingers. See you in a few."

Snatching his hat from where he'd tossed it on the room's loveseat, Shane set it on his head, then collected his keys, wallet, and cell phone from the desk. He almost ran over Paige as he hurried out into the hall and grasped her arms to keep her from falling backward. "Shit, sorry, Paige."

"No worries. Is something wrong?"

"Yeah, sounds like Tuck might have a busted ankle. Got thrown from his horse, then got stepped on."

Her eyes widened. "Oh, no! Do—do you need help? I could go with you."

Smiling, he shook his head. "Nope. I'm not going to subject you to his foul mouth right now. I'm taking the truck out to get him. Jamie and I can get him in it without a problem. The closest X-ray machine is about twenty minutes away. I'll call you as soon as I know what the verdict is. Do me a favor, though. Don't mention it to Arianna. She gets spooked at the mere mention of a doctor unless it's for her own checkups. I guess she still remembers all of Sarah's appointments and hospital stays, even though she was only four, almost five, at the time."

"Okay," she said while nodding. "I'll just tell her you had to go out on business or something. But call me if you need me."

"Count on it." He couldn't stop the wink he gave her, and despite his worry about Tuck, he was thrilled to see her blush.

Ten minutes later, he parked a few feet from where Tuck was lying on the ground and climbed out of the driver's seat. Tuck's face was contorted in pain, and he was still cursing. "About goddamn time. Get me up."

"Think it's broken?" Shane asked, squatting down to look at his husband's foot. They'd wisely left the boot on, keeping the swelling in check for now, but the Tony Lama might have to be cut off. Tuck would have a fit if it came to that. They were his favorite pair of work boots—Sarah had given them to him on their last Christmas together.

"I'll be surprised if it isn't."

"Is Rowdy okay?" Shane glanced at Tuck's horse, grazing nearby, and then at Jamie Dalton.

"Yeah, he's fine. Once I killed the rattler, he calmed down."

He took a deep breath and let it out. "All right. Let's stabilize Tuck's foot. Then you can help me get him up and into the passenger seat. If he complains, feel free to call him a little girl."

Tuck growled. "Fuck you, Shane."

Shane retrieved a heavy wool blanket he kept in the back for Arianna to use during the winter, then found some rope in the toolbox in the truck bed, directly behind the cab. He held the folded blanket around Tuck's ankle, cushioning it, while Jamie tied it in place. With Shane on one side and Jamie on the other, they put Tuck's arms across their shoulders, then stood as gently as they could, taking him with them.

"Fuuuuccck." He hissed through gritted teeth. "Goddamn, that fucking hurts."

Shane could only imagine—Tuck wasn't one to complain about injuries or if he was feeling sick.

It took a little maneuvering, but they got him settled into the passenger seat. Shane climbed into the driver's seat, leaving Jamie to get Rowdy back to the barn. He drove across the pasture as slowly as possible, watching out for any dips that would cause the truck to rock. It took twice as long to get back to the house, but once he hit the road, the smooth pavement allowed him to accelerate to a normal speed.

He glanced over at Tuck and noticed his pale face. Reaching over, he grasped his husband's hand and squeezed it. "Did you hit your head at all?"

"Nah. Just didn't roll fast enough, and the damn horse stepped on me. Shit, I'm going to be useless if they cast it."

"Don't worry about it. We'll assign a driver to

chauffeur you around on the golf cart." They had a souped-up one that could handle the rough terrain and pull a flatbed cart attached to it. Once again, Tuck gave him the finger.

Shane chuckled. "Anytime, babe."

As he drove to the clinic, Shane hoped the injury wasn't serious, but a part of him wondered what would happen if Tuck was laid up for a bit and had to hang out with Paige at the house. Maybe he'd open his eyes and see they had a second chance at love with a woman —that is if Paige was willing to try a ménage relationship with them.

Chapter Fifteen

A knock had Tuck growling lowly before bellowing, "Who is it?"

As if he didn't know. Arianna was at school, Shane was out with the ranch hands, and Lila was working, so no one else but Paige could possibly be knocking on his bedroom door at 9:00 in the morning. All day yesterday, she'd knocked whenever she brought him a meal or his pain meds or just poked her head in to see if he needed anything. And each time, he asked the same surly question. And each time, her response was the same.

"May I come in?"

"Yeah," he answered with a sigh. His foot wasn't broken, but it was badly bruised, and the ankle was still swollen. The doctor had ordered him to keep it elevated for several days, icing it on and off for the first two to reduce the swelling. Tuck couldn't get a boot or even a sneaker on right then. He was stuck on crutches until he could bear weight on the foot. Yesterday, he'd slept most of the day, thanks to the pain pills. They made him stoned out of his mind, and he hated it, but his foot throbbed. Shane gave him a pill before he headed out about fifteen minutes ago, but it hadn't fully kicked in yet. Hopefully, by tomorrow, Tuck could get by on just Tylenol.

The door swung open, and Paige stood there in a pair of faded jeans, white sneakers, and a blue V-neck T-shirt. Her hair was in a ponytail, but he found he liked it better when it was down. Pushing the unwanted thought from his mind—it shouldn't matter to him how she wore it—he tried to concentrate on what she'd just asked.

How am I doing? I'm bored out of my fucking mind. "I'm fine, thanks. You don't have to keep checking up on me."

She frowned. "You must be bored out of your mind. Why don't I help you out to the couch? That way, I can clean your bathroom and in here, then throw the sheets and towels in the washing machine."

He knew she had a schedule she'd been following—a list of chores she did on certain days—and he didn't want to inconvenience her. Maybe a change of scenery would do him good, not that he'd be any less bored on the couch than he was in here. Even though he didn't watch much TV, it was better than lying in bed staring at the ceiling. Sarah hadn't wanted a television in their bedroom—she'd said there were many more entertaining things they could do in there—and after her death, neither Shane nor Tuck had thought of putting one in.

"Um. Yeah. But you don't need to help me. I can get there on my own."

Stepping into the room, she spied his crutches, leaning on the other side of his nightstand, and retrieved them for him. She stood next to the bed, holding them in place. "I'd rather help. You were a bit wobbly on these yesterday. I don't want to have to call Shane and tell him you took another header."

He scowled—he didn't need a babysitter—but her expression told him she wasn't taking no for an answer. Forcing the breath from his lungs in exasperation, he flung off the covers. Thankfully, he had on a pair of sweatpants, but then again, it would have served her right if he'd been in his boxer briefs or nothing at all. He thought he saw a flash of interest at his bare, sculpted chest, but she glanced away too quickly for him to be sure. It wasn't something he hadn't seen before when women, and even some men, saw him without a shirt on—heck, Sarah had said his bare shoulders were one of the first things she found attractive on him. He'd been shirtless when she arrived at their annual barbecue all those years ago after someone had accidentally spilled their beer on him.

Pushing off the bed, he stood on his good foot and grabbed the crutches before he lost his balance. Once he was steady, Paige stepped back and gestured for him to precede her. Rolling his eyes, he thrust the crutches forward, then followed with a hop. Slowly, he made his way out to the family room with Paige on his heels. He was surprised at how strenuous it was to move with the aluminum supports. When he reached the couch, he carefully turned and then sat. Leaning back, he brought his leg up to lie length-wise on the cushions.

Paige gently placed a pillow under Tuck's foot. "Is that okay?"

He grimaced as he tried to get comfortable. "Yeah, thanks."

"I'm sure the pain meds will kick in soon." She gestured toward the television and then the bookcases. "Do you want to watch TV or would you prefer to read?"

"The TV is fine, I guess—I don't watch it often. And I don't read at all." When she raised a curious eyebrow at him, he clarified, "I've got dyslexia. I can read invoices, signs, and simple sentences enough not to be a problem, but the paragraphs in books and magazines drive me nuts. I can't concentrate enough to enjoy them." Why he'd told her any of that was beyond him, but he was starting to agree with Shane—Paige was easy to talk to.

"I'm sorry. I didn't know."

"No apologies needed. I didn't expect you to know. When I was little, my mother was a teacher-turned-stay-at-home mom. She recognized early on that I had a reading disability and taught me how to work around it. Then, when I was old enough, she got a job at one of those learning centers, so I got free help with all my other subjects. I was able to pass my classes, but in some of them, I barely squeaked by. That's one of the reasons I prefer to work with my hands and let Shane deal with all the paperwork that goes with running this place."

He pointed at the bookcases. "All those are either Shane's, Sarah's, or from Shane's mother's collection. Helen loved the classics, and her husband, Peter, would gift her leather-bound copies for almost every holiday. Shane and I continued the tradition for Sarah, but I've never read any of them."

"I—" Paige held up a finger before striding toward the hallway leading to her suite. "Hang on. I've got an idea."

His eyes narrowed in confusion as he wondered what she was up to. Moments later, she returned with one of her Kindles in hand. Was she going to read to him? He wasn't entirely comfortable with that. Yes, he could admit his disability, but he didn't want to be catered to as a result of it.

"I'm guessing you'd be a suspense/thriller fan . . . hmm, let me see what I've got on here." Her finger swiped across the screen several times. "Ah, here's a good one by Brad Meltzer that I think you'll enjoy."

"Uh, you're not going to read to me, are you?"

"Nope. I've got a ton of laundry to do." She reached into the pocket of her jeans, pulled out a pair of earbuds, and then plugged them into the e-reader. "This has a text-to-speech feature. It's digitally generated, so it's a little monotone but still enjoyable. If you find you like listening to books, there's a huge variety of audiobooks with different narrators for you to try. Just let me know, and I'll help you pick out some good ones I've already read."

Paige handed him the device as he sat there, dumbfounded. He'd barely been civil to this woman since she'd gotten to the ranch, and here she was doing something incredibly sweet for him. Not even Sarah had thought about trying to get him into audiobooks—she'd simply accepted that reading wasn't his thing, although she often gave him a summary of a book she'd read and loved.

Tuck stared at Paige with new and appreciative eyes. Yes, it wasn't hard to see why Shane, and all the ranch hands for that matter, found her attractive, but there was so much more to her than her pretty features and curves. In some ways, she reminded him of Sarah, but in other ways, the women were completely different and unique. Sarah's words came back to him out of nowhere—had their wife really sent them someone else to love? Would Paige be comfortable in a relationship with two men? Could Tuck open his heart to her and let her in?

When she leaned down, he could smell her shampoo. It was light and fresh—just like her—and caused a stirring in his groin. She pointed to the e-reader's screen, and he forced his eyes to follow. "Just tap here to start and stop, and if you missed something—I zone out every once in a while when I'm listening—you can go back just by sliding this button here." She straightened and smiled. "Can I get you anything else before I tackle the laundry and plan dinner?"

"Um, no." Before she could step away, Tuck reached out and grabbed her hand. "Thank you, Paige." He held up the Kindle. "This was very nice of you."

"It was my pleasure. If you can't get into that book, you can look through my library for something else. Although, I must warn you, about three-quarters of the books on there are romance." She shrugged. "What can I say? I'm a sucker for a happy ending, even if I didn't get one."

Tuck still had her hand in his and gave it a squeeze. "Your husband was an ass."

"Yeah, that's putting it mildly. But, honestly, when we first started dating, and even when we first got married, he was different. Well, he had aspirations like everyone else, but when I think of us as a couple back then, there were a lot of good times. I'm not sure what made Myles change—greed, I guess—but there was a point in his life when he'd been a good and decent man, and that's how I try to remember him."

Of that, Tuck had no doubt. He couldn't imagine Paige falling for someone who wasn't good and decent. He felt bad about what she'd gone through but was stunned at her resolve to remember the happier times and not dwell on the sad. Tuck should take a page from her book. Despite everything, she was determined to start over and find her place in the world once again.

Chapter Sixteen

Leaning against the door jamb, Shane stared at Tucker in stunned silence. His husband was stretched out on the couch, one pillow under his head, another under his foot, and his eyes were shut. He wasn't asleep, though, as he drummed his fingers softly where they rested on his chest. Shane hadn't believed Paige when she said Tucker was relaxing and listening to her Kindle read a book to him. The man wasn't a fan of TV shows, only watching the occasional movie with Arianna or Shane, and with his dyslexia, he didn't read books or magazines. But here he was, apparently, enjoying the story he was listening to.

"Holy shit."

Shane's eyebrows shot up at Tuck's murmured words. There were no signs of distress, and his eyes were still closed, so Shane had no idea what'd prompted the curse. Striding over, he squatted next to the couch and set his hand on top of Tucker's. His husband startled, and his eyes flew open. "Shit! Don't do that!"

Tucker fumbled with the Kindle as he tried to shut it off, then yanked the earbuds out. Shane chuckled in amusement. "Sorry, didn't mean to scare you."

Sighing, he flopped his head back down on the pillow. "I just found out who the murderer is, and he's about to kill again. I didn't hear you come in."

"I thought Paige was joking when she said you've been listening to a book all day."

Tucker sat up and pushed down on his hands, grimacing as he did so until he rested against the back of the couch. "I thought she was kidding when she suggested it, but I'm really enjoying it. I'd be further into it, but I fell asleep after lunch for about an hour. How was your day?"

"Good. We finished fixing the fence in the west pasture, and everything's set to start moving the herd tomorrow. I'm going to hop in the shower, and then we'll have dinner. Paige made homemade pizza, so we can eat in here. Sound good?"

"Sounds great." He sniffed the air, and his stomach growled. "Smells good too. I'm starving."

"So am I, but she made plenty." Shane stood. "How's the foot?"

"Throbbing, but not as bad as it was earlier. Paige gave me another pain pill about an hour ago."

"Good. Oh, and Lila's here—she's eating with us too." He paused, studying Tuck's face. There was a sense of peace there he hadn't seen in a long time, and he didn't think it had anything to do with the narcotics. Whatever had happened between Tuck and Paige during the day had changed the man. Maybe he'd started to realize Paige was someone special—the woman who might finally heal them. Their three-way attraction was growing, and if Tuck was done fighting his feelings, he and Shane could start seducing their sweet house manager. Neither man would ever forget Sarah—she'd always have a place in their hearts—but there was room to love another woman, and if Shane had his way, she'd be Paige.

An hour later, Shane, Tuck, Arianna, Lila, and Paige were scattered around the family room, on the L-shaped couch and two recliners, watching the animated version of *Beauty and the Beast* for what felt like the one-millionth time to Shane. However, Arianna laughed and oohed and aahed as if it was the first time she saw it—just like she always did. With the little girl sitting between them, the two women chatted about various things, mainly about the town, its history, and the upcoming Rodeo Bonanza. Paige had agreed to help out that day for a few hours, and Nicole assigned her to the ticket booth with Lila.

Out of the three thin-crust pizzas Paige made from scratch, two had been completely consumed by Shane and Tuck. The ladies split the third one between them. Shane had been amused when his husband repeatedly raved about how good his pizza was—that was the most he'd heard Tuck say to Paige in one sitting. Add that to him telling Shane about the book he'd been listening to, and Tuck was a bit of a chatterbox that evening. Even Lila had stared curiously at her brother a few times. It had been a long time since the man was as cheerful as he was right then. Shane also didn't miss the somewhat discreet glances Tuck gave Paige and the ones she gave both of them. Her cheeks had been tinged pink several times over the past hour, and he wasn't sure if it was from the compliments and attention or if she recalled what'd happened in the barn a few nights ago. If he had to guess, it was probably a mix.

Yup, things are going to get mighty interesting around here.

When Lila got up to use the restroom, Arianna also stood and put her empty paper plate on the coffee table. "Daddy, can we play Jenga?"

"Sure, pipsqueak." He got to his feet, happy to have his daughter interested in anything other than watching the movie. "Let me clean off the table while you put your pajamas on and then get the game."

As Arianna ran upstairs to her bedroom, Paige jumped up and began to gather the paper plates and the empty pans she'd cooked the pizza in. "I'll do it."

Grasping her hands, he gently guided her back to her seat. "You did enough today—I've got it."

"Um . . ." She stared up at him, and his cock twitched in his jeans. Damn, he could get lost in those eyes of hers. "O-Okay. I mean, I can help."

"Nope. You can sit there and relax." It took all his

willpower to let go of her hands and not look to see if Tuck was watching their exchange. If he saw the interest he hoped was on his husband's face, he'd toss Lila out the door and Arianna into her bed, just so they could have Paige to themselves.

Not yet . . . but soon.

They played the wooden block game for about an hour, laughing and teasing each person who tried to make their move without toppling the tower over. After Tuck lost for the second time, Lila stood and stretched. "It's getting late. Thanks for dinner, Paige. It was delicious."

"Any time.

Shane placed his hand on the back of his daughter's head. "Time for you to go to bed, sweetheart."

"Please, can I stay up for a little while longer?"

Her pleading eyes usually had him caving, but he shook his head. "Uh-uh. You're already up past your bedtime, and it's a school night. Kiss everyone goodnight. I'll come tuck you in in a few minutes."

"Okaaayyyy." The adults all chuckled at her adorable pout as she gave each of them a hug and a kiss.

Getting to his feet, Shane walked Lila to the door, then waited until she got into her car and put it in Drive before he turned off the porch light. Meanwhile, Paige had finished putting the Jenga blocks back into the box, collecting the empty dinner glasses, and bringing them into the kitchen. Now that she was alone with them again, she avoided looking directly at either of them. Tuck's brow was furrowed as if he were trying to figure out what was wrong while silently watching her. Well, Shane wasn't filling him in—not yet.

Shane stopped at the bottom of the stairs. "After I read Ari a book, I'll help you back to bed, Tuck." He'd taken another pain pill a little while ago and had been unsteady on his feet during a trip to the bathroom.

"I can do it," Paige said as she returned from the kitchen. "I got him out here without a problem. He did most of the work, anyway."

He glanced at Tuck, who nodded. Shane shrugged. "Okay. Just pray Ari doesn't pick *Beauty and the Beast* for me to read again. I'm so sick of that one."

Paige's chuckle was a delight to hear, and it tickled his groin as he ascended the stairs and entered his daughter's room.

"Here, Daddy. *Beauty and the Beast.*"

Using the crutches, Tucker advanced down the hallway a little slower than earlier. He felt spaced out from the drugs. Paige trailed behind, just as she'd done each time he'd moved around the house today. Despite his injury and earlier resistance, he'd kind of liked having her fuss over him.

Hobbling into his and Shane's bedroom on one

foot, he managed to move over to the bed as Paige set her e-reader on his nightstand. He tried to turn around to sit on the bed but lost his balance. In a reflexive reaction, as he felt himself start to fall, he released the crutches, reached out, and grabbed Paige's arm. She was caught by surprise, so instead of stabilizing him, she was yanked off her feet. Tucker fell back onto the bed with her on top of him, almost knocking the breath from his lungs. "Shit! Are you okay, Paige?"

"Oh, my God. Did I hurt you?"

"No, I'm fine. I'm sorry, I turned too fast." He froze when their current positions registered in his brain. She was sprawled over his chest and abdomen, and her hips were nestled between his thighs. His dick didn't mind at all when every ounce of his blood rushed to it. He knew the second she realized she was in his bed . . . with him . . . in a suggestive manner . . . with his very hard cock between them. Her gorgeous blue eyes grew wide, but she remained as still as he was. It was as if she couldn't figure out how to get up without making things worse. His heart rate sped up as he stared at her mouth, which had rounded into an "O." All he had to do was lift his head a scant two or three inches, and he could kiss her.

"Ahem. Am I interrupting?"

The spell was broken at the sound of Shane's low and amused voice, and Paige scrambled to get off Tuck. "No! No. Um . . . it's not what it looks like, Shane!"

Her wiggling against Tuck's thick erection didn't help matters, and he squeezed his eyes shut while she managed to get her feet on the ground and push off him.

"Well, that's disappointing."

Tucker didn't have to look at his husband to know he was grinning and as hard as Tuck was.

"What? No. I-I was helping Tucker, and he—he moved too fast and fell. I-I tried to keep him from falling, but he's so big . . . I mean, height-wise, not . . . um . . . I mean . . ."

Opening one eye, Tuck dared to take a peek. Her blushing face was full of mortification and worry that Shane thought something was going on between them. He could have told her his husband probably hoped there *had been* something going on. Tuck bit his upper lip to keep from cracking up and embarrassing her more.

"That's all that happened, I swear . . ." She glanced at Tuck and then back at Shane before hurrying toward the door. "I'll just go to bed . . . um . . . alone . . . my own bed . . . good—goodnight."

Both men tried their best not to laugh as she practically ran out of the room after Shane stepped to the side to let her pass. He then stuck his head out the doorway to watch her hasty retreat before turning back and closing the door behind him. He leaned against it and crossed his arms, chuckling as he did so. Tuck put his hands behind his head, relaxed into the mattress, and stared at Shane. "She won't be easy to convince."

Shane didn't ask what he was talking about because

he already knew. After tonight, they both wanted her—that was obvious, at least to them. Tuck may have been a little slower to get on board, but he was definitely there now, a fact Shane was thrilled about. "I think she might surprise you."

"Why do you say that?"

Pushing off the door, Shane strode across the room and picked up the Kindle from the nightstand. He booted it up and lay on the bed next to Tuck, who watched as he scrolled through the list of e-books in her library. He stopped when he found what he was looking for, then turned the device so Tuck could see the screen better. Stunned, he gaped at a bunch of book covers that had two men and one woman on them, all half-dressed and in sensual poses.

"I overheard her and Nicole talking about some books they'd read. Apparently, ménage romance has a huge following nowadays."

"Holy shit!" Tuck took the e-reader and scrolled down further. They weren't all ménage, but there were quite a few. She hadn't lied when she said she favored romance books.

"Uh-huh."

Tuck frowned at him. "But reading it and living it are two different things, Shane. I mean, if we screw this up, Arianna will be heartbroken if Paige feels it's our way or the highway."

Rolling onto his side, Shane ran a seductive hand up and down Tuck's torso. "Then we'll have to make sure we don't screw it up. Although she tries to hide it, she's interested in both of us. We made Sarah a vow—if we had the chance to let someone else in, we'd take it. I want that someone to be Paige, but we do this together or not at all. Are you in?"

Briefly, he studied Shane's handsome face and then the sexy book covers on the device in his hand. Finally, he glanced at the closed door before nodding. "Yeah, I'm in."

Chapter Seventeen

Paige watched as Tucker eased himself down to the couch in the corner of the "L," then lifted his leg and rested his foot on the pillow she'd set in place for him. She still hadn't been able to look into his face this morning, her mortification from last night still coursing through her. It'd been an accident and nothing more—and Shane hadn't been mad when he'd walked in on them in the compromising position. In fact, he'd had a sense of humor about the whole thing. Paige just wished she could laugh it off as easily as both men had. She also wished she couldn't remember how hard Tucker had been against her lower abdomen. It had to have been a natural response. A guy's cock got hard if anything warm, soft, human, and the right sex brushed against it . . . right? *Oh, Lord.*

"Hey, Paige? Sit, please. I want to talk to you for a minute." With warm benevolence in his eyes, he patted the cushion next to him. Well, he didn't look like he was going to fire her, so that was one less worry on her mind.

She sat, ensuring there was enough distance between them, and turned toward him, her knee resting on the couch, adding a small barrier. "What's up?" She hoped the question sounded nonchalant, but his eyes narrowing a bit told her she hadn't quite pulled it off.

Reaching out, Tucker gently took her hand, and it was hard not to concentrate on anything but how her body responded to his simple touch. "I just wanted to apologize. I haven't been the nicest guy to be around lately, and honestly, I know it sounds cliché, but it wasn't you—it was me. When Hannah was here, she was a grandmother figure for Ari, so it didn't feel like she was taking Sarah's place. But having you here has been hard on me."

"I'm—"

He squeezed her hand. "No, let me finish." When she nodded, he continued. "Again, you didn't do anything wrong. I've been grieving Sarah's death for over two years now, and I guess . . . well, I guess I was afraid if I stopped, I'd forget her. I'd be admitting in my heart what my head already knew—she's gone and never coming back. But then you walked in, a breath of fresh air—one I desperately needed but still fought against. I didn't want to like you because it felt like I was betraying her. Shane—well, he likes everyone—always has. But me . . . it takes me a while to warm up to people, and I know that can put many of them off.

It's just my nature. Anyway, what I'm trying to say is I'm sorry if I made you feel uncomfortable or unwelcome in our home. You've been great the last few weeks, and I'm really glad you're here."

Tears threatened to well up in her eyes as she swallowed hard. This was the real Tucker—the one she hadn't met yet—the one she really, really liked. The one she could . . . *Oh, hell.*

"Um . . . I'm glad I'm here too. Thank you for taking the time to explain everything to me." As she spoke, his thumb started to caress the back of her hand in a soft, back-and-forth motion, and her mind went blank. All she could do was stare at him as he stared right back at her with an intensity that caused the butterflies in her stomach to take flight. Electricity crackled throughout the room. Time stood still. When Paige gulped, then subconsciously licked her lips, Tucker's gaze shot to her mouth, and heat flashed in his eyes. *What's happening here?*

The backdoor opened and closed, snapping her out of the trance. Snatching her hand from Tucker's, she jumped to her feet a split-second before Seth walked into the room. "Paige, are you ready?"

Tucker's eyes narrowed as he frowned at his handyman. "Ready for what?"

Taking a step back, Paige hitched a thumb toward Seth. "To go into town. Um . . . Seth's been driving me for my grocery runs."

Her boss's face hardened, and she couldn't figure out why. "Didn't Shane give you the keys to the SUV?"

"Uh . . . yes, he did. But I didn't know my way around town at first, so Seth volunteered to take me. Since then, we've just made it a weekly thing."

"Really?"

Paige didn't like how Tucker had said that one word, as if it dripped with venom, nor the nasty look he was now giving Seth. If he could've stood on his injured foot, she wouldn't have been surprised if he flew across the room and tackled the other man. "Um . . . is—is something wrong?"

"Well, I hate to tell you this, Paige, but Seth's intentions haven't all been pure and good. He's been trying to figure out how to get you into his bed without you eventually wanting a white dress and a legal document."

What? She glanced at Seth, who now had a sheepish expression on his face. Then he shrugged. "What can I say? I'm a man-whore and proud of it."

Rolling her eyes, she silently chastised herself for mistaking his offers to help as just that and not something with altruistic intentions. Yeah, she was out of practice when it came to recognizing when a guy was flirting and hitting on her. "Sorry, Seth, but one-night stands aren't my thing."

"Who says it has to be one night only?" he asked with a huge grin. "Two or three nights is fine with me."

Despite Tucker's low growl, Paige knew Seth was only teasing her. He was an easy-going guy, without a mean bone in his body, as far as she could tell, and she did enjoy his company on their trips into town. He just wasn't her type—although she wasn't even sure what her type was anymore.

"Well, either way, it's not going to happen. Thanks for helping me, but I think I can get to town and back now without a problem." Striding past him, she smiled and patted his shoulder. "Nice try, though."

Entering the kitchen, she snatched the keys to the SUV from a hook near the pantry and stepped over to the table where she'd placed her purse earlier. Hanging it on her shoulder by the strap, she paused when she heard Seth's voice coming from the other room. "So, that's how it's gonna be, huh?"

"Yup," Tucker replied with no hesitation.

"Jeez—you and Shane get all the good ones."

"Damn straight—and don't you forget it."

Now what the hell did that mean?

STROLLING UP AND DOWN THE AISLES, PAIGE SEARCHED for what she needed amid the limited supply of staples the Stop & Go stocked. Whenever Shane or Seth had to go to Garden City for any reason, she'd go online and order everything she couldn't get at the small grocery store from Walmart, and they'd pick it up for her.

As she shopped, her mind kept returning to what happened in the family room that morning. She tried to convince herself the heat she'd seen in Tucker's eyes when he stared at her had only been her imagination. But then she remembered that same look in Shane's eyes the night before when he'd walked in on them . . . in bed . . . together . . . *oh, boy.*

"There you are! I thought I saw you walk in." Marla Oberman walked toward Paige with a small, familiar-looking box in her hand. "That tea you said you loved came in."

She smiled at the gray-haired older woman and took the box of herbal tea from her. "Oh, thank you, Marla. I really appreciate you ordering it."

While Walmart carried the brand, there were so many different flavors, and they didn't carry the one she liked in the store. She would have to order it from them online and have it delivered to the ranch, so she'd taken a chance and asked the owner of Stop & Go if she could stock it for her.

"My pleasure. Are you finding everything else okay?"

"Yes. Oh, and I made a roast the other night with the recipe you gave me, and it was a big hit."

The woman patted Paige's forearm and winked. "The fastest way to a man's heart is through his stomach, my mother always said."

Her eyes bugged out. "Um . . . I'm not after anyone's heart, Marla."

"Hmm." There was skepticism in her eyes and tone. "But you have to admit, those Wilson boys are yummy. I loved their wife, Sarah, even though some biddies around here turned their noses up at her. Honestly, I think they were all just jealous. I wouldn't mind two hunks like that lovin' on me. Especially since my Albert has lost interest, the old coot."

Paige choked on a combination of a laugh and a snort. She wondered if Shane and Tucker knew they had a secret admirer and if Albert knew his wife had a kinky side.

"Anyway, let me know if you need anything else." She started to walk away, then paused, lowering her voice to a near whisper. "Oh, by the way, there's a sale on condoms in the next aisle. You know . . . in case you need any."

That time, Paige couldn't hold back her laughter at the woman. It looked like she had a fairy godmother in her life, whether she wanted one or not.

Once she'd finished her shopping and checked out, Paige waved goodbye to Marla through the window of the woman's office at the front of the store, then headed out to the small parking lot. As she placed the grocery bags into the backseat of the SUV, she heard footsteps approaching her from behind. Glancing over her shoulder, she groaned inwardly as she shut the door. Somehow, she'd managed to avoid Bridget Kline during her occasional forays into town before today. The woman was smiling, but it was obvious to Paige it was forced. Her bleached-blonde hair had been teased to the point of absurdity, and Paige was tempted to tell her the hairdo had gone out of style in the 1980s. Add the makeup job that belonged on a Hollywood set, long, blood-red nails, and tight clothing, and the woman's looks practically screamed "vamp." However, her diamond earrings, platinum necklace, and designer labels turned the scream into "rich vamp."

"Hi, you must be Paige. I'm Bridget Kline." She held out a hand in a way Paige hated. The "I'm better than you" limp offering that, in olden days, men would just have to lift an inch or two to kiss it. Back in California, she'd known many women who shook hands that way —and most of them had been snotty bitches.

Paige gave the hand a tight squeeze before letting go, happy to see the woman wince slightly. "Nice to meet you." Yeah, it was anything but. With narrowed eyes and that fake smile, she knew this wasn't a "let's be friends" connection the woman was trying to make. "I guess everyone knows I'm working at the Red River Ranch by now."

"That's what happens in small towns—everyone knows everyone else's business, especially when someone not from around here is hired as a new housekeeper. Where are you from?"

Her eyebrows ticked upward, but she ignored the disdain she heard in the other woman's voice when she uttered the word "housekeeper." Paige straightened her back. "I'm originally from Nebraska." It wasn't a lie— she just left out the years since then.

"Oh, that's nice." She reached into her purse and pulled out an envelope addressed to Paige's employers. "Would you be a doll and give this to Shane and Tucker for me?" she purred. "It's a private dinner party I'm inviting them to."

In other words, Paige wasn't welcome to join them. In fact, she wondered if anyone other than Shane and Tuck was being invited. She took the envelope and gave her own phony smile. "Sure. I'll give it to them while we're having dinner—together." Score one for Paige when Bridget's glare cooled considerably. "Or maybe over dessert—they both have a sweet tooth."

The woman's gaze dropped and took in Paige's frame, then returned to her face. Her distaste was evident but didn't garner the response she probably wanted. "Don't get too cozy, dear. I've been waiting a long time for them to get over their dead wife. They'll be mine soon enough."

"Oh, really?" Paige crossed her arms. "Do they know that? Because if that was the case, I'm sure one of them would have mentioned it . . ." She paused for effect. ". . . when we were in bed together last night."

Well, technically, only Tucker and Paige had been in bed together. It was an accident, and they'd been fully clothed, but Shane had only been a few feet away watching them—with amusement and heat in his eyes. Oh hell, why had that popped into her brain again?

So, she'd stretched the truth quite a bit, but it was worth it when Bridget's mouth puckered and her eyes flared—the woman was speechless. Score another point for Paige.

After pulling the driver's door open, she climbed in. "It was really nice meeting you, Bridget. I'll be sure to let Shane and Tucker know about your intent to seduce them. They could probably use the laugh after a hard day's work. Have a nice day."

Without waiting for an answer, she shut the door, started the engine, and then backed out of the parking space, leaving behind the red-faced woman who was sputtering in disbelief and rage. Paige had barely made it to the exit of the lot before she burst out laughing, tears rolling down her cheek. She'd forgotten how much fun living in a small town could be. Now, she just had to get back to the ranch and let Tuck and Shane know what happened. She was pretty sure they'd be laughing right along with her, but she had to beat the gossip mill first.

Chapter Eighteen

"You really should be resting on the couch," Paige said to Tuck for the second time after Shane handed him a bunch of silverware to dry before it got put away. Since he still couldn't stand on his injured foot, he sat at the kitchen table while Paige washed the dishes and Shane dried most of them. The only good thing about that was he had an eye-level view of both their asses. Shane was wearing the black sweatpants Tuck loved—the ones that molded around his muscular glutes and thighs. Meanwhile, Paige's faded jeans fit her like a glove—one he wanted to slide his hand into.

"It won't hurt my ankle if I sit here and dry a few things, darlin'."

It'd been an interesting day. After she returned from her grocery shopping trip, Paige had handed him an envelope and then, with pink-tinged cheeks and quite a bit of giggling, told him about her run-in with

Bridget. At first, he was stunned by the audacity of the woman who'd been making it obvious she wanted to get into Shane and Tuck's bed for a while now. In fact, the divorced mother of two bratty daughters started hitting on them not long after Sarah's funeral, and all it did was turn the men off more than they'd already been when it came to the stuck-up bitch.

Bridget had been one of Shane's one-night-only indiscretions back in high school, and she'd been trying for a repeat ever since. She did have her standards, though—as greedy as they were. She'd never given Tuck a second glance when he'd first gotten hired as the foreman of Red River—the job didn't pay enough to satisfy her. She only became interested in him after the Wilson ménage relationship had gone public.

It wasn't long before Tuck had been laughing right along with Paige, and after Shane came back to the house for lunch, as the men had planned, the three of them were in stitches. Needless to say, neither man would attend the "private dinner party" they'd been invited to. They were pretty certain the table would only be set for three. Even if they hadn't set their sights on Paige, there was no way they would've said yes to Bridget's request.

Tuck watched as Shane took a half step closer to Paige and smiled. They'd devised a plan to woo her that included brushing against her, crowding her a little, teasing her, using terms of endearment, and flat-out flirting with her. This seduction would be different than the one they'd gone through with Sarah. Before

Shane came up with the idea of the ménage relationship with her, he and Tuck almost came to blows when they realized they both wanted the same woman. At first, Tuck thought his boss would fire him to ensure he got the girl, but then he thought the guy was crazy with his inane suggestion, which eventually benefited all three of them. One woman. Two men. Seriously? But the more Shane had explained and talked about it, the more Tuck wanted to try it. He'd known Shane was bisexual—pretty much the whole town did by the time Tuck had taken the job a half hour from where he'd grown up. Shane had assured him that his only intention was to give Sarah the love and attention she deserved. Little did Tuck know that'd been a white lie. Shane had definitely wanted a full ménage relationship, meaning everyone did everyone.

While the two of them had seduced Sarah, Shane had also been seducing Tuck. The first time Shane kissed him, they had been alone in the barn, arguing about something Tuck couldn't even remember. Things got heated, and the next thing he knew, he was shoved up against a stall, and the other man's mouth smashed into his. The only thing burned into his brain was how stunned he'd been. Not so much at the fact Shane had been kissing him but at the instant hard-on that resulted. Shane had known what he was doing, though. He'd given Tuck the space he needed for a few days after that, yet not letting him get too far away. By the time the two men finally had sex, with Sarah's consent and enthusiastic voyeurism, Tuck wanted

Shane as much as he'd wanted the woman they both fell in love with. It was several more months after that before Tuck allowed Shane to drag him out of the closet.

While there had been numerous attempts at public shaming, they were no more than what he'd already faced being involved in the threesome in the first place. His parents and sister had been his rocks since the beginning—while the relationship was unconventional, they saw how happy he was and had given him their blessing.

Once the dishes were all put away, Tuck reached for his crutches. He waited until Paige stepped over to wipe down the table, as she always did. Pushing off the chair, he stood then wobbled, "accidentally" falling toward her.

"Oh, Tuck!" She lunged at him, one strong yet soft hand landing on his chest, the other at his waist as she steadied him.

It was all he could do not to groan at her touch. Over Paige's head, he saw Shane silently chuckle and wink at him.

"Are you okay?" she asked.

"I'm fine now, darlin'." The concern in her eyes flared to heat when he covered the hand on his chest with his and gave her the lopsided grin Shane had always told him was sexy. "Thanks for rescuing me."

He could have sworn she stopped breathing as she stared into his eyes. No one said a word. Shane just watched the exchange and shifted his hips to give his growing hard-on some room in his briefs. Tuck was tempted to do the same.

Paige licked her lips, then dropped her gaze to the floor. Pulling her hands back, she bent over to pick up the crutches from where they'd fallen at his feet. The polite thing to do would have been to hop backward a bit when she ended up at eye level with the bulge in his sweatpants. Yup. There was no way to hide that.

When she stood again and handed him the crutches, her face was beautifully blushed, and Tuck wondered if her nipples were the same color.

"Um . . . Shane, would you . . . um . . . help Tucker back . . . um . . . to the couch? I-I'll finish up in here." She didn't look at either of them as she snatched up the sponge she'd been using to wipe the table and began to use it again.

Instead of doing her bidding, Shane closed the distance between them, gently grabbed her wrist, and took the sponge before tossing it back into the sink. "The kitchen is clean enough, Paige. You're done for the night. C'mon into the family room and relax. We can watch an adult movie tonight since Ari is sleeping at Nicole's." Two Friday nights a month, the two young girls had a sleepover, alternating houses.

Paige's eyes widened when Shane said adult movie, causing Tuck to laugh. "Shane didn't mean that kind of adult movie, darlin', but if that's what you want to watch, we're more than willing to accommodate you."

With amused expressions, both men raised their

eyebrows while awaiting a response. Her blush deepened.

"Uh . . . n-no. I'll just . . . um . . . go to my room and read for a bit."

Shane rolled his eyes as he grasped her shoulders and turned her toward the door to the family room. "He's only kidding, sweetheart, but I wasn't. You've been working hard all week and deserve some downtime. We'll even let you choose the movie."

As his husband urged Paige into the other room and to sit on the couch, Tuck followed, hobbling on the crutches. His foot was feeling better, and he'd switched from prescription painkillers to over-the-counter ones. Taking his usual seat on the couch, he brought his foot up to rest on the pillow he'd been using. Meanwhile, Shane steered Paige to sit to Tuck's left and then sat down on the other side of her, sandwiching her between them yet giving her a little space.

Picking up the remote, Shane turned on the TV and then scrolled through dozens of movie channels. "Let me know when you see something you like."

At his words, Paige seemed to relax a little into the cushion. Had she thought they were going to jump her? Hell, no. The plan was to make her come to them. They'd let her know soon enough what they wanted, then would pray she didn't run on them. What they had in their favor was that she hadn't freaked out when Shane told her about their wife and the fact that Paige had read a lot of ménage books. And damn, some of them were really hot! Tuck had selected a few on the

Kindle during the day and skipped around to listen to some of the sexier scenes. Talk about hard-ons! When Shane returned to the house just before dinner, Tuck followed him into their bedroom on his crutches and practically begged him for relief. His husband had been all too happy to help after a thirty-second shower to rid himself of the sweat and grime covering him.

Tuck was surprised when Paige pointed at the TV screen. "Oh, James Bond! Let's watch that one."

"Really?" Shane asked, even though he clicked to select the channel.

Smiling, Paige nodded her head. "Yup. My dad loved Sean Connery as Bond, but I'm a total Daniel Craig fan." She jumped to her feet, and both men started, wondering what she was doing. "I'll be right back. I can't watch double-oh-seven without popcorn."

The husbands glanced at each other and grinned. They were coming to like Paige more and more as each hour passed. Tuck hoped it wouldn't take long before the time was right to try to push her out of her comfort zone.

PAIGE COULDN'T CONCENTRATE ON THE MOVIE EVEN with Daniel Craig standing there, shirtless. She was hyperaware of the strong, handsome men sitting on either side of her. Something had been different today.

Both, especially Tucker, had seemed to be . . . well, flirting with her. While Shane had always been friendly and even a little flirtatious, today it'd felt like a . . . seduction? No, that wasn't the word . . . or was it?

She sighed to herself. It'd probably been inevitable. After she'd worked for them all these weeks, a friendship had developed between them, and they were more comfortable around her now, as she was with them. That was all there was to it.

If you're so comfortable around them, then why are your shoulders so tense? Why did your heart pound in your chest when Shane put his arm along the back of the couch behind you? And why did you get all those funny feelings deep in your core every time Tucker's hand brushed against yours when they ended up in the popcorn bowl at the same time?

Ordering her subconscious to shut the fuck up, Paige stood as the ending credits began. "I think I'll turn in."

"Okay," Shane replied as if her statement had been expected.

And why are you so disappointed with his response?

Oh, shut up!

She had to leave the room before she started verbalizing the conversation ping-ponging around in her head. Shane's bare feet rested on a small pillow he'd placed on the coffee table, so Paige had to go the other way. As she rounded the corner, she stubbed her toe on the leg of the table.

"Ouch!" Cringing at the pain, she stumbled . . . right into Tucker's lap. Again.

How the hell do I keep doing that?

His arms wrapped around her to prevent her from sliding off onto the floor as Shane jumped up. "Are you all right?"

Without waiting for an answer, he knelt beside them and lifted her left foot. He took off her fuzzy sock, with the safety-grip bottoms, before she could stop him and inspected her toes. His touch was gentle and mesmerizing. "Doesn't look like you broke any." Not letting go of her foot, he glanced up and grinned. "I like the hot-pink polish. It's sexy."

His gaze bored into her, and she suddenly realized Tucker's hands were slowly caressing her arms. Paige gulped. She couldn't look away. Couldn't stand. Couldn't deny the tingling sensations she felt at their combined touches.

"Paige."

With great effort, she turned her head toward Tucker. His gaze was as searing as Shane's. Ever so slowly, he leaned forward. It wasn't hard to figure out what he was doing once his eyes zoomed in on her mouth. He gave her every chance to back away—to say no, she didn't want this. But that was the last thing she wanted to do—at least, she thought it was. The heat from his body under hers was dizzying. From his position next to them, Shane did nothing but watch and run his hands over her foot and ankle.

Tucker's face stopped a scant inch from hers. "I want to kiss you, darlin'. Will you let me?"

She gaped at him, unable to formulate a response.

Shane moved forward and whispered in her ear. "Let Tuck kiss you, baby. I'm dying to see his mouth on yours."

Her gaze dropped for a fraction of a second before returning to Tucker's face. Her clit was throbbing just from their nearness and words. What she wouldn't give to have one of them touch her there. It'd been a year and a half since she'd kissed a man . . . since she had a man in her bed. Her marriage was over the moment she realized her husband was a criminal. She'd taken her wedding ring off the night he'd been arrested when she knew she'd never be able to look at him the same way again. Yes, she'd grieved when he'd committed suicide, but aside from court and on the news, she hadn't seen him since his arrest.

Tuck waited. Clearly, if she wanted this kiss to happen, she'd have to close the last bit of distance between them. If she did, though, it would change everything. It was a huge risk. If she took it, what would happen next? Her sex drive knew what it wanted to happen, but was she just a new toy for them? No. Nicole had told her, as far as everyone knew, Sarah had been the only woman who'd ever been in bed with the two men simultaneously. This wasn't just a fling they were asking of Paige, but could she handle more than that? Two men? Yeah, it happened in many of the books she read, but this was real life.

She had no idea how much time had passed before Tucker raised his hand and lightly cupped her jaw, his thumb brushing her cheek. "Some other time then,

Paige. The offer will stay on the table until you're comfortable taking it."

His gaze held no disappointment, just understanding, but she still felt the need to apologize. "I-I'm sorry."

Shane set her foot down and took her hand in his. "There's nothing to be sorry about, sweetheart. We didn't expect this to happen so soon. We wanted to . . . well, seduce you a little bit. But fate decided to step in. When we hired you, we had no idea we'd come to want you, but we do. You've brightened our lives in the short time you've been here, but you're not ready, and we understand. You might never be. Just know whether you say yes or no, your job here is safe. Having a relationship with us is not mandatory." A wicked grin spread across his face. "Although, it would definitely be worth it." He stood and helped her to her feet, but before he let go of her hand, he bent down and placed a soft kiss on her forehead. "Sleep well."

As if I could fall asleep at all after everything that'd happened today.

Chapter Nineteen

After taking the saddle off his horse, Rufus, Shane let him loose in the small paddock near the barn, then strode toward the house. The only thing that could make doing the Monday paperwork bearable was seeing Paige. Three days since their shared movie night, and she still hadn't given them an answer. Then again, it'd been busy around the ranch. A brush fire, probably from a carelessly tossed cigarette, had kicked up across the main road on Saturday and spread quickly. All available personnel from Triple-R, and the surrounding farms and ranches, had joined the volunteer fire department to put it out. If it hadn't been for their quick response, once someone had spotted the smoke and an evening rainstorm, it could have spread out of control. As it was, it'd taken a few hours to put it out.

Then, yesterday, Arianna hadn't been feeling well. She'd picked up some sort of stomach bug and had spent the morning puking and then the rest of the day sleeping on the couch or watching the TV. They'd taken turns cuddling with her, which she'd loved. Shane had thought she'd need to stay home this morning, but she'd woken up looking and feeling fine and had wanted to go to school. With no fever, and a healthy appetite at breakfast, she'd gotten dressed, and Paige had escorted her to the road for the bus.

Tuck was walking around again, albeit gingerly, and he'd headed out to work using one of the ranch's ATVs instead of his horse. After joining him for a bit, Shane had gone back to do the dreaded paperwork.

He stopped and collected the files that were waiting for him on Nicole's desk and carried them into the house. Paige was busy dusting the living room, which they rarely used, and the vacuum stood next to the couch. Once again, he noticed the small changes she'd made around the place. He thought it was nice how she'd managed to keep many of the details Sarah had lovingly put into decorating the house yet give everything an updated look. He glanced around and felt a kick in his gut. There were photos of Sarah everywhere. What did Paige think of them hitting on her in a house so full of memories of a dead woman?

"Hey. You okay?"

Her question caught his attention. Damn, she was so pretty. They hadn't planned on letting their feelings be known the other night, it'd just happened. Since Paige hadn't taken off running, they figured they still had a chance with her. "Uh . . . yeah. Sorry. Just daydreaming."

She smiled. "Happens to me all the time."

With a wink, he said, "I'd love to know what . . . or *who* you're daydreaming about."

"I'm sure you would, but my lips are sealed." Her eyes were dancing as she teased him right back. "Now, go do your paperwork. I've got cleaning to do. My bosses are slave drivers."

A full belly laugh erupted from him. "Yes, ma'am. Wouldn't want to get you in trouble with your bosses, now, would we?"

Shane was halfway through his paperwork when he heard the doorbell. He wondered who it was but didn't get up. Paige would let him know if he was needed. He heard her footsteps in the hall and then the foyer. An alarmed cry and the door slamming had him jumping up and running out to her. With wide eyes, he took in the sight before him. Paige was paler than a ghost. She'd slid down the back of the door into a squat, and her hands trembled.

He rushed toward her. "Baby, what's wrong? Who is it? Tell me what's wrong."

Her eyes were huge, and tears rolled down her cheeks. "They—they found me. I'm so sorry, Shane. They're outside."

Whoever it was, he was going to kill them for terrifying her. "Who are *they*, Paige?"

"The press. Reporters out there with cameras and . . . and . . ."

"Shh." Taking hold of her shoulders, he helped her up. He ignored the doorbell as it rang a few times in succession, but the sound had Paige nearly jumping out of her skin. Stepping back, away from the door, he pulled her with him. "Shh. It's going to be okay. Go into my office and call Tuck on the radio. Tell him to get back here as fast as he can. Where's Seth?"

Her whole body was shaking. "He—he went into town—to the feed store. I'm sorry, Shane. I never meant—"

"Hush. Go in my office and call Tuck," he repeated. "I'll take care of these assholes." He'd fucking rip them apart. "Go."

He gently shoved her toward the hallway and waited until she disappeared around the corner before turning around and yanking open the door. Two men and one woman immediately shoved voice recorders and microphones at him. Two cameramen stood behind them, filming the whole thing.

"Where'd Paige Winthrope go?"

"Is she working here? What does she do?"

"Did you know her husband swindled their friends out of millions?"

"Is she really your housekeeper?"

With rage on his face, Shane stood to his full height and stepped forward, forcing them to move back. He didn't know what the hell was going on or how these people found out Paige was there, but he wasn't letting them anywhere near her. "Get the fuck off my property! You're trespassing, and around here, we shoot trespassers."

Apparently, the threat was one they'd heard before because they ignored it and continued with their rapid-fire questioning.

"Are you aware of who you hired?"

"Where's Paige? We want to ask her some questions."

"You're Shane Wilson, right? Are you and your husband in a relationship with Paige?"

Seth's white truck pulled up, and he jumped out, taking in the chaotic scene with narrowed eyes. The female reporter gestured to him. "Is that your husband?"

Shane took another threatening step forward. "Get the hell off my property! Seth, call the fucking cops. Tell the chief he's gonna have to arrest me for assault when he gets here. Make sure he confiscates the cameras and recorders as evidence."

"Sure thing, boss," his employee replied, taking his phone from the holster on his hip.

That threat and his tone of voice seemed to get through the predators' heads finally. The two male reporters and the cameramen hurried down the steps, their devices still recording.

Tuck came flying around the side of the house on an ATV and slammed on the brakes, skidding to a halt. Apparently, he hadn't been too far away when he'd gotten Paige's SOS. "What the hell's going on?"

"These assholes are trespassing." He scowled at a

microphone being held only inches from his chin. "And I've never hit a woman before, but if you don't get that damn thing out of my face, there's a first time for everything."

The female reporter's eyes rounded before she hastened to join the others getting into their vehicles. She glared back at him before shutting the passenger door of a van and said, "We'll just get the story in town —people love to talk. Look for yourselves on KHBR-California's website."

"Bitch," Shane muttered under his breath as Tuck approached and climbed the steps to the porch, still limping a little.

"What the fuck was that?"

He was still glaring at the retreating vehicles. "I don't know, but we'll find out. First, we have to take care of Paige. She freaked when she saw them."

"Shit."

"Seth, make sure they don't come back. Let me know when the police get here." Shane followed Tuck inside and closed the door behind them. "She's in the office."

When they walked into the room, Shane's heart almost broke. Paige sat on the small loveseat with her arms wrapped around her midsection as she cried her eyes out. She jumped to her feet when she spotted them. "I-I'm so sorry—"

"Shh. It's all right, sweetheart," Tuck said as he pulled her into an embrace. Her arms automatically went around his waist as she buried her face into his chest, sobbing.

Shane shut the door before stepping closely behind Paige, his chest to her back. He ran his hands up her arms, then moved her hair from her shoulder so he could whisper in her ear. "It's okay, baby. They're gone, and we won't let them anywhere near you again." She rubbed her forehead back and forth on Tuck's chest, and Shane's gaze met his husband's. He tilted his head toward the small couch, silently communicating what he wanted Tuck to do.

When Shane moved back, Tuck bent his knees and swept Paige's feet out from under her, lifting her into his arms and then sitting with her on his lap. The fact she didn't protest, only crying harder, had them both worried. Shane held up a finger to Tuck, then opened the door and walked out of the room. He returned moments later with a lowball glass half-filled with whiskey and shut the door once again. Kneeling in front of Tuck, he held the glass up to Paige. "Here, sweetheart. Take a sip."

She hiccupped, then reached for the glass with a trembling hand. Shane didn't relinquish it but held it for her as she drank from it. "That's it. Take some more."

They watched as she downed the rest of the amber liquor. After swallowing, she murmured her thanks. Shane set the empty glass on an end table, then took Paige's hands. He brought them to his mouth and kissed her knuckles. Meanwhile, Tuck rubbed her back with one hand and her shins with the other. They remained quiet, giving the whiskey a few moments to work and Paige a chance to collect herself.

Finally, she released a long, deep breath. "I'm sorry."

Shane kissed her knuckles again. "Nothing to be sorry about, baby. You didn't do anything wrong. Do you have any idea how they knew where to find you?"

"No." She sighed heavily again. "Quinn and my friend Marcella are the only two who knew I was coming here. Marcella wouldn't have told a soul—she's just as protective as Quinn is." That was saying a lot. Shane's cousin would have laid down his life before putting a witness or former witness in jeopardy.

"You've called her, right?" Tuck asked. "Maybe someone tapped her phone."

Paige shrugged. "Could be. I usually call her cell, but sometimes she calls me from her house phone."

"Well, we'll figure that out later. For now, we want to make sure you're all right."

Her gaze lifted to Tuck's. "I'm fine, thanks to both of you."

Shane watched as Tuck cupped her jaw. This time, when he brought their mouths within inches, Paige closed the final distance. Tuck let her lead for a moment, merely taking his cues from her. She brushed her lips against his several times, then moaned. That was all the encouragement Tuck needed. He buried his hand into her thick hair and held her head where he wanted it. Shane's cock hardened at the sight. Lifting her hands again, he took one of her fingers and sucked it into his mouth. She gasped, and Tuck used it to his advantage, plunging his tongue between her lips. He tasted and teased her for several minutes before releasing her. Staring down at her with eyelids at half mast, he held her chin between his thumb and forefinger. "Let Shane kiss you, darlin'. He's been waiting quite a while now and should be rewarded for his patience."

When she faced Shane, Tuck shifted her on his lap until her back was against his chest. He put her legs on the outside of his own and then spread them. Shane crawled between their knees, his gaze never leaving Paige's, which was filled with the same lust that was in Tuck's. Shane wanted to memorize everything about their first kiss to easily recall it years from now. Leaning forward, he caressed her lips with his own. The familiar taste of Tuck, combined with the smooth whiskey, was on her, and it fueled his desire. When she opened for him, he didn't hesitate, thrusting his tongue out to tangle with hers. The sexy, little noises she made spurred him on. His hands went past her hips and clutched Tuck's. It'd been so long since they'd had a woman between them, but they still ensured they were also attached to each other.

Shane's eyes fluttered shut, and when Paige tilted her head to the side, he knew Tuck was nibbling on her neck as his hands came up to cup Paige's breasts. She thrust her chest forward, crushing his hands between her and Shane, and hummed in delight.

A knock at the door had all three starting—they

hadn't heard anyone approach. No surprise there. Shane hadn't been aware of anything other than Paige and Tuck in the last few moments.

"Shane? The chief's here."

Shit. Lousy fucking timing. "I'll be out in a minute."

"'Kay." Seth's footsteps faded down the hall.

After giving Paige a final, brief kiss, Shane reluctantly got to his feet and then adjusted himself. He winked down at her blushing face. "I'm never going to hide what you do to me when we're alone, sweetheart, so you better get used to it. Now, let Tuck take care of you while I talk to the chief." He glanced at the clock that sat on one of the bookshelves. "I'll get Ari off the bus—I don't want you anywhere near the road where those bloodsuckers could ambush you."

She nodded, seemingly still out of sorts, but his guess was it was now due more to the last few minutes than from the reporters showing up out of nowhere. "Okay. Thank you."

"No, thanks necessary, sweetheart. Take care of her, Tuck. I'll be back."

Opening the door, he strode out and prayed the incident with the press had been a one-time-only thing, but he doubted it.

Chapter Twenty

Tuck strode into the kitchen, where Shane sat at the table, checking Arianna's homework. Their daughter looked up at him with worry in those big, blue eyes she'd inherited from her mother. "Is Paige going to be okay, Papa?"

He gave her a reassuring smile. "She's going to be fine, sweetheart. She's just taking a nap. Nothing to worry about."

"I didn't make her sick, did I?"

"Nope, not at all. You had a stomach bug. Paige has a . . . um . . . headache. She'll feel better when she wakes up."

While Shane talked to the sheriff, Tuck had picked Paige up in his arms and carried her to her room despite her protests because of his foot. Honestly, any pain that was there hadn't even registered in his brain as he'd snuggled her close to his chest. After laying her down in the middle of her bed, he'd pulled off her sneakers, kicked off his boots, and climbed in next to her. He'd spooned her, and a thrill coursed through him when she hadn't objected. He'd slowly caressed her arm and leg, urging her to fall asleep for a bit. It hadn't taken long for her body to go lax as slumber overtook her, with assistance from the whiskey. He hadn't been able to get up right away after that. Once he had her in his arms and tasted her luscious lips, there was no turning back for him. Shane had been right—Paige would be theirs. It felt right.

A half-hour later, he'd eased from her bed, picked up his boots, and quietly left the room. As he'd passed through the family room on the way to the kitchen, he paused at an array of photos in small frames on the bookshelves, focusing on his favorite one of Sarah. Her eyes sparkled as if she'd been laughing at something silly when he took the candid shot of her early in her pregnancy. The vow she'd demanded of them floated through his mind. It was time—he was certain she'd sent them someone who could love them both, knowing it didn't mean they loved her any less. His heart expanded in his chest. It wasn't pushing his wife out but making room for someone new.

Taking a deep breath, he'd let it out slowly, then murmured, "Thank you for sending Paige to us, sweetheart. She's beautiful in every way, just like you. You knew I wasn't ready until now, didn't you? Thanks for not giving up on me. I'll thank Shane later for the same thing. He deserves to hear it too."

As Tuck got himself a glass of water, Shane handed

Arianna back her homework. "You got them all right, Ari. Good girl. What do you say we give Paige a break tonight and get takeout after your dentist appointment? You and I can run over to Bar None and get some mac and cheese for you and lasagna or something for us. Okay?"

"Yay!"

"Shh, Ari, not so loud, Paige is sleeping," Tuck reminded her. "Go change out of your school clothes. Your shirt's dirty."

She glanced down at the red stain on her belly, then shrugged. "I spilled my juice on it at lunch."

"That's okay, it happens. Just go change and brush your teeth, then Daddy'll take you to your appointment."

After their daughter skipped out of the room, Tuck leaned against the refrigerator and eyed Shane. "Glad you remembered the dentist was this afternoon because I forgot. What did Chief Hughes say?"

"He showed up with Lane." Officer Lane Myers was a childhood friend of Shane's, who'd returned to the town they'd grown up in after twelve years and four tours overseas with the Marines and joined the eight-man police department. "On their way here, they passed the three vans heading into town."

"Making good on their threats to talk to others. The good thing is Paige has made some friends since she's been here. On the flip side, there're more than a few people who are going to be slinging bullshit just to get their faces on TV."

Shane nodded. "Yup. Lane and the chief said they'd do their best to run them out of town, but legally, nothing can be done unless they commit a crime. Before I go to Bar None, I'll stop by the station and sign a formal complaint that's being prepared for me. Lane will round up the reporters, identify them, and tell them, in no uncertain terms, that if they step foot on our property again, they'll be charged with trespassing and harassment. He'll also see if he can find out how they knew Paige was here. Hopefully, when they realize they're not going to gain access to her, they'll climb back under whatever rock they crawled out from."

"I'll assign one or two hands to work with Seth out front to make sure no one gets close to the house. I also think one of us should be here at all times for the next few days, just in case."

"I agree."

"I'm ready, Daddy." Arianna ran back into the kitchen, wearing a clean shirt, then spun around and headed for the front door. "Let's go."

Getting to his feet, Shane made sure he had his keys, wallet, and cell. As he strode past Tuck, he paused and whispered, "I can still taste both of you on my tongue."

Heat flared in Tuck's eyes as his cock swelled. Shane winked at him and then laughed as he left the room, knowing full well he'd just given his husband a hard-on with the only relief in sight coming from his own hand, at least, until later. Having Paige in their bed tonight was not going to happen. It was far too soon, and she'd still be upset over the reporters. When she came to them, they wanted what would happen between them to be drama and stress-free. But as soon as he got his husband alone later, Shane would be bottom this time if Tuck had his way.

HER EYES STILL CLOSED, PAIGE STRETCHED THE KINKS out of her entire body. She didn't even remember falling asleep and wished she could say the same about what'd transpired earlier. The reporters, not what'd happened in the office with Shane and Tucker. Nope, that she never wanted to forget. Was it wrong to want two men at the same time? Years ago, she might have said yes, but the books she'd read had eased her into accepting the subject—although that was only fiction. She found ménage romances enjoyable and hot as hell. However, this was real life, and it involved her.

She thought back to the conversations she'd had with some of the residents of Hazard Falls since she'd moved there. A few people obviously found the Wilson men distasteful and perverted and probably thought she was already sharing their bed if the turned-up noses she'd encountered were any indication. Meanwhile, others, like the men and women who worked at Red River or were friends with the couple, were more than comfortable with their relationship and the one they'd had with Sarah. Paige couldn't deny she was attracted to both men, but could she handle a three-way romance? Part of her was scared to try, while the other part of her, the one that hadn't had sex in over a year and a half, was screaming for her to take a chance. What if it didn't work out, though? There was no way she could stay at the ranch, working for them, if a romantic relationship between them failed. Arianna would be heartbroken if Paige left, and vice versa.

Sitting up, Paige removed the lightweight quilt Tucker must have laid over her before he'd left her sleeping. She'd been surprised when he'd climbed into bed with her but had been too upset over the reporters to think more about it. Then he'd put his arms around her, and she'd felt things she hadn't felt in a long time— safe and cared for. She'd relaxed into his embrace and had drifted off within minutes.

Paige glanced at the clock on her nightstand and realized it was past time to start dinner. After a quick trip to the bathroom, she removed her jeans and pulled on a comfortable pair of yoga pants. She then shoved her feet into her black, fuzzy slippers instead of her sneakers and padded out to the family room. No one was there, but she heard someone in the kitchen. The smell of something baking, and maybe even burning a little, made her stomach growl. When she entered the room, Tucker glanced over his shoulder as he pulled an aluminum sheet filled with chocolate chip cookies out of the oven. "Hey."

His eyes roamed her body, warming her from head to toe and back again before he gestured to the cookies. "They're not from scratch like yours, but I found a container of the spoon-and-drop kind in the fridge."

She gave him a sheepish smile. "Well, that's what I use when I make mine. I kind of fibbed when I said I make them from scratch. I can cook many things, but baked goods aren't my forte. My cookies always come out too dry and cake-like."

Shaking his head, he chuckled. "Now I don't feel so bad—well, actually, I still do. At least you don't burn them around the edges." He set the tray on the stove, then tossed the oven mitt he'd been using on the counter and strode toward her. "How do you feel?"

"Better. Where're Shane and Ari?"

"The dentist, then they're stopping at Bar None to bring home dinner."

Paige's gaze shot to the calendar they kept on the refrigerator. "Oh, no! I forgot all about her dentist appointment."

Clasping her shoulders, Tucker got her attention. "Relax. We've got it covered. After what happened this afternoon, I forgot all about it too. Shane was the one who remembered. It happens. No big deal. Okay?"

She paused, then nodded, grateful Tucker wasn't mad at her. "Okay. Did you just say they were getting dinner too?"

"Yup. You have the rest of the day off."

"I'm sorry about the reporters—"

Catching her off guard, Tucker pulled her close and lifted her chin so she could look up at him. "No one's blaming you, Paige, so stop saying you're sorry. It's not like we didn't know about the shit storm you got caught up in, thanks to your ex-husband. We're not letting you go because of a little bump in the road. Shane and I have been the talk of the town many times before. The gossipers go crazy for a bit and then set their sights on fresher meat. You know how small-town rumor mills go. But . . . if you want to leave . . . if you think Shane and I can't protect you—"

"No! I-I don't want to leave. For . . . for the first time in years . . ." She glanced away and then quickly returned her gaze back to him. ". . . I feel . . . well, I feel like I really belong. I liked California, but honestly, I never felt like I fit in there. Here, I do."

As his body relaxed in obvious relief at her words, the corners of Tucker's mouth curved upward. "Good. Because we feel like you fit in here too."

Lowering his head, he kissed her, and Paige melted into his arms. His tongue teased her as he backed her up against the pantry door until there was no room between their bodies. Tucker held her head at the angle he wanted so he could devour her. When he ground his erection against her lower abdomen, she moaned and lifted her knee to his hip in a desperate attempt to climb him. Tucker reached down and cupped her ass, then dragged her up his length until she could wrap her legs around his slender hips. Her hands clutched the hair at the back of his head. When his cock pushed and rubbed against her clit, Paige gasped. "Oh, God, yes!"

Leaving her mouth, Tucker kissed along her jawline until he reached her ear. "Damn, Paige, you feel so good. You don't know how much I want to take you into my bed and make you scream my name as I fuck your sweet pussy—"

"Yes!"

He chuckled. "You're not ready for that, baby—not yet. Besides, the first time I take you, Shane will be there too."

Paige froze, and Tucker pulled back to see her face. She stared at him, completely mortified, her cheeks turning beet red, and his eyes narrowed. "What's the matter, sweetheart?"

"I—" How did she say that she'd been so wrapped up in a near-sex-induced fog that she hadn't even thought of Shane? It wasn't that she didn't want him, too, she just—

Tucker kissed her forehead, interrupting her thoughts, then said, "Hey, it's okay. It happens. I'm kind of glad I can get you so revved up that everything else disappears from your mind—even Shane. There'll be times when it's just you and me or just you and him— hell, even me and him. We'll want our alone time with you as much as we'll want all three of us together. That's how this works. That's why I don't think you're ready just yet. Okay?"

Her heart pounding, Paige nodded slowly, trying to

shift gears mentally. She'd been so close to begging him to take her right there. "Okay."

When she tried to put her legs down, he tightened his hold on her, keeping them up. "Uh-uh, sweetheart. Just because I'm not taking you to bed right now doesn't mean I'm not going to give you a taste of what's to come."

Using his trim hips, muscular thighs, and one hand to hold her in place, he brought his other hand up and cupped her breast, thumbing her nipple through her light T-shirt and barely-there bra. Paige's eyelids fluttered shut as she savored his touch. He plucked the peak, then ran his hand down her abdomen. Her head fell back against the pantry door with a thud when she realized his intent. His thumb found her clit through the thin cotton barrier and brushed over it, causing her to buck against him. With slow, purposeful circles, he slowly drove her to the brink of insanity. Her hands clutched his broad, muscular shoulders, clenching and releasing in time to his sensual ministrations. A climax began to build within her. She panted and squirmed, wanting more. Wanting it all. One of her slippers fell off her foot and plopped onto the floor—she didn't even notice.

"Please . . . oh, please, Tucker."

He increased the pressure against her clit. "That's it, baby. Damn, you're beautiful. Come for me, Paige. That's it. Let it go."

Using his thumb and forefinger, he pinched her sensitive bud and sent her flying. Her scream was cut off by his mouth slamming down on hers, and his fingers rubbed hard, drawing out her release. Her legs shook, but she was safe in his arms. As the orgasm began to ebb, Tucker brought his hand back around to cup her ass and hold her tightly against his rigid cock. He nuzzled her neck, allowing her to draw in gulps of air to her oxygen-deprived lungs.

When Tucker lifted his head, Paige's eyes opened in narrow slits. He was grinning like a schoolboy who'd just gotten his first car or blowjob—she couldn't decide which. Either way, it was sexy as hell.

He let her slide her legs down, and after her feet touched the floor, he waited until he was certain she could stand on her own. Squatting down, he grabbed her fleece slipper, then curved his hand around her calf and lifted her foot so he could slide it on. He looked up at her and winked. "A perfect fit, Cinderella."

In post-orgasmic bliss, Paige had a sappy, satisfied smile on her face. If this was what one Prince Charming did to her without ever taking off a stitch of her clothing, what would happen when the second one joined them and they stripped her naked?

Chapter Twenty-One

Paige wiped her mouth with a napkin, then sat back in her chair and sighed. She'd been hungrier than she'd expected, putting away a large helping of lasagna, two pieces of Italian bread with herb butter, and a small salad. "That was delicious, thank you."

"Wo're wewl-comb," Arianna answered, her cheeks full of the last spoonful of mac and cheese from her bowl.

"Ari, what have we told you about talking with food in your mouth?" Tuck stood and collected the adults' empty plates from the table.

The little girl swallowed. "Sorry. Can I have some cookies now?"

"May I?" Shane, Tucker, and Paige chorused.

"May I?"

"After a bath, my stinky, little brat." Shane leaned

toward her, inhaled deeply, then held his nose. "Pee-yew."

Arianna giggled. "Daaadddy! I don't stink. You stink! Pee-yew. Pee-yew. Pee-yew."

Reaching over, he scooped her out of her chair and onto his lap. Her giggling increased tenfold as he tickled and teased her. Paige could tell he was being mindful of the fact Arianna had just eaten, but it was still fun to watch.

Tucker strode back into the dining room and smirked. "She pukes, you're cleaning it up, Shane."

Sighing, the other man relented and set Arianna on her feet next to him. He gave her nose a tweak. "Papa spoils all the fun. Go take your bath, and then we'll have cookies."

As Tucker followed Arianna down the hall, Paige stood from her chair, intent on making a cup of tea—she'd been forewarned she wasn't allowed to lift a finger to help with the cleanup. The men had said they'd take care of everything tonight—she was officially off the clock until tomorrow. She stepped toward the kitchen but didn't get any further than that when Shane's hand shot out and snatched her arm. With a quick tug, he pulled Paige onto his lap, causing her to let out a brief yelp. One arm wrapped around her waist, holding her closely. As she gaped at him, his eyes twinkled. "So . . . I've heard you're freaking gorgeous when you come. I'm disappointed I missed it."

Her cheeks flamed. Grinning, Shane ran a hand up

her shin, over her knee, to her thigh. "What are the chances of getting an encore performance?"

Paige's breath hitched, and, holy hell, her clit began to throb. If his touch hadn't already sent her hormones into overdrive, his huskily-voiced question would have. She couldn't tear her gaze away from his face as heat flared in his eyes. His hand made lazy circles over her thighs before sliding between them. His other hand went to the nape of her neck, and he pulled her toward him before brushing his lips against hers. Paige melted into him. His taste was similar to Tucker's yet different —she couldn't have explained it if she'd tried. All she knew was she liked kissing both of them.

Shane licked and nibbled his way to her ear, his hot breath sending shivers down her spine. "Spread your legs for me, sweetheart. I want to watch you shatter from my touch."

She stiffened when a noise at the other end of the house reminded her they weren't alone. Tucker clearly wasn't a problem, but what if Arianna walked in and saw them? Shane seemed to read her mind. "Don't worry. Tuck will keep Ari busy for a while. We'll have enough of a warning to make sure she doesn't see or hear anything."

"You—you both planned this?" she asked, not really caring if they had. Her eyes fluttered shut. She could barely think straight as he nuzzled the pulse at her neck, and his thumb found her clit through her yoga pants.

Shane leaned her back on his lap, forcing her to

fling her arms around his neck, even though he wouldn't let her fall. The new position gave him better access to her breasts. "Mmm. Not exactly, but you must have missed the little signal I gave him before he left the room."

"I-I guess I did. I'll have to learn to look for the super-secret signals, so I'm not caught off guard next time."

"I kind of like you off guard. I also like how you said, 'Next time.' Rest assured, there will *be* a next time —with Tuck joining us. But for now, you're all mine, and I want to taste what's mine."

The possessiveness in his voice did things to her she hadn't felt in years—if ever. However, somehow, she knew that if she said the word "no," Shane would back off immediately. He'd be disappointed—so would she, for that matter—but he would respect the single spoken word.

He lowered his head and molded his lips to her breast. Despite the fact her T-shirt and bra were between her skin and his mouth, the heat engulfed her, distending her nipples to the point of pain-induced pleasure. The hand at the juncture of her legs dragged upward until it reached the elastic waistband of her spandex pants. It probed under the fabric, returning to where it had been giving her undeniable gratification, but this time, there was nothing but skin against wet and wanting skin. Paige squirmed on his lap, wanting more. His lips found hers again, and he murmured against them, "Do your best to stay quiet, sweetheart.

Not only do we not want Ari to overhear you scream my name in ecstasy, but your restraint will make your climax more explosive. You'll find I like giving orders while giving mind-blowing orgasms—just ask Tuck."

"Oh, God," she gasped, barely above a whisper, as his words were punctuated by his fingers plunging into her wet core. Her eyes fluttered shut.

"He can't save you now, sweetheart. Just go with it. You're so tight. So wet. Your walls don't want to let go of my fingers. That's it. Good girl. Ride my fingers."

Paige did just that. While controlling what was happening between them, he let her wriggle on his lap, trying to take everything he was giving her and silently demanding more. She bit her lip to keep from screaming when the heel of his hand pressed against her clit as his fingers continued their torturous assault. Mews and whimpers escaped her as she raced toward completion. Her nails gouged into his muscular shoulders.

"Yeah, baby. Mark me, so every time I feel where your nails dug into me for the next few days, it'll remind me how you looked and felt in my arms as I watched you come apart. Look at me, baby. Let me see those beautiful eyes as you come for me."

It took a monumental force to do as he'd commanded, but she somehow managed to lift her lids and find his gaze with her own. It was as if a volcano had erupted within him, his eyes burning with desire as he drove her further and further to the point of no return. His cock was big and hard against her hip. The thought of him fucking her with it like he'd fucked Tucker's mouth in the barn sent her over the edge. Her lips opened to cry out in complete rapture, but before a single note could be uttered, Shane covered them with his own—claiming her orgasm as his and his alone. She shattered, just like he'd demanded. His fingers played deep within her, drawing out her climax. Her mind spun like a tornado. All thoughts except how amazing she felt had fled. Her body liquified as she came down from the blissful high and sagged against him. Shane's fingers and mouth slowed before coming to a stop. Lifting his head, he stared at her as he pulled his hand from her pants and brought it to his lips. He sucked on each digit that'd been inside her, moaning at the taste of her pleasure, his gaze never leaving hers until he'd licked them clean.

Lifting her back upright on his lap, he lazily kissed her, letting her taste herself on his tongue. She was in a post-coital, euphoric zone for the second time that day, and that was the only reason she didn't protest when he'd stood and carried her into her room. As Tucker had done earlier, Shane placed her in the middle of her bed, then climbed in behind her, spooning her. With her eyes closed, she snuggled against him. She subconsciously reached out and was surprised at her disappointment when she realized her hand came up empty. Without even thinking about it, her body had expected Tucker to be on her other side, sandwiching her between him and Shane. It was as if the two men were halves of a whole, and it was weird to have only one in the bed with her even though she'd never been with both.

In actions almost identical to his husband's, Shane caressed her arm, hip, and thigh until sleep overtook her.

UNDER A CLOUDY SKY, TUCK HELPED SETH UNLOAD some groceries from his pickup truck. With the reporters still snooping around town, Paige had made Tuck a list of what she needed since he refused to let her drive to the store, even with an escort. As he'd suspected, the gossipers were in full form, and rumors abounded. Marla, who'd always been a sweetheart and rooted for the underdogs in life, had filled him in while he strode up and down the grocery store's aisles. She was one of the first people in town who'd had Sarah's back when the news of the ménage relationship had lit up the phone lines.

On his way back to the truck for the final few bags, Tuck noticed a vehicle coming up the driveway, kicking up dirt. He relaxed when he spotted the blue-and-red light bar on the roof. Putting his hands on his hips, he waited for Lane Myers to park his police department-issued SUV and climb out. "Hey, Lane."

"Hey." He shook Tuck's proffered hand. "Any more problems?"

"No. But I'm sticking close to the house with Seth, and Paige is staying behind closed doors. We didn't want anyone taking photos of her with a camera's high-powered zoom lens. Any idea how they found out she was here?" Last night, Shane called Quinn, who'd gone to Paige's friend's apartment. Marcella had let him check her place for bugs, and as far as the marshal could tell, there were no taps on either her cell or land-line phones, nor did he find any listening devices or cameras. So, they still had no idea how the bottom feeders had found Paige.

Lane sighed as he leaned against Tuck's pickup. "Could have been a few ways. Someone could have tracked her social security number—she used it to open a checking account in town—or her checking account back in California. She deposited a check for a few thousand dollars from that account into the new one here, then closed the old one. But her last state-ment from the old account would show where the check was deposited. From there, they probably asked around and found out where Paige lived."

Another car coming down the drive stopped the next question that'd been on Tuck's tongue. Both men's eyes narrowed until the vehicle was close enough to recognize. Lane crossed his arms. "What's Lou doing here?"

Tuck had no idea, but he looked forward to the fire-works that went off every time Betty Lou and Lane got within twenty feet of each other. They let everyone within earshot know they hated each other, but the sexual tension was off the charts between these two. From what Shane had told Tuck, the pair had dated for a few months during their senior year in high school, but the romance had ended when Lane enlisted and left town without warning. Apparently, he'd left Lou a letter, and whatever it'd said had caused a huge rift between the two, which still hadn't healed after all this time. But while their minds, and possibly their hearts, told one story, their bodies told another. They were hot for each other, but neither dared admit it.

Lou parked her pickup next to Lane's SUV, then climbed out and approached them. Of course, as usual, she refused to look at or acknowledge Lane's presence. "Hi, Tuck."

The corners of his mouth ticked upward. "Hey, Lou. What's up?"

She stopped a few feet in front of him. "Came across some info I figured you'd be interested in, considering the clueless cops still have no idea how the press found Paige."

If the rest of her statement hadn't been about what he was trying to find out, he might have laughed at the blatant dig aimed at Lane. "What'd you hear?"

"Apparently, they got a tip from Bridget."

His eyes widened, and he barely kept his temper in check. "What?"

At the same time, Lane asked, "How'd you find that out?"

Lou's gaze flickered to the man she was trying to avoid, then shot back to Tuck. "Two of the cameramen came into the bar late last night. A few shots of tequila and their lips loosened." She shrugged. "I asked, they answered."

"In other words, you flirted with them, got them thinking they had a chance, then kicked them out of the bar after you got what you wanted."

Rage flared in the woman's pretty, brown eyes. "Screw you, Lane. Don't you have jaywalkers to hassle or a cat that's stuck in a tree somewhere?"

Lane smirked. "Nope, no jaywalkers today, and cats in trees are the fire department's problem. Not mine."

She shook her head in disgust. Damn, Tuck wished he could be a fly on the wall when the inevitable fireworks started between those two. Before Lane moved back to town and took the job with the police department, Lou had been fine. But now, just a glimpse of the man had her jaw clenching and her right eye twitching, and no one seemed to know why. On the other hand, Lane seemed to take great pleasure in pushing Lou's buttons. Tuck didn't know why they didn't just hit the sheets because he was sure it would be explosive for both. "If you two are done, can we get back to Bridget? Are you positive?"

With a final nasty glare at Lane, Lou turned back to Tuck. "Yeah, he showed me an email that was forwarded to the reporters. The bitch had done an internet search of Paige's name, and it didn't take long for her to find out who she was.

"Did her husband really swindle their friends out of millions and then hang himself in jail?"

Tuck frowned and crossed his arms. "Yeah. Paige was the one who turned him into the feds when she found out about it. After his arrest, she filed for divorce —long before it went to trial and he was found guilty. He only lasted a day into his sentence before he committed suicide." Tuck normally didn't give out information like that—he hated gossip, having been on the other side of it often enough—but any idiot with a computer would find out the same information. He was sure the reporters had been telling everyone about it, anyway, while putting their own perverse spin on it.

"Well, when you let Bridget have it, make sure I have front-row seats. I hate that conniving bitch."

So did Tuck.

Chapter Twenty-Two

Three nights later, sitting in the family room, Paige folded Arianna's laundry while Shane finished the dishes, and Tucker put their little girl to bed. Paige was still in shock that Bridget had contacted the press. As far as she knew, the woman had no idea the word was out she was behind the reporters invading Hazard Falls, and, for now, Shane and Tucker wanted to keep it that way. The only others in the loop were Lane and Nicole. The latter had been told because Shane had her doing a little research for him. He was hell bent on a little revenge, and, honestly, Paige was happy about it. She knew he wouldn't harm Bridget, but there were other ways to retaliate—ways that would make the woman regret ever putting a target on Paige's back.

After the basket was empty, Paige noticed some of Ari's homework was still sitting on the coffee table. She picked up the girl's knapsack from the floor and put the pages into their proper places. Pulling out the teacher's communication folder, Paige checked to see if there were any new notifications. There was a consent form for an upcoming class trip that either Shane or Tucker had to sign. Reading through it, Paige noticed the school wanted volunteer chaperones to accompany the class to a place called the Native American Village, about fifty minutes away from Hazard Falls. It looked like a fun trip. Apparently, it was an indoor and outdoor museum of sorts, showing the students how the Native Americans had lived before they lost their land to the settlers who'd taken over. There were teepees and artifacts, basket weaving and cooking demonstrations, and plenty of other activities and sights for the children to learn from.

Leaving the consent form on the table, Paige stood and walked into the kitchen but stopped short when she saw Tucker and Shane making out by the sink. Damn, that was so fucking hot to watch.

Over the past few days, the men had been seducing Paige—that was the only way to describe it. Whenever they could, one or the other had cornered her, kissing her, getting her all hot and bothered, and making her scream in ecstasy, but never at the same time. Shane told her they wanted her to be comfortable with them as individuals before taking her as a couple. She highly suspected the men were having sex with each other every chance they could because neither had sex with her, despite her begging. They'd driven her crazy with passion but had only gotten her off with their hands and mouths. Neither had let her return the favor. And damn it, she wanted to. She wanted more. Never in her life had she thought of being with two men at once—in reality, not a fiction-induced fantasy—but now she could dream of nothing but.

Shane's big hands were in his husband's hair as he held his head where he wanted it. His tongue fucked Tucker's mouth, eliciting soft moans of delight. Meanwhile, Tucker's hands clutched Shane's hips as he ground their groins together. Paige was frozen in place, feeling herself grow wet as she stared at the erotic scene before her. Her nipples hardened, almost to the point of pain.

As if sensing her in the room, Shane lifted his head, and his lust-filled gaze found hers. Tucker's wasn't far behind. Shane grinned at her. "Like what you see, darlin'?"

Unable to find her voice, Paige just nodded. Both men had shifted their stances, and the sweatpants they wore did nothing to hide their mutual arousal.

"Want to join us?"

Fuck, yeah! She wanted that more than anything right now.

She didn't verbally answer, and she wasn't sure if she'd given him a non-verbal response either, but his smile widened. Taking a step back, Shane gestured toward Tucker. "Come and take my place."

Her eyes narrowed. *Was he going to leave?* She didn't want him to.

Apparently, reading her mind, Tucker chuckled.

"Don't worry, sweetheart, he's not leaving. You'll find Shane likes to watch for a bit before joining in on the action. Come here."

When he held his hand out to her, she found her feet moving toward him. She placed her hand in his and felt a jolt of electricity. With one final glance at Shane, Paige stepped into Tucker's embrace. His mouth descended on hers, and she was instantly transported to Heaven. His smooth lips were a combination of soft and hard. She moaned when his tongue darted out and demanded entry into her mouth. When she parted her lips, he didn't hesitate, sweeping in to taste her. His hands caressed her back on their way down to her ass. But instead of settling over her yoga pants, he dipped his hands below the waistband, finding her bare cheeks separated only by the lacy thong she was wearing. Kneading her ass, he groaned into her mouth, then ground his pelvis against hers. His cock was firm against her abdomen, and she wanted to climb his body to get that piece of solid flesh where she needed it the most.

Paige lost track of time as Tucker devoured her. Suddenly, she felt another hard body behind her. Shane's erection settled at the small of her back. His hand pushed her hair to one side before his mouth latched onto her neck. He nibbled and licked his way to her ear. "You have no idea how fucking sexy it is to watch the two of you. We want you, Paige. We want you in our bed, pleasing you, fucking you, making you spiral out of control. Tell us you want that too."

His words and hot breath sent shivers down her spine. Tucker's mouth left hers, and he stared down at her. "It's your choice, sweetheart. No pressure. If you want some more time, we'll give it to you. Just know that if we can't enjoy your body yet, we'll enjoy each other while imagining you between us."

Paige groaned at the image that flashed in her mind. Damn, they knew the fine art of seduction and used it to their advantage. Swallowing hard, she placed one hand on Tucker's chest and the other on Shane's hip. "I want you . . . both. But I'll admit, I'm nervous. I've never . . . with two—"

"We know, sweetheart," Shane said while running his hands up her flanks to the underside of her breasts. He tested their weight. "We'll ease into this. If something scares you or you're unsure of anything, just say so. We can't read your mind. While we'll be able to read most of your body language, it's best if you come right out and tell us something's wrong. The last thing we want to do is hurt or frighten you. Understood?"

She glanced over her shoulder, and her gaze met Shane's. The combination of tenderness and lust she saw there threatened to unravel her. Paige knew every single one of his words had been the truth. Trusting them to take care of her, she nodded. "Yes, I understand. I promise I'll tell you if I'm scared or unsure."

"Good."

Tugging on her hips, Shane coaxed Paige to take a step backward. He then bent down and swooped her up into his arms. She let out a startled squeak and clutched his shoulders. "Shane!"

"Shh, sweetheart," he replied as he strode toward her bedroom, with Tucker following. "We don't want to wake Ari."

Once the three of them were behind the closed door, Shane set her on her feet again, then sat in a rocking chair that occupied one corner of the room. Volcanic heat emanated from his eyes. "Stay perfectly still, Paige. Undress her, Tuck."

A smile spread across Tucker's handsome face as he closed the distance between him and Paige. "Told you he likes to watch. He also likes to give orders."

The corners of her mouth curved upward despite her nervousness. "I can see that."

Tucker grasped the hem of her oversized T-shirt. "I like to give a few orders too. My first one will be no more big shirts on you, darlin'. I like it when I can see your curves." He dragged the shirt up her torso and over her head before tossing it aside. "And that did nothing but hide them." Trailing his knuckles down her chest and across one bra-covered nipple, he licked his lips. "Now, this is more like it. If I had my way, you'd be walking around in nothing but lacy bras and panties all day long. Unfortunately, that's not feasible, so I'll have to settle for times like this."

Swaying under his touch, Paige's eyes fluttered shut as she grabbed Tucker's upper arms to steady herself. Just that simple caress had her feeling lightheaded.

"Open your eyes, darlin'. I want to see all the passion inside you directed at me."

When she forced her eyelids to lift again, she found Tucker staring down at her. He was drinking her in, and her skin flushed with warmth everywhere his gaze wandered. Reaching up, he lowered her bra straps until they were wrapped around her elbows. Instead of turning her around, Tucker moved behind her and unclasped her bra. He peeled it off her and let it drop beside her shirt before cupping her breasts and pulling her flush against his hard chest. She could feel the thickness of his cock nudging her lower back. Lifting her hands, he placed them around his neck, which caused her back to arch and her chest to thrust forward.

"Damn, that's a pretty sight." Shane remained seated but shifted to adjust his erection. "Pluck those gorgeous nipples, Tuck."

The man didn't hesitate, rolling and tugging on the tender peaks while Paige moaned. Her clit was throbbing, begging for attention. She rubbed her thighs together, trying to garner some friction. It was the weirdest thing—Paige had thought she'd be embarrassed having one man watch while another stripped her clothes off and did naughty, delicious things to her. But with these two men, it felt right. Yes, she was still nervous, but in the past, she was nervous the first time she had sex with any of her boyfriends. Many women were self-conscious during sex with a new partner. Questions such as, Do I look okay? How do I sound?

Am I doing it wrong? and other questions flew through their minds.

"Where'd you just go, darlin?" Tucker whispered in her ear, sending a shiver down her spine. "I must not be doing this right if your mind is wandering."

Before she could think of an answer that wouldn't offend him, Shane got to his feet and sauntered toward her. "She's wondering if we'll find her lacking in any way." She was shocked he'd read her mind.

"Never," Tucker responded, kissing along her shoulder, his hands kneading her breasts. "You're incredibly beautiful, Paige. Inside and out. Let us show you."

Shane dropped to his knees in front of Paige, hooked his fingers into the waistband of her pants and thong, then slid both down her legs, baring her for his viewing pleasure. "Mmm. So damn pretty. Did you know her pussy is waxed, Tuck?"

"My fingers knew, but I haven't seen it yet. I was afraid I wouldn't be able to stop myself if I did." His hands roamed downward as Shane helped Paige step out of her clothing. Tucker squeezed her ass cheeks. Her stomach quivered when Shane ran his tongue along the crease of her hip.

Paige began to pant as they touched her everywhere with their mouths and hands, causing goose bumps to pop up all over. "Oh, God! You—you two are overly dressed."

Lifting his head, Shane smirked at her. "That we are. Turn around and undress Tuck while I nibble on your delectable ass."

Heated desire flashed through her, and her pussy wept with need. Pivoting, she gave Shane her back before her hands dipped under Tucker's T-shirt. His intense stare had her heart pounding against her ribs. He swallowed hard, and his nostrils flared as she removed his shirt. Tossing it to the floor to join her own clothing, she focused her attention on his sweatpants. Pulling the string, she loosened the waistband and then shoved the garment downward. In the meantime, Shane was still on his knees behind her, doing what he'd said he would do—nibble on her ass. His hand snaked between her legs, and his fingers teased her swollen pussy lips, sending shockwaves through her entire body.

Once Tucker was as naked as Paige, he grasped her hair, drew her to him, and fused his mouth to hers. Their tongues dueled as Shane's fingers eased into her core. Bending her knees slightly, she swayed her hips, trying to get him further inside her. She explored Tucker's hard chest and sculpted abs with her hands. He took her breath away, and she gladly gave it to him. The two men's combined assault on her senses caused all thoughts, other than how good they were making her feel, to flee from her mind.

Chapter Twenty-Three

od damn it! Shane was going to come in his pants if he didn't get ahold of himself soon. But Paige's body was so warm, so delicious, so . . . perfect, he was finding it hard to stay in control. The last thing he wanted to do was scare the living daylights out of her by acting like a caveman. With Tuck, he could do that. The man loved it rough, and Shane enjoyed it just as much. It was part of how their three-way marriage had worked so well for them.

Placing one last kiss at the base of Paige's spine, Shane withdrew his fingers from her tight passage, then got to his feet. "Tuck, lay on the bed and let Paige straddle your hips and that fucking thick cock I love so much. Don't you dare slip inside her until I tell you to."

His husband's eyes shined with unadulterated lust as Shane shed his own shirt and pants. While there were times Tucker liked to take control of their sexual encounters, more often than not, he preferred to let

Shane top him. It'd been that way since the beginning of their relationship, and Shane didn't mind one bit. He'd had a lot longer to come to terms with his bisexuality than Tucker had.

Once Tuck was in position, Shane helped Paige climb on top of him. With one knee on either side of Tucker's hips, she lowered herself until the man's cock touched her core. Shane watched as she slowly humped the hard flesh between her legs while Tucker resumed his sensual invasion of her mouth. Placing his hand between Paige's shoulder blades, Shane urged her to relax against Tucker's chest. "Down you go, baby. I want access to both of you."

Shane dropped his knees to the floor between Tucker's legs, which hung off the side of the bed, and pushed them outward, giving himself more room. After taking a moment to admire the way Paige's pussy was nestled against his husband's shaft, Shane leaned down and licked Tucker's balls, the root of his cock, and then Paige's swollen labia, all in one pass. When the two of them moaned in tandem, he did it again and again. Grabbing Paige's hips, Shane lifted her enough that he could fuck her with his tongue. When she held herself up for him, he cupped Tuck's balls in his hand, rolling and squeezing them.

Retreating a little, Shane gathered up some of the cream seeping from Paige's pussy and brought it down to the crack of Tuck's ass. He used it to lubricate the man's tight hole. Shane planned to screw Tuck while his husband was buried deep inside Paige, knowing he couldn't be gentle enough for her the first time he came tonight. But once he took the edge off, Shane intended to find out just how good it felt to be inside the sweet woman he was falling in love with. He couldn't tell her that yet—hell, he couldn't even tell Tuck that yet—but he knew it was happening. This beautiful woman was easily worming her way into his heart, and he had more than enough room to let her in. He just had to wait until he was sure she and Tuck were both on the same page as him before making any declarations of love.

As he finger fucked Tucker, Shane returned to feasting on Paige's ripe flesh. She squirmed against his lips and tongue, gasping and moaning. He took her higher and higher, urged on by her mewls disappearing into Tucker's mouth. Shane impaled her with his tongue and was thrilled when she came for him. Her entire body shook with the impact, and he continued to lap at her juices until she settled back down on Tucker's chest, gasping for air. But the night was far from over. That was just the first of many orgasms they planned to give her tonight.

Tucker shifted Paige, dragging her up his torso so he could give her breasts the attention they deserved. Her new position gave Shane access to his husband's cock, and he sucked it into his mouth, reveling in the familiar, masculine taste.

Tucker's hips bucked. "Fuck, yeah, Shane! Suck me! Harder!"

Rolling to one side and lifting her leg so she didn't

hit Shane in the head, Paige watched him pleasure the other man, desire evident in her eyes. His gaze held hers as he took Tucker to the back of his throat repeatedly. For his part, Tucker writhed on the bed, but he could still reach up and cup Paige's head. "Help him, baby. I want both of your mouths on me."

Paige crawled over to join Shane, and he released Tucker's cock from his mouth and held it upright for her. "Lick him, sweetheart."

She leaned closer, and her perfect, pink tongue made long strokes from root to tip. Shane's own dick hardened to the point of pain. "Fuck, that's so damn hot. Take him in your mouth and blow him."

As she did as instructed, Tucker muttered a bunch of lust-filled curses while Shane climbed up on the bed. He laid down next to Tuck in a sixty-nine position, never taking his gaze from Paige's cock-filled mouth. Tuck's hand closed around Shane's erection, and seconds later, his husband began to suck him. A groan escaped Shane as he leaned forward and licked Tuck's cock as Paige withdrew it from her mouth.

They soon became a moving mass of human flesh and bones. Hands and mouths went everywhere they could reach. Grabbing Paige's leg, Tuck brought it to the other side of his head, so he could indulge himself with her delicious pussy. Shane and Paige tortured him and each other with their lips and tongues, fueling the passion filling the room. Extending her hand, Paige found Shane's thick shaft, and when her fingers closed around him, he nearly blew his load right then and there. He moved out of her reach before that could happen.

Crawling to the edge of the bed, he looked down and located his sweatpants, close enough to snatch up from the floor. He removed the two condoms he'd tucked in the pocket earlier and tossed one on the nightstand. Opening the other one, he put it on Tuck, eliciting an anguished groan from the man while Paige watched intently.

"Paige, sweetheart?" Shane waited until her gaze met his. He leaned over and brushed his lips across hers. "Tuck's going to fuck you while I fuck him. Are you okay with that?"

While she hadn't had any objections before now, he wanted her to know she could still back out. If she wasn't ready to have sex with either of them, that didn't mean they couldn't let her watch if she wanted to. Hell, it wouldn't be the first time she'd seen the two men go at it like rabbits. Only Tuck still wasn't aware of that fact.

"Yes, I'm very . . . okay with that," Paige responded breathlessly.

"Come with me, then." Shane held out his hand and helped Paige stand before leading her over to the chaise he knew she liked to stretch out on when she was reading. He adjusted a throw pillow at the head of the lounger. "Lay on your back and spread your legs wide."

After she did as he'd ordered, Tuck handed a bottle of lube to Shane, then knelt between Paige's legs. With his latex-covered cock in his hand, he rubbed the tip of it over the wet lips of her pussy. With one hand on her knee, holding it so she was completely exposed to his view, Shane watched as his husband's dick slid between her folds, disappearing into her tight channel. Paige gasped as she raised her hips, inviting Tuck to go deeper. The man slid in and out, moaning with pleasure.

"Damn, that's so fucking hot," Shane said, his gaze glued to where Paige and Tuck were joined. "How does she feel, Tuck?"

The other man's eyes were shut, and Shane knew he was probably trying not to go off like a rocket. Tuck groaned. "Fucking awesome. She's so tight, Shane. So damn hot. If you want to join us before I blow it, then you better get in my ass now."

Shane took one last look at Paige's face. He saw nothing but pure pleasure there. No hesitation. No second thoughts. No regrets. Her desire-filled gaze met his. "Please, hurry. I'm not going to last, either. Oh, God, that feels so good! Please!"

That was all the encouragement he needed. Flipping the lid of the tube in his hand, he squeezed a small amount of lube into the crack of Tuck's ass. He'd taken his husband enough times over the years that there was little need to prep him, but Shane still used his fingers to work the slick liquid past the man's sphincter quickly. Tuck's hips slowly moved back and forth. "Shit. Hurry, Shane. Damn, sweetheart, you're like a vice. Feels amazing."

Bending his knees, he positioned himself at the entrance to Tuck's ass, then eased his cock inside. It only took a moment or two until he was fully engulfed by his husband's familiar, hot, tight walls. As Shane pulled out again, Tucker did the same, easing from Paige's pussy. Shane thrust forward, hard and fast, sending Tuck deep into Paige once more. They did it over and over, working in tandem, with Shane fucking Tuck and Tuck fucking Paige. Her gasping, moaning, and begging, combined with Tuck's, was music to Shane's ears.

Paige's whimpers became louder and climbed several octaves, and Tuck's ass clenched around his husband's cock. "She's about to come, Shane, and shit, she's gonna take me with her."

"Do it. I'm right behind you." He had no doubts that when Paige's orgasm sent Tucker over the edge, he wouldn't be able to stop himself from falling into the abyss right after them.

Both men increased the pace and depths of their thrusts as Shane clutched Tuck's hips. The erotic sounds of flesh hitting flesh filled the room, combined with muttered pleas and curses. Shane felt his balls draw up into his body. His eyes slammed shut as he tried to stave off the inevitable for a few more seconds, wanting both his lovers to come before he did.

"Oh, God!" Paige cried out as her body shook with the impact of her climax.

Tuck plunged into her once, twice, then stilled as he emptied himself into the latex barrier. But there was nothing between the two men, and when Shane ejaculated, he filled his husband's ass with his seed.

As carnal bliss fell over the trio, Tuck collapsed on top of Paige, both gulping for oxygen. Shane staggered backward until his legs hit the bed. He flopped onto the mattress, his lungs heaving. Rolling his head to the side, he stared at the two bodies still entangled on the chaise and wished like hell it wasn't a Sunday night. It sucked they had to get up early in the morning because he wanted nothing more than to fuck both of them all night long in every position they could come up with.

But the night wasn't over just yet.

Chapter Twenty-Four

Two weeks later, Shane held Paige's hand as he escorted her to the admission booth set up at one of the two entrances to the rodeo grounds. As far as he could tell, the reporters had given up on trying to interrogate him, Paige, and Tuck after being snubbed for over a week. They'd interviewed everyone in town, or at least tried to. Shane had read a few of the resulting articles online but had finally stopped because Paige was afraid of his blood pressure spiking. Apparently, his face turned red, his jaw clenched, and his temple throbbed while he read them. He was still livid at Bridget for inviting the tabloid trash into Hazard Falls, knowing the turmoil that would result, but he and Tuck were biding their time, waiting for the right moment to get their revenge. They wouldn't harm her, at least not physically, but they would make sure a heavy dose of karma came her way. Shane was tossing a few ideas around in his head, and hopefully, one of them would get the desired results.

In the meantime, even though the reporters and cameramen had checked out of the motel they'd been staying in, Shane wasn't taking any chances that one or more of them would circle back into town. Anytime Paige left the ranch, she'd be accompanied by either Shane, Tuck, or Seth. The latter, though, was only to be used in emergencies. Shane trusted his employee to keep Paige safe but was still pissed the dog had been trying to seduce her. Not that he blamed the man for trying, but Shane was keeping that to himself.

The Rodeo Bonanza didn't start for a few more hours, but the grounds were bustling with activity. Bulls, horses, and sheep were being herded into their respective pens—children would ride the smaller animals during mutton-busting events. Food was being prepared. Cowboys—Tuck and Seth among them—and cowgirls were checking their equipment and shining their saddles. Equine manes and tails were being combed, braided, and decorated. Last-minute fencing and gates were being put into place, and plenty of other chores were being done. Thank God this only happened once a year because it was a huge under-taking for the residents of Hazard Falls. However, everyone enjoyed it, especially owners of the restau-rants, bars, and shops, who, on average, more than quadrupled their sales for the month, thanks to the two-day event.

As they approached the southeast entrance, Nicole

and Lila spotted them and waved them over. Tucker's sister grinned when she noticed Paige's hand enveloped by Shane's larger one, but she didn't mention it. "Well, hi, you two. I assume my brother is over by the stables. Where's Arianna?"

Shane dropped Paige's hand and kissed Lila, then Nicole on the cheek. "Seth took her to the petting zoo pen. You'd think she has enough animals to dote on at the ranch."

"That girl is going to be a veterinarian someday. I guarantee it."

"That's fine with me, as long as she doesn't want to open her practice in my barn."

Nicole smiled. "You say that now, but when she's ready to go off into the great big world on her own, you'll do everything you can to keep her here."

He shrugged. "Damn straight. But if she needs to spread her wings and fly, we'll let her. Of course, we'll probably attach a tracking device to her somehow."

The three women laughed out loud.

"Shane! I need your help over here, please!" The grocery store owner was setting up one of the many food tents a short distance away from the entrance.

"Coming, Marla!" Shane looked at Paige, then tilted his head toward Lila and Nicole. "You're in good hands. Call my cell if you need anything or if you see any of the reporters or cameramen. I'll be helping out all over the place, but I won't be far away."

"I'm sure I'll be fine."

Surprising himself, Paige, and the two other

women, Shane leaned down and gave Paige a brief but intense kiss on the lips. When he stood straight again, he grinned at her shocked expression. After giving her a wink, he hurried off to help Marla with whatever she needed to be done. Shane was certain Tucker would get word of that kiss faster than a spreading wildfire. It was a good thing they were now all in agreement that the trio wouldn't hide their new relationship. They'd talked about it last night after Paige had given Arianna a bath and put her to bed. While none of them had uttered the L-word yet, Shane knew his husband had fallen as hard for Paige as he had over the few past few weeks. And, if his suspicions were correct, she was falling for them too.

Up until last night, the two men made sweet love to their woman or just cuddled with her in her bed for a few hours before returning to their own, long before Arianna awoke. They hadn't wanted to get the little girl's hopes up before they knew the ménage relationship would work. The men also had wanted time to clear the last of Sarah's ghost from their bedroom. While her clothing had been donated to a women's shelter in Garden City, per her wishes, other things remained. It'd been little things they couldn't bring themselves to move into other parts of the house until recently. Her jewelry box was now tucked away in a closet in the office to be given to Ari when she was old enough to appreciate the contents and not lose them. Things like Sarah's toiletries and hairbrush, which had been scattered throughout the master bath's drawers and cabinets or in her dresser, had finally been removed. Any pictures with Sarah in them had been taken from the bedroom and distributed about the house after Paige had told them it didn't bother her that their late wife's image was in almost every room. She'd said she respected the woman who'd brought Tuck and Shane together and given them their daughter and liked to think they would have been friends if they'd known each other.

Last night, once the master suite no longer resembled a shrine, Tuck and Shane had brought Paige into their own bed, where they'd made sweet love to her for hours. When the sun had risen this morning, and the toilet in Arianna's bathroom had flushed, Shane had gotten up, leaving his two lovers cuddling in their sleep, and plodded out to the kitchen to have breakfast with his daughter. Ari didn't seem surprised when Tuck and Paige emerged from the same hallway a half hour later—in fact, she'd been too busy talking about everything she planned on doing and seeing at the rodeo to even really notice.

A threesome was still very new to Paige, but both men made sure they had some one-on-one time with her, as well as with each other. They wanted her to know them as individuals as well as a couple. Sometimes Shane would stay after breakfast and talk with Paige as he helped her with the dishes or join her for lunch on his paperwork days. Tucker liked to take walks around the ranch in the evenings, and he'd invited Paige to accompany him on a few occasions.

More than once, their duet interludes had involved sex or a make-out session—well, more often than not, at least in Shane's case—but many times, they didn't. It was dating small-town-ranch-and-ménage style.

As for the employees of Red River Ranch, Shane was sure they had their suspicions about the ménage, but no one, other than Seth, had questioned it or mentioned it to him. Tuck and Shane had wanted to give Paige time to be certain this was what she wanted before the rumor mill went into production, so they'd avoided PDAs. They'd told her all about how Sarah had handled things, what her snappy comebacks had been whenever someone tried to insult her or snub her because she had two husbands. If their wife ever felt depressed about being bullied by the snobs of the town, she'd never let anyone know it, not even Shane and Tucker. Whenever they'd asked her about it, she'd always said the love she felt for them squashed any negativity that came her way. On her deathbed, she'd told them that she had never regretted her decision to love two men—and Shane believed her with all his heart.

While Sarah and Paige were both strong women, their personalities were different. Where Sarah had tended to be more reserved, laughing at jokes but never really telling one, Paige was very outgoing once she felt comfortable around someone new. The ranch hands had been delighted when she'd joined in the friendly barbs being thrown around the ranch, especially at breakfast. The men and women who worked at Triple-

R were so much more than employees—they were family. It wasn't often a new position opened at the ranch since those that occupied them usually stayed for a very long time.

Shane hoped Paige was willing to stay with them for a very long time, too—in fact, for the rest of their lives. She belonged there, and he didn't think he and Tuck would ever be able to let her go.

As Shane walked away, Paige's gaze stayed glued to his back—actually, to his perfect, denim-clad ass—as she tried to ignore Lila's and Nicole's open-mouthed stares. Tucker, Shane, and she had discussed not hiding their relationship anymore. Still, she hadn't expected Shane to kiss her right in the middle of the rodeo grounds, announcing to everyone that there was plenty of hanky-panky going on at the Red River Ranch.

Her cheeks flamed as she turned to face her two new friends. She'd gotten to know them both well over the past few weeks, and she really liked them. But she wasn't prepared for the onslaught of questions that were surely coming her way. Paige cleared her throat. "So . . . tell me what I'll be doing in the booth."

"Oh, no, no, no, girl," Nicole chastised, wagging a finger at Paige as her eyes brimmed with amusement and curiosity. "Work can wait—the ticket booths don't open for another hour. You've been holding out on us.

Lila crossed her arms and cocked her hip to the side, but the broad smile on her face belied her attempt to appear pissed. "Apparently, my brother and brother-in-law have also been holding out. Damn, Paige, you cost me fifty dollars!"

Her eyes grew wide. "What? What are you talking about?"

"Betty Lou and I had a bet. We both agreed you were perfect for Tuck and Shane, but I said it would be three months before y'all realized it. Lou said two months." She glanced around. "Shit. Too many people saw that kiss for me to ask you to hide for another month." Her mouth turned into a frown. "And the tittle-tattling has already started. Bridget is madder than a wet hen, and she'll be the first one slinging the mud, *bless her heart*. You should smack Shane for not looking around first before planting a big one on you. Well, that was actually a small one, as kisses go, but it was enough to light off some fireworks."

Paige followed Lila's gaze across the gravel parking lot. Sure enough, the blonde bitch's eyes were cold as she sneered in their direction. There was no doubt Bridget and her brunette friend, who Paige had never seen before, were talking about the kiss they, and others, had seen. Refusing to give them the satisfaction of thinking they'd upset her—which they hadn't—Paige put on the biggest smile she could . . . then waved at her rival. "Hi, Bridget. Nice to see you again. So sorry

Shane and Tucker couldn't make it to your dinner party—they were otherwise occupied."

When the other woman's face turned an angry red, her cold eyes went absolutely frigid. Paige expected to see steam rising from her bleached-blonde hair. Lila and Nicole burst out laughing. The latter looped her arm around Paige's elbow and pulled her toward the booth they'd be working in. "Sometimes I forget you know how to play the small-town game. You'll fit in just fine, my friend. But don't think you got out of telling us the details behind that hot kiss!"

Two hours later, the three women were busy taking money, handing out admission tickets, answering questions, and giving directions. Each had their own window built into the side of the structure, which also contained a small table and a safe that had been brought in and bolted into the floor for the occasion. Every half hour, Nicole would close her window for a moment, then take a portion of the larger bills from each till and put them in the safe. Later, the money would be transferred to the bank under the watchful eyes of the manager, a clerk, and two of the local deputies.

Today was for the amateur events, then tomorrow, the professionals would take over the competition. It wasn't a televised event, but there were still many pros in attendance since the event was held on a weekend that didn't have many other options for them in the national circuit. Over the years, the organizers had tried to keep it that way, and high-ranking participants from the PRCA—Professional Rodeo Cowboy Association—liked having a small-town event to ride in for a change.

The kids' mutton busting had finished, and one of the junior events for teens had started a few minutes ago. There was already a large crowd to cheer them on. Tucker's bronc-riding contest was scheduled to start in a little over an hour while Seth was calf-roping later in the afternoon. Meanwhile, Lou had entered the barrel racing, and two of Red River's ranch hands would be riding bulls for the coveted buckle in the highlighted event that evening. Paige realized how much she'd missed the rodeo days held in some of the larger towns surrounding Johnsonville, Nebraska. It'd always been a big weekend party when the rodeo rolled in.

After taking Ari to the petting zoo and watching the mutton busting, Seth had brought her to the little hut that housed the admission booth, so Paige could watch her for a while. Nicole's husband, Hank, had also dropped off Joey, so the two girls were sitting on the floor, playing jacks—another fond memory from Paige's childhood. Growing up in a small town meant not having access to many things most kids in the cities and suburbs took for granted. The children of places like Hazard Falls and her hometown of Johnsonville still played outside and made their own fun and games instead of living in their rooms on computers.

Paige handed another customer his tickets, then waited for him to move away before realizing no one else was waiting behind him.

"Hi, Mrs. Mathers. Is Joey around?"

Peeking out her window, Paige saw a little blonde-haired girl about Arianna's age standing on her tiptoes, looking earnestly at Nicole. With her was a teenage couple who looked about eighteen or so. The young woman wore designer short-shorts that barely covered her ass cheeks and a tight, pink tank top. Her blonde hair and facial features were similar to the little girl, so they had to be related. The guy standing beside her, with his hand on her ass, was bad news. Paige could see that from a mile away, thanks to his long, dirty-blond hair, beady eyes, and the cigarette tucked behind his ear. His white, sleeveless T-shirt over torn jeans, crude arm tattoo, and a smirk that seemed permanent sealed the deal. In fact, his date looked way out of his league.

"Yes, she is, Brooke," Nicole replied to the little girl as she handed three tickets to the older one. "She's in here with Ari playing jacks. Would you like to join them?"

"Yay!"

"No!" The teenage blonde glared at the young girl in distaste. "You're staying with us. Mom said you can't play with that little brat."

Paige froze at the venom in the teenager's voice in addition to her words. Beside her, Nicole bristled, her eyes narrowing. If there weren't a wall between them, she'd probably be in the teen's face. "And which 'little brat' are you referring to, *Brenna*?"

The teen sneered, her face turning ugly, and, at that

moment, Paige knew who their mother was. *Bridget.* Figured.

"I'll tell Daddy," Brooke whined.

Her sister ignored Nicole's question. "You think I give a fuck?"

"But I wanna play with them."

"Shut the fuck up, you little brat!" Without acknowledging Nicole's question, Brenna pointed at Paige, surprising her. "Ty, that's the slut I told you about, screwing the two guys who also screw each other."

Ty eyed what he could see of Paige through the window. He licked his chapped lips, which disgusted her. "Guess neither is man enough to satisfy you, huh? Whatta you expect from fucking queers? I'd be more than happy to show you what a real man can do, babe."

Anger scorched Paige. The strong plexiglass was the only thing preventing her from flying through the window and smashing the repulsive leer off the punk's face. Instead, she crossed her arms and scowled at him. "Considering you'll never be a real man and don't even know what one is, I'll pass."

He shrugged his shoulders. "Your loss."

The two teens laughed as they walked away, dragging the now-crying little girl with them. Paige glanced at Ari and Joey, who'd missed the exchange as they played, before turning back to Nicole and Lila. There was a lull in the ticket line.

Lila shook her head. "*Those* were Bridget's girls."

"I figured that out," Paige replied. "The apples didn't fall far from the tree, huh?"

"Actually," Nicole chimed in. "They're like night and day—two different fathers. Brenna's was Bridget's first husband—a bull rider from out of town—but her father made sure the marriage was annulled after learning the guy couldn't keep it in his pants. Brooke's dad is a really nice guy, which makes you wonder what he saw in Bridget. That marriage lasted about three years, if I remember correctly. Thankfully, he lives in the next town over and is very involved in Brooke's life. She takes after him, so I have no problem with Joey playing with her as long as it's not around Bridget or Brenna."

"I hope she stays a good kid and her mother and sister aren't a big influence on her as she grows up."

"So do I. Anyway, I wonder what Brenna would say if she knew her mother wanted to get horizontal between Shane and Tuck."

Several people approached the windows, and the women's unscheduled, two-minute break was over. Pushing the unpleasant encounter from her mind, Paige got back to work.

Chapter Twenty-Five

"Let's go, Tuck! Ride 'em, cowboy!"

In the bleachers above the ring, Shane put his pinkies in his mouth and whistled loudly as Ari and Paige sat next to him, cheering. Tuck was down in the chute, settling into his saddle on the bronc that would try its damnedest to buck him off. He was the last participant in this event and needed a score of seventy-seven on his eight-second ride to win the competition. Shane knew it was possible, Tuck's best score in the past had been an eighty-one. In fact, the man could have gone pro years ago, but that would have meant being on the road constantly, moving from state to state, with no guarantee an injury wouldn't end his career before he'd seen the big money. So, instead, he stayed in the amateur ranks and did it for fun. He'd won numerous times and had a bunch of gold and silver buckles to prove it. Tuck had put the money that came with them in the bank for their daughter's college fund. There was a tidy sum in there, and it would be enough for tuition for any number of schools, depending on what Ari wanted to study.

The aromas of chili, popcorn, fried foods, leather, hay, and dung wafted over the rodeo grounds. A few airhorns went off, and a rodeo clown joked with the crowd while waiting for the signal indicating the next rider was ready.

When the announcer called out Tuck's name over the loudspeaker, it was met with applause and hollers supporting the local boy. As the guy in charge of opening the chute prepared to pull the rope attached to the gate, Tuck finally signaled he was ready. When the horse was released into the ring, all four hooves left the ground as Tuck held on for dear life. As required, his spurs touched the horse above the shoulder when the hooves landed for the first time with a thud in the ring. One hand held onto the reins attached to a halter, while the other hand was above his head for balance as he quickly found his rhythm with the bucking mass beneath him. His feet remained in the stirrups as he was tossed about. The horse spun, twisted, and kicked its hind legs high in the air, trying to throw its rider. Dust and dirt were sprayed into the air whenever the horse's hooves hit the ground. The crowd got to their feet, yelling and whistling as the seconds ticked by. Tuck's cowboy hat flew from his head, but he stayed glued to the saddle.

No matter how often Shane had watched his husband compete, he still held his breath until the buzzer sounded. As she stood beside him, Paige's lungs didn't seem to be working either. Her hands were clasped under her chin as she watched the action with wide eyes.

Eight seconds felt like eight hours, but when the time was finally up, the buzzer went off loud enough for Tuck to hear. He let go of the reins and not-so-gracefully dismounted, rolling and stumbling out of the way of the still-bucking horse. The rodeo clown and a few cowboys got between Tuck and the animal, which began to calm down after noticing his rider was gone. Cheers filled the air as Tuck picked up his hat and flung it into the air in celebration. It'd been a great ride, but how great depended on the judges. Fifty points were based on the rider, while the other fifty rated the horse's attempt to rid itself of the man on its back.

All eyes were on the giant electronic scoreboard on the opposite end of the ring. If this had been one of the bigger rodeos, there would have been a replay of the ride on a jumbo screen. There, all they could do was wait. Tuck's gaze was on the board as he strode toward the section of the bleachers where his family sat, his recovered hat back on his head. Meanwhile, the prancing horse had been ushered out of the ring. Tuck put one boot on the bottom rung of the fencing and hoisted himself up, still staring at the scoreboard.

When the digital numbers lit up, announcing a score of seventy-nine, he jumped back into the ring, throwing his hat and hands in the air as the crowd went wild. Shane suddenly found Paige plastered against his chest, her arms around his neck. He picked her up and hugged her tightly before setting her down again. Swinging Arianna up in the air, he hurried down a few steps to where Tuck was now waiting for them. Shane handed over their daughter, and Tucker walked a short victory lap around the center of the ring with her on his shoulders. He'd done it every time he won since she was eleven months old.

Shane put his arm around Paige's waist and tucked her into his side. She was breathless and placed a hand on his chest. "Oh, my God! That was amazing! I knew he could ride, but actually watching him is a totally different thing!"

He couldn't help but bend down and whisper in her ear. "I prefer watching him ride you, sweetheart."

Her cheeks burned bright red, and he busted out laughing. *Damn, I love this woman.*

Pulling Paige into his arms, Tuck did a simple two-step to the music as they made their way around the dance floor. Several large tents had been set up on the rodeo grounds, and cold beer, good food, country music from a live band, and loud conversation were on everyone's agenda tonight. The competitions were over, and the buckles and prize money were all awarded. Tuck wore his new gold buckle on his belt.

He stared down at Paige. "I know I said this earlier, but you look beautiful tonight, darlin'." It was the first time he'd ever seen her all gussied up in a dress, and he'd be damned if it was the last time. The retro, ivory-lace garment draped over her curves, stopping just below the tops of her vintage button-up boots. Two thin straps held up the dress. Not for the first time that night, he leaned down and kissed the exposed skin where her neck and shoulder met.

"Thank you. You're looking mighty handsome tonight too." She smiled as she brushed her hand over his chest before returning it to the spot just above his clavicle. "Because of you and Shane, I've been getting a lot of jealous glares." Both men wore their best snug jeans—black for Tuck, dark blue for Shane—crisp, white western shirts, cowboy boots, and black hats. Tuck wouldn't exactly call himself handsome, but his husband looked downright fuckable. Even after all the years they'd been together, it still amazed Tuck that Shane was the only man he'd ever been attracted to. Not that he planned on straying. In fact, if something happened to his husband, Tuck doubted he'd ever have another intimate relationship with someone of the same gender ever again.

He winked at her as he steered her around a slower couple. "Let 'em be jealous. We've only got eyes for you." Hell, he loved it when her cheeks were splashed with pink.

"The feeling is mutual."

His cock stirred in his jeans at the husky tone of her voice. He looked forward to taking her and Shane home and fucking them both silly tonight. Arianna was sleeping at Nicole's house with the woman's mother babysitting for the evening, so the trio could be as loud as they wanted throughout the night, which Tuck planned on doing. As they always did the day after the annual Rodeo Bonanza, the owners and employees of Red River Ranch would take the day off, for the most part. Only the bare minimum of work needed to be done, like feeding and watering the animals. Coins had been tossed to see who would handle the morning feedings and who'd take care of the evening ones. Shane had to get up early with Seth and a few other hands before returning to Tucker and Paige in their extra-large, king-sized bed.

Most of the residents of Hazard Falls would be too exhausted from the hectic weekend, so only a few businesses would be open. Years ago, the local school district declared the Monday afterward a holiday of sorts so that the students would be off as well. During the following week, the townsfolk would work together to take down the tents, other temporary structures, and fencing at the rodeo grounds. Everything would be stored away until next year.

A couple moved in next to them, and the guy hip-checked Tuck. Pulling his gaze from Paige, he laughed when he saw it was Shane, taking Betty Lou for a spin around the dance floor. The two men had taken turns dancing with their woman all evening, which had obviously caused a stir. Word had spread about the kisses and hugs Shane and Tuck had exchanged with Paige over the past two days.

The men had never been big on public displays of affection between themselves unless it was during small gatherings with their friends and family, but with Sarah and now Paige, PDAs had become a normal occurrence. But there were plenty of Hazard Falls residents and even a few tourists who'd eyed them with disgust over the past forty-eight hours. Shane and Tuck had made sure that at least one of them was available to come between Paige and anyone who wanted to insult her for being with two men. If she needed to go to the ladies' room, Lila, Nicole, or Lou went with her, although Paige hadn't figured out yet that her lovers had asked the other women to watch her back. It wasn't that they thought Paige couldn't defend herself—they were sure she could— but some of the women in the small town could be downright nasty, especially if they teamed up. Again, they wanted her to become more comfortable in their relationship before she was exposed to its only downside.

The two-step music changed over to one perfect for line dancing. Shane and Tucker lined up with everyone else and put Paige in between them. Lou ended up on the other side of Shane, but she stormed off the dance floor after Lane sidled up next to her. Tuck chuckled when the police officer grinned and shrugged his shoulders before shifting to get between two blonde twenty-somethings.

When the song ended, Shane went to grab three beers from the bar while Tuck and Paige stood off to the side, trying to cool off. The night air was still humid but seemed to be letting up a bit. Paige waved her hands in front of her face, trying to create even the slightest of breezes. "What's up with Lane and Betty Lou? She won't say, and Nicole and Lila said they don't know the whole story."

Tuck took her hand and led her over to a table that'd just opened up. After they settled into two of the four folding chairs, he said, "I honestly don't know what's going on with them. Nicole probably knows more than I do. She grew up here like Lou and Lane did. All I know is what Shane told me—they dated their senior year of high school, then broke up after gradua- tion. Lane went and enlisted while Lou stayed in Hazard. She never gave anyone an explanation, to my knowledge, but was really pissed when he came back to town and took a job with the police department." He grinned. "But the sexual tension between those two is freaking unbelievable. I can't wait to see what happens when it comes to a head."

"Me too. She talks and acts like she hates him, but she has a hard time keeping her eyes off him when she thinks no one's watching."

"I've noticed that too."

"Noticed what?" Shane set a beer down in front of

each of them, then took the seat on the other side of Paige.

"Lane and Lou," his husband answered, simply knowing Shane would understand what he was referring to.

A broad, amused smile spread across Shane's face. "Oh, to be a fly on the wall when that shit hits the fan."

"Right?"

Tuck's sister strode over, frowning. "Hey, guys, Seth sent me to get you. Some asshole slashed the tires and keyed the passenger side of Shane's truck."

"What?" Shock then rage coated Shane's face as he jumped to his feet. "Motherfuckers!" He hurried toward the far side of the rodeo grounds, where he'd parked the vehicle earlier in the day.

Tuck stood to follow, then stopped, glancing down at Paige. She was having such a good time, and he didn't want the vandalism to disrupt it. Lila patted his shoulder. "Go. I'll stay with her. Make sure he doesn't kill anyone."

Despite his sister's offer, he still wanted to ensure Paige would be okay without them. "Paige?"

There was worry in her eyes, but she nodded. "I'm fine. Go with Shane. As Lila said, make sure he doesn't kill anyone."

Leaning down, he brushed his lips across hers before whispering in her ear, "No worries. I have dirty plans for the two of you later, and they don't involve Shane sitting in a jail cell."

And there's that blush I love to see.

Chapter Twenty-Six

As Lila took the seat Shane had vacated, Paige watched Tucker follow the same path his husband had taken through the crowd. "Who would do such a thing?"

The other woman shook her head. "Not sure, but I have my suspicions."

Paige eyed her. "Bridget?"

"Or her teenage brat's boyfriend. Shane had a man-to-dickhead chat with him yesterday."

Her gut clenched. "Shit. I knew I shouldn't have said anything to them about that."

"They would have been pissed if you'd kept it from them." Lila reached over and patted her forearm. "Listen, Paige. One thing I'll say about Tuck and Shane is that they're extremely protective over who or what is theirs. Yes, they care about you as a woman, but even if you weren't in a relationship with them, you're also their employee, and the results would have been the same. They take care of their own."

A sigh had her relaxing a bit. "I know that." It was obvious to anyone who knew Shane and Tucker well that they were good men.

"Hey, darlin', how about a dance?"

With a beer gut and the stench of chewing tobacco and sweat emanating from him, a tall, half-drunk cowboy grasped Paige's arm and attempted to haul her to her feet without waiting for a response. She slapped her hand on the table, trying to gain balance, before yanking her arm from the creep. "Uh, no, thanks."

"Back off, cowboy," Lila warned as she stood.

The jackass ignored Tuck's sister as he leered at Paige. "C'mon, darlin'. I saw you spreading the love with those two guys earlier. Wh-what's one more?"

His eyes were bloodshot, and his speech was thick. He was drunker than Paige had initially suspected. She didn't recognize him and didn't think Lila did either, so he was probably one of the many cowboys who'd rolled in with the rodeo.

"Let's dance, honey." He reached out to take her arm again but was suddenly jerked backward.

Lane Myers had him by the back of his shirt, pulling him away from Paige. The police officer towered over him by almost six inches and was in a lot better shape. Instead of his button-down, white uniform shirt and the shiny gold shield he wore most of the time he was on duty, tonight, Lane wore a white polo shirt with the department logo on it. His duty belt, with his gun, handcuffs, keys, and a bunch of other things, sat on his hips over his navy blue cargo pants. "What'd I tell you earlier about asking permission before laying your hands on a woman? You really want to spend the night in jail before you leave town tomorrow?"

"Naaaw, *occifer*," the man slurred as he swayed on his feet, the alcohol dragging him down. If Lane wasn't still holding him by the shirt, he might've fallen on his ass. "What I really want is a—a sssoft bed and f-fine woman. Nuttin' wrong with that, isss there?"

Lane shook his head and rolled his eyes. "Not at all, Darren, but you're supposed to chat with them first, then romance them a bit before you ask for permission to touch them. You're going about it all wrong, man. Now apologize to the ladies."

The drunk finally had the sense to appear sheepish. He took his hat off. "S-sorry, ma'am . . . ma'ams. But the blonde over there . . ." He gestured with his forefinger over the opposite shoulder and almost poked Lane in the eye. ". . . said you wanted to dance and get down and dirty with—with every guy here. Guess that's not true, huh?"

"No, it's not." Although Paige couldn't tell who Darren pointed to, she had a pretty good idea it was Bridget who'd sent the man over. The woman was really getting on her nerves. Paige wondered if the bitch *did* have something to do with Shane's truck being damaged.

"Sorry, ma'am," he repeated as he settled his hat

back on his head. "Won't happen again. *Occifer*, can you point me in the direction of my—my truck?"

Lane snorted. "Nope, but I can give you a lift to your motel."

The man pivoted and almost lost his balance but managed to stay upright with a little assistance from Lane. Darren slapped the lawman's shoulder. "Sounds good, but I gotta take a piss first."

"I'll find you a tree along the way. Let's go."

Crossing her arms, Lila shook her head as the two men sauntered away—well, one sauntered, the other staggered. "One guess who the blonde was."

"Don't need to guess. I've had it up to here with her." Paige brought her flat hand above her head.

"With whom?"

She spun around to see Tuck had returned. Knowing it was best to tell him what happened before he heard it from anyone else, she laid it all out as Lila stepped away to talk to a friend of hers. As Paige spoke, Tuck's eyes narrowed.

"Are you okay?" he asked when she was done, running his hands up and down her arms. She could see he was clenching his jaw.

"Yeah, I'm fine." He didn't look like he believed her. "Really, Tucker, I'm fine. The guy apologized, and Lane's taking him to a motel."

"Good. It'll keep me from decking him." He took a deep breath and let it out slowly, obviously curbing his anger. "Shane and Seth are changing the two tires, using the spare and the one from the ranch truck a few of the hands drove over. I think we better head home. Shane will bitch about this all night if we let him, so we need to get his mind off it and onto something else."

Paige had a good idea what that "something else" was, and she was all for it. They'd had a great time over the past two days, and she didn't want the last hour to be the only thing they remembered. "Okay. But what about Bridget?"

Gently taking her upper arm, he led her toward the parking lot. "Don't worry. She'll get what's coming to her."

SHANE'S JAW WAS TIGHT AS HE FOLLOWED TUCK AND Paige into the house. He was beyond livid but didn't want to take it out on them, so he'd tried to get himself under control during the entire ride back out to the ranch. Between the flat tires, keyed doors and panels on the truck, the drunk cowboy who'd dared to touch their woman, and the bitch who'd probably been behind it all, Shane needed an outlet for his anger. But he was worried he'd scare the hell out of Paige if he took Tuck the way he wanted to. She'd seen them fuck before, but never as intensely as it could get between the two of them.

Shutting the front door behind them, he hung his hat next to Tuck's on the coat rack in the foyer. It was the same one his father had used for most of Shane's life after his mother had found it in a little antique shop just outside of Garden City.

Without saying a word, Paige took his hand and then Tuck's before leading them down the hall to the primary bedroom. She released them, then sashayed across the room and sat on the chaise. Shane raised his eyebrows. "Whatcha doing over there, sweetheart?"

"Tonight's my night to watch and give orders. I don't get to see everything when I'm in the middle."

He chuckled at her playfulness as his hands went to the buttons on his shirt. "You saw everything that night in the barn."

"Huh? What are you talking about?" Tuck leaned on the bed and was in the middle of pulling off his boots when he froze and looked at the two of them in confusion.

It was time to come clean. Shane took off his shirt and tossed it in the hamper just inside the walk-in closet. "The last time you and I fucked in the barn, our little woman here was up in the loft, getting an earful and probably an eyeful."

"You bastard," Tuck said, but there was no anger in his tone. He shook his head and went back to getting undressed.

Shane shed his boots, jeans, and boxer briefs. Striding naked across the room, he stopped in front of Paige, who eyed his erection. He held out his hand. Her brow furrowed as she took it and let him help her stand. He grasped the skirt of her dress and drew it up her body. "If you want to watch, that's fine. But I want to watch you get yourself off as you do. Is that what you did in the barn, baby? Did you masturbate up there while we were fucking each other?"

He pulled the dress up and over her head. Her pink cheeks answered his questions before she said anything. "Um, yeah."

"Thought so." He removed her strapless bra and then shoved her panties down her legs until she could step out of them. "Leave your boots on. They're sexy."

"I thought I was the one issuing orders tonight."

He gestured for her to take her seat again. "Nope, you're issuing *suggestions*. I'll be issuing the orders. Before you start, let me just do something first."

In another corner of the room was a standing mirror. He picked it up and put it next to the chaise at an angle. Meanwhile, Tuck had rid himself of all his clothes and walked over to stand in front of Paige. She licked her lips as she glanced back and forth between the two men's groins. "Promise me something, though?"

"Anything," Tuck responded, his voice thick with desire and need as his gaze roamed her body.

Shane repeated the word. "Anything, baby."

Her eyes met Shane's and held them. "Don't hold back." When he tilted his head to the side, she added, "I know you've been gentler with me between you. Show me what happens when you don't hold back with each other."

She was more perceptive than he'd known, but it

didn't surprise him. And she was right. Even that night in the barn, while it had been a damn good fuck, it still wasn't as potent as it could be between him and Tuck. When anger and frustration were thrown into their lovemaking, it was explosive, and tonight, he was both angry and frustrated—but not at either of them. "Are you sure?"

"Yes." There had been no hesitation in her answer and no uncertainty in her expression. She wanted to know everything about them, inside and out, no matter how overpowering it could be. Nothing had chased her away yet, so maybe she could also deal with this.

His chin dipped once in acquiescence. "As long as you masturbate for us."

Her gaze dropped to the floor. They'd taken her many different ways, except for her ass, but that was going to change tonight. Shane had picked up a set of anal plugs on a trip into Garden City the week before. Paige had been nervous initially, but she'd consented to using them. After a week's preparation, she was ready to take one of them in her ass while the other was in her snug pussy. The only other thing she hadn't done yet was get herself off in front of them.

Biting her bottom lip, she slowly dropped her hand to her bare sex. Shane hadn't thought he could get any harder than he already was, but holy hell, that was hot. Her hand stilled. "I *suggest* you start because I won't until you do."

Tuck barked out a laugh. "Yes, ma'am." He turned to his husband. "You heard the lady."

Shane closed the distance between them and clutched Tuck's head before smashing his mouth down on his. Their tongues dueled. One of Tuck's hands clasped the back of Shane's neck while his other hand cupped his jaw. Both men battled for dominance, something they did on occasion, neither willing to give in immediately. Shane knew Tuck was pissed about the incident with the truck and the drunk hitting on Paige, but that didn't scratch the surface of how Shane felt. He reached down and gripped Tuck's cock as tightly as possible, and the man moaned into Shane's mouth. Tuck kissed him along his jaw, then sank his teeth into Shane's shoulder. That spurred him on. He grabbed his husband's long locks, reveling in the fact he could use them to control him. He pulled, exposing Tuck's neck, before running his tongue over the pulsating artery and corded muscles. But he didn't stop there.

Shoving Tuck against the wall to face Paige, Shane dropped to his knees. "Hands behind your head," he growled. He was done playing.

After Tuck did as he was told, clearly understanding Shane needed to be in control this time more than he did, Shane deep-throated his thick cock. There would be no slow seduction. No gentleness. Nothing but a deep-seated need to take what was his and do as he pleased.

Shane sucked and licked, his gaze trailing up the taut abdomen and chest above him before shifting to the left. The mirror was in the perfect position to let him see Paige. Her eyes were glued to the blowjob he was giving Tuck. Her fingers stroked her wet pussy. *Damn, that's so fucking hot.* Her legs were spread wide, giving them both one hell of a show. Shane wouldn't disappoint her and redoubled his efforts to return the favor.

Releasing the cock for a moment, Shane spit on his fingers, then returned to sucking his husband's erection. His hand went between Tuck's legs, and he started to prep the hole he planned to fuck. But there were other things to take care of first. He worked a finger past Tuck's sphincter, and the man bucked his hips forward, moaning loudly as he did so. Shane loved it when no one else was around to squelch Tuck's vocal responses to the pleasure he was receiving. With Arianna home, Shane rarely got to hear Tuck lose control.

"Fuck, Shane! Do that again. Oh, please."

That's what he wanted to hear—Tuck begging.

Shane took him to the back of his throat again and swallowed around the tip of his cock, as he finger-fucked Tuck's ass. Cupping and rolling the man's balls with his other hand, Shane sped up his assault, silently demanding his lover's orgasm. Male and female moans filled the air. Shane claimed them both as his.

Tuck gasped. "Oh, shit! Come with me, Paige. I'm going to fill Shane's mouth."

"Yessss," she hissed. "Oh, God, I'm close!"

Without letting up, Shane watched Paige in the mirror. Her fingers rubbed her clit as fast as they could go. Her other hand was at her breast, tugging and rolling the nipple. Feeling the sac in his hand draw upward, Shane thrust his finger as far as it would go into Tuck's ass, setting off the man's climax.

"Oh, shit!" Tuck shouted as streams of cum shot into Shane's mouth, and he swallowed every drop.

Paige's orgasm hit her hard. "Oh, God!" Her eyes slammed shut, her body quivering.

As Tuck sagged against the wall, heaving for oxygen, Shane left him and crawled over to Paige. He grabbed the wrist of the hand still between her legs and licked every digit before moving it out of his way. He lapped at her cream-coated pussy, adding her taste to what was still on his tongue from Tuck. It wasn't long before she climbed again, then screamed as she went over the edge.

Now that both of his lovers were taken care of, it was Shane's turn to find his release. Getting to his feet, he shoved Tuck face down over the edge of the bed, not worried if it seemed harsh. Tuck had submitted to Shane many times before. It would be rough, carnal, but utterly consensual. With their woman, they could be gentle and loving, with some mild kink thrown in there for good measure, but then the two men could unleash the beasts within them when it came to screwing each other.

Dropping to his knees again, he spit on and tongued Tuck's asshole, making sure he'd be able to get in without hurting him. His fingers dug into the man's muscular ass cheeks, spreading them wide.

Squirming under the attack, Tuck fisted the covers. "Fuck me, Shane! Fuck my ass, now!"

He slapped his husband's ass as he stood, leaving a pale-red handprint. Fisting his hard-on, he spread the pre-cum that'd pearled at the tip around the head of his shaft. Lining up with Tuck's back hole, he eased in, fighting the urge to thrust hard. That would come in a moment, but first, he had to get all the way in.

Both men groaned as Tuck's body yielded to the invasion. "Oh, shit, Shane! More!"

"Getting there, babe." He rocked his hips back and forth, gaining ground with each pass. His eyelids fluttered shut as he slid home. Finding a rhythm, he fucked his husband hard and fast. Gone were the thoughts about his truck, the drunk, Bridget, the reporters, and everything else. Feelings of passion and ecstasy had replaced them. His lovers were happily sated, and now he could join them in orgasmic bliss.

Moaning and cursing, Tuck clenched around Shane's cock, making him see stars. From her perch on the chaise, Paige murmured, "That is so freaking hot. I've got to watch more often."

Shane was more than willing to oblige her anytime she wanted to observe. His eyes opened in mere slits as he glanced down to where he disappeared into Tuck's body. Yup, that was freaking hot. Grabbing Tuck's hair again with one hand and his shoulder with the other, Shane pounded into his ass with such force that the bed inched across the floor beneath them. Wanting a different angle and to see Tuck's face, Shane pulled out. "Flip over."

Within seconds, he was buried balls-deep again. Tuck bent his knees and brought them to his chest, giving him room. Shane reached up and tweaked the man's nipples, causing Tuck to tighten around the dick in his ass. "Fuck!"

Even though he'd orgasmed just moments ago, Tuck grew hard. Shane wrapped his hands around the stiff flesh and pumped it in time to his own thrusts. "You're gonna come again, babe. I'm taking you with me."

"Yes! Oh, shit, Shane! Hurry!"

Shane felt a tingle race down his spine and tightened his grip on the cock. When the climax hit him, he roared his release, emptying himself inside Tuck. A split second later, streams of semen shot onto Tuck's abdomen and chest as he came for the second time. "Fuuuuuucccckkkk!"

Completely spent, Shane collapsed on top of Tucker, keeping some of his weight on his forearms, as the two struggled to catch their breath. After a few moments, he felt the bed dip, then Paige's lips were on his. Opening his mouth, he let her tongue find her and Tuck's taste in his mouth. Still deep inside his husband's ass, Shane felt his dick begin to recover and prepare itself for round two. If he had his way, they'd be fucking all night, and there was no doubt neither Paige nor Tuck would argue with him.

Chapter Twenty-Seven

While Shane had a blanket under his arm, Tuck carried the picnic basket as they walked into the local park adjacent to the little league baseball field. The town had sprung for one of those huge, inflatable screens and a movie projector and held movie nights twice a month during the late spring through early fall when the weather was nice. Every other Friday night alternated between G-rated movies for the whole family and PG-13 for the older crowd. Tonight was the latter, and for the first time in a long while, Tuck was looking forward to the show. It was guaranteed to be the talk of the town for weeks to come.

"Paige! Over here!"

The trio headed toward where Nicole was waving them over. There was an empty spot next to her and Hank. On the other side of the couple sat Lila and the guy she'd just started dating. Gavin Zeller had been a year ahead of Tucker in high school, which made him four years older than Lila, who'd been in the same class as Gavin's sister, Gabby. Lila had run into the sister and brother at the Rodeo Bonanza two weeks earlier, and Gabby had introduced Lila to Gavin. He'd never met her before since he graduated the year before Lila was a freshman. The divorced father of two, who lived about half an hour away from Hazard Falls, and the single teacher had hit it off and had gone on a few dates since then. Tuck thought Gavin was a nice guy—just as he'd been in high school—and he didn't mind his sister hooking up with him.

There were hugs and handshakes when the three-some joined the other two couples. Shane spread out their blanket and then held Paige's hand as she lowered herself to the ground. The two men sat on either side of her. Within a few minutes, drinks and sandwiches had been handed out.

Tuck glanced around. The park's lawn was filled with the usual who's who of the town and surrounding county, and, as expected, the mayor and his family were in attendance. Over the years, movie night had become a social event. Some people brought lounge chairs, while others preferred blankets. Wine and beer were allowed but no hard liquor. People could bring their own food or purchase popcorn, hot dogs, hamburgers, and other snacks from a concession stand that was also open during little league games.

Tonight's feature was supposed to be *The Princess Bride*, but Tuck and Shane knew the town was in for a little surprise. After the Rodeo Bonanza, Shane came up with the idea of hiring a private detective from Garden City to delve into Bridget Kline's past. What the man had uncovered was going to be sweet revenge. With the help of Jack Mueller, an electrician who ran the projector for each event, the scheduled movie had been swapped out for one that was a little more risqué, starring the mayor's daughter.

Apparently, Bridget had been a very naughty girl while vacationing with friends a few years ago in Corpus Christi, Texas. After a few martinis and shots of tequila, she and two of her girlfriends had ended up at a "gentlemen's" club, where they'd proceeded to do a bit of pole and lap dancing, among other things. Two guys they'd hooked up with earlier in the evening had somehow managed to film some of the show. How the private detective had gotten his hands on it, Tucker had no idea, but it didn't matter. With Jack's computer knowledge, they'd blurred out a few faces and private parts, but there would be no mistaking who the blonde was and what she was doing.

No one else in the crowd, including Paige, knew what was about to happen. Just in case, the disc had been wiped clean of fingerprints, and Jack had conveniently been away from his setup for about twenty minutes to run home and grab something he'd "forgotten." Any number of people, who'd arrived early to get a good spot, could have swapped out the disc in his equipment after he'd left it out in the open. Small-town residents tended to be too trusting at times. Tsk. Tsk.

Shane reached around Paige and nudged Tuck, who looked in the direction his husband indicated with a tilt of his head. The guest of dishonor had arrived just in time to see the start of the show. Bridget and some rich-looking dude Tuck had never seen before were making their way toward her parents, who'd set up their usual elaborate table and chairs in the center of the field. Yup, this was going to be good.

From the look of things, there were about 150 people in the audience from throughout the county. It would be a long time, if ever before Bridget's high-brow reputation recovered from tonight's humiliation, but Tuck and Shane didn't regret it one bit. Nobody fucked with their woman.

At nine o'clock on the dot, the park lights dimmed, and the oversized screen came to life. Instead of *The Princess Bride*'s opening credits, the inside of the strip club appeared with pulsating music and catcalls filling the air. Tuck tried to look as confused as everyone else, but it was damned hard not to laugh out loud.

The picture jumped around for a moment, then zoomed in on a blonde who'd already removed her top and was gyrating against a stripper pole in only her bra and miniskirt. Murmurs began to spread throughout the crowd until some guy shouted, "Holy shit! That's Bridget Kline!"

Laughter and whistles were aplenty, but they didn't cover the shriek of humiliated outrage that came from Bridget. "Turn that off! Jack! Oh, my God! Turn it off!"

The stunned mayor somehow got to his feet and

rushed over to where Jack was cackling his ass off while the video continued to play. Richard Kline yelled at the man to shut it off, but Jack was bent at the waist, trying to breathe. The scene had shifted, and Bridget could be seen grinding against some guy in a drunken lap dance while her skirt was up over her hips, showing off her black thong underwear.

The crowd roared. And in the middle of it, a red-faced Bridget scanned the area until she spotted Tuck, Paige, and Shane. At least now, Tuck didn't need to hold in his laughter. In fact, his sides hurt, and tears were rolling down his cheeks. He couldn't remember the last time he'd howled that hard. Again, there were no regrets.

Bridget stormed toward them. Her hands were clenched, and her lips were curled back in a snarl. "You bastards! I know you did this!"

Shane jumped to his feet, but Tuck was a little slower since he was holding his sides and rolling around on the picnic blanket. He couldn't look at Bridget because it just made him laugh harder, but he did manage to get himself between her and Paige, who was also gasping for air. Beside them, Nicole, Hank, Lila, and Gavin were not faring any better.

"You fucking bastards! How dare you!" She poked a shaking finger in Paige's direction. "That cunt put you up to it, didn't she?"

That stopped both men cold. Shane took a threatening step forward and growled before dropping his voice several octaves. "You refer to Paige one more time using anything else but her name or a pronoun, tonight will look like a Sunday school lesson. She had nothing to do with this. Clearly, you pissed off someone else. I don't know where that porn video of you came from . . ." Technically, that was the truth. ". . . but I'd like to shake the hand of whoever found it. Looks like your elite status dropped a few pegs, and you're down here with the rest of us peons. Now, you might want to go help your mother since it looks like she fainted, and by the way, your date is heading for his car."

Bridget spun around, and then, with a backward glare, she ran after her date. Nice to know where her priorities lay.

The mayor had finally gotten Jack to turn off the video. An off-duty EMT cared for Alice Kline, who hadn't fainted but probably wished she had. Richard hurried back to his wife as the correct movie began to play. The crowd was still chuckling and talking, but they began to settle down to watch the scheduled show.

A hand on Tuck's arm had him turning around. As she eyed Tuck and Shane, who stood next to him, Paige's face was filled with mirth. "Thank you."

"For what, sweetheart?" Shane managed to ask with a straight face.

"You did this, didn't you?"

"Nope."

Tuck shook his head and glanced at his husband

before looking back at Paige. "We have no idea what you're talking about, darlin'."

Her eyes narrowed—clearly, she didn't believe them. "Uh-huh." After a moment of them not confessing, she placed one hand on Tuck's chest and the other on Shane's, as a saucy grin appeared on her pretty face. "Well, then, if you happen to find out who *did* do it, tell them I owe them one. You know, in case they ever want to collect."

She went up on her tiptoes and kissed Tuck and then Shane on the lips with a little tongue swipe. Suddenly, all Tuck wanted to do was take her and his husband home and spend the rest of the night in bed with them, completely naked.

Chapter Twenty-Eight

After double-checking that the first graders all had their seatbelts on, Paige sat next to Nicole in the front row, behind the driver of the school bus. Across the aisle was the students' teacher, Melanie Dwyer, who was about twenty years older than the two other women. Her salt-and-pepper hair was styled in a short pixie cut, and she was super sweet. Her students clearly loved her.

Their driver, Clem, who just happened to be Melanie's husband, shut the hinged door before putting the yellow vehicle in Drive and pulling away from the curb in front of the school. The fifteen first-grade students, with Joey, Arianna, and Brooke among them, were cheerfully chatting away, excited about the field trip, which was getting them out of the classroom for most of the day. Paige remembered how that felt—it was the best feeling in the world for kids that age, aside from the last day of school and Christmas.

"So, have Shane and Tucker confessed to the video yet?" Nicole asked, keeping her voice low to not be overheard by the multiple ears around them.

Paige shrugged. "Nope. Tight-lipped bastards that they are. But I will say their eyes sparkle whenever I ask about it." She'd been trying to get them to admit it for the past two weeks, but she couldn't get a straight answer out of them.

"All Jack will say is he had the correct CD in the player before he ran back to his house."

"Which, put that way, could mean the correct CD was *The Princess Bride* or the amateur porn video. And women think they're the sneakier sex when it comes to revenge."

Nicole snorted. "True that."

They'd been on the road not even ten minutes when Arianna called Paige's name from a few seats back on the other side of the aisle. She glanced over her shoulder and answered some questions Ari and Joey had as the bus rounded a curve on the two-lane back-road they were on. It was the fastest route to the Native American Village, where the kids would learn what it was like in Kansas before white men came and took over.

Paige felt the bus begin to slow.

"Uh-oh," Clem said. "Looks like someone drove into the ditch. Better stop and make sure they're okay."

Leaning to the right, Paige looked out the wind-shield and saw a beat-up Cadillac partially blocking their lane. The right front tire was off the road, and the vehicle was tilted a bit as the tire had started to go into the ditch. No one was in sight, and she couldn't see through the Cadi's dirty windows with the sun's glare.

The bus came to a stop, and Nicole stood with Clem. "I'll go with you. Hopefully, they're not hurt and just need a tow truck.

Clem opened the door and stepped down. Nicole was right behind him, but before she got out, she froze on the bottom step. Paige looked at her friend in confusion, but then Melanie's gasp and "Oh, my Lord" caught her attention. Paige turned her head, and what she saw had the blood draining from her face.

Nicole backed up the stairs slowly and into the aisle, her eyes wide in terror and her hands up in the air. Following Clem back into the bus were two men pointing big, black, ugly handguns at him and Nicole. Paige had never seen the first guy before—he was about eighteen or nineteen, with dark, greasy hair and wearing a nose ring and brow stud. But the other one, Paige recognized right away—Brenna Kline's scuzzy boyfriend, whatever his name was. Both punks were dressed in black shirts, jeans, and construction boots. What scared Paige the most, besides the guns, was the fact neither was hiding their face. That never boded well for witnesses in movies and TV shows.

The greasy-haired guy shoved Clem into the driver's seat while Ty—somehow, his name popped into Paige's head—pointed his gun at Nicole. Her hands started to shake. "I don't know what—"

"Sit down and shut up!" When she hesitated, he barked, "Move! Now!"

Nicole had moved back enough in the aisle that she ended up taking the seat behind Paige.

The door to the bus slammed shut, and Clem was ordered to follow the Cadi, which was back on the road heading toward the Native American Village, but Paige doubted that was their destination now. Behind her, the children were eerily quiet, and she glanced back. Their eyes were wide with fear, and a few had tears rolling down their cheeks. Arianna's petrified gaze met hers. Paige tried to smile as she mouthed the words, "It's going to be okay."

The bus jerked forward, and Paige had to throw her hand out in front of her, against the back of the driver's seat, for support. She'd taken her seatbelt off when the bus had initially stopped, and for now, she left it that way. If she had to react quickly, she wouldn't be able to do it with the restraint. Across the aisle, Melanie was pale, and her hands trembled, but from her expression, Paige knew the woman would do anything to protect her students. The four adults in charge would have to wait to find out what was happening and how they would get themselves and the children out of it.

"Where are we going? What do you want?" Nicole asked, fear and loathing combined in her tone.

"Shut! Up!" Ty growled. "You'll know soon enough."

God, Paige hoped she'd told Ari the truth when she'd said everything would be okay. Tucker and Shane would both shatter if they lost their little girl. The whole town would be devastated if anything happened to *any* of the children. Paige didn't know why, but suddenly she found herself praying—not to God, but to Sarah.

Please don't let them take her from Shane and Tucker. She needs to stay here with them because you couldn't. Watch over her, and while you're at it, please watch over the rest of us too.

Chapter Twenty-Nine

Lane Myers grinned. His day had just been made. Every shift he worked, and many of the days he was off duty, he found a way to get an eyeful of Betty Lou. Not that she was happy about it. He smiled. She frowned. And he got a big kick out of it. One of these days, the stubborn woman would finally admit she wanted Lane as much as he wanted her. He always had. If things hadn't blown up between them at the end of his senior year of high school, they probably would've been married with a few teenage kids by now. He'd never stopped loving her, and he was certain if he finally managed to knock the chip off her shoulder, she'd realize they still belonged together, even after all these years.

He leaned against his department-issued SUV and crossed his arms, waiting for Lou to come back out of the bank. He'd parked right next to her pickup truck, and she'd have to walk right up to him to get in. Her only other option was to get in the passenger side and slide over, but he knew she'd never do that. That would make her appear weak, and Lou was anything but. She ran Bar None with an iron fist. She took no shit from her customers or employees, and, damn, if most of them didn't love her for it. On more than one occasion, she'd threatened to bash a cowboy's head in for starting trouble in her place. Ninety-nine percent of the time, they backed down, especially when the regulars started laying down bets on how many bones she'd break if she started swinging.

The door to the bank swung open, and out strode Lou, looking incredibly delicious. Faded jeans molded to her curves, while a blue tank top showed off her tanned shoulders and hugged her breasts. Those puppies had filled out more since the last time he'd had his mouth and hands on them, and his palms itched to get at them again.

She'd been almost to the tailgate of her truck when she spotted him and slowed her stride. That pissed-off glare she'd perfected when it came to him appeared on her face. Her hazel eyes flared in annoyance.

"Morning, doll-face. Beautiful day isn't it?"

Her jaw tightened. "It was until a few seconds ago."

She reached for the door handle, but Lane stepped in front of her, preventing her from opening the door. She growled. "Get out of my way, Lane." When he didn't move, she rolled her eyes. "What do you want?"

"Just thought you might want to thank me."

Her eyes narrowed. "For what?" she spat.

He shrugged. "For taking out the trash last night." It'd been one of the few times a ruckus had gotten a little out of control at the bar. A drunk had hit on another drunk's woman, and shit had gone downhill very quickly. Lane had been heading home from his father's house when he spotted the brawl in Bar None's parking lot. He'd called it in on his radio as he'd pulled in, then hopped out of his vehicle. With his military training, it hadn't taken him long to incapacitate both men—the fact that they were extremely intoxicated and exhausted from beating on each other had helped just a tad.

"I didn't need or ask for your help. Now get out of my way, or I'll tell the chief you're harassing me again."

Lane smirked. "Didn't do you any good the last time you complained to him."

Graham Hughes was a wise man and knew when to placate the residents of Hazard Falls and when something really needed his attention. After all, he'd been chief of police for over fifteen years.

"Move, jackass," she huffed. "I've got things to do. Go write a ticket or something, will ya?"

He was about to respond with a snarky remark when his cell phone rang. With his father's health declining, he never hesitated to check the screen in case of an emergency. He pulled the phone off his hip and saw the call was coming from the station. His brow furrowed. Why were they calling him on his phone instead of the radio, which always had better reception than the cellular network in some parts of the town?

Stepping away from Lou's vehicle, he answered the call, disappointed when she took advantage and hopped into the driver's seat and started the engine.

"Myers."

"Lane, are you nearby?"

Caitlyn Wells's voice sounded a bit frantic, and Lane was instantly on alert, ignoring Lou's truck pulling out of the parking spot and driving away. "Yeah, I'm by the Stop & Go, what's wrong?"

"Need you back at the station as fast as you can get here and stay off the radio. No lights or sirens, but hurry."

Shit. Whatever's up can't be good.

Minutes later, he strode into the police station with another officer, Tad Winslow, on his heels. Apparently, he'd also gotten the SOS. Chief Hughes stood behind Caitlyn at the call desk, frowning. He waved Lane and Tad over. The dispatcher's face was pale, and she was wringing her hands together.

"What's wrong?" Lane asked as he and Tad joined the other two.

Hughes gestured toward the computer setup that was part of the county's 911 system. During the day, one of two department dispatchers answered the phones and assigned calls to the on-duty officers. At 4:00 p.m., the county dispatchers took over until 8:00 a.m. the following day. "A call came in on the non-emergency line that you have to hear. Play it again, Caitlyn."

The three men and one woman were quiet as a phone call recording played back.

Caitlyn's cheerful voice was the first they heard. "Hazard Falls Police Department, how can I help you?"

"Caitlyn, it's Nicole Mathers." The hair on the back of Lane's neck stood up at the quiver in the woman's voice. The call sounded like she'd made it through a speakerphone feature. "I need you to listen very carefully. I'm on a school bus with Clem and Melanie Dwyer, Paige Merritt, and fifteen first-graders. The bus has been hijacked, and we're being held for ransom. At the moment, we're all okay." A gasp came over the speakers, and Lane assumed it had been from Caitlyn reacting to the information, but the dispatcher had wisely not interrupted. "There's three of them—"

There was the sound of a scuffle, then a male mumbling something unintelligible.

"Ow! All right already!" Nicole snapped.

"Nicole! Are you okay? What's happening?"

There was a pause before the other woman came back on the line. "Yeah, Caitlyn, I'm okay. I'm just supposed to tell you what they told me and nothing more. They have guns and want two hundred thousand dollars in unmarked bills, or they'll . . . they'll kill us all. They have a police radio, so they'll know if you call the sheriff's department to help. I'll call back in an hour and tell you where they want the money delivered."

"Nicole, how—"

The call had been cut off before Caitlyn could finish

her question. Shutting off the recording, she looked up at the three stunned lawmen.

Winslow spoke first. "What the hell do we do?"

Running a hand down his face, Hughes shook his head once, then started barking out orders. "Caitlyn, get on the phone with the school principal and find out exactly who is on that bus and where they were headed. Lane, call the sheriff's department—we'll need backup. Tell them complete radio silence and have anyone who can respond here. After that, call Shane, Tucker, and Hank. Tell them to get over here—we may need their help. We'll need to let the rest of the parents know their kids are in danger—shit, those are phone calls I'm not looking forward to.

"Tad, call Willard Knutt over at the bank and tell him to get his pathetic ass over here and to keep his mouth shut. I'll call the fucking mayor. If we have to come up with some money as a way to trap these assholes, Knutt's not going to do it without Kline's okay."

Everyone jumped into action. Lane's first call was to the sheriff's department, which covered the towns in the area that couldn't afford their own police force, as well as any county-owned properties and roads. He then notified the other few police departments and got all available hands covertly heading toward Hazard Falls. It was easy for anyone to pick up a police scanner and enter the local radio codes to listen in. Finally, he made the second worst call of his life—the first being to a good friend and fellow

Marine's parents after they'd been notified he'd been KIA.

The call rang twice in his ear before it was picked up. "Hey, Lane, what's up?"

He took a deep breath and let it out. "Shane, I need you to listen to me. Grab Hank and Tuck and get down to the police station. We received a call from Nicole. She and Paige are on a school bus with a bunch of kids, and they've been hijacked for ransom."

There was a long pause on the phone, and for a moment, he thought they'd been disconnected. "Shane?"

The man's voice was low and threatening. "Tell me this is a really sick joke, man."

"I wish I could. All we know is that at the time of the call about ten minutes ago, everyone was unharmed. Nicole said they were all okay for now. Just get down here and keep it quiet. Supposedly, they're listening to the police radios."

"Fuck! I swear if anything happens to Ari or Paige— Lane, you better cover my ass for the murders I'll commit."

Shane disconnected the call before his friend had a chance to answer, and Lane hoped like hell he wouldn't have to cover the guy's ass.

About forty minutes later, they were no closer to figuring out where the kids and their chaperones were. Officers and deputies from around the county had responded, and many of them were now in unmarked vehicles, borrowed from the parents of some of the missing children, driving around the area trying to spot the big, yellow bus. A few state troopers had also arrived after being notified their assistance was needed. So far, everyone had maintained radio silence unless it had to do with anything other than the hostage situation. Shane, Tuck, and Hank stood in the corner of the reception area, having refused to wait in the American Legion Hall next door with the rest of the shocked parents. They'd been warned not to contact anyone else and reveal what happened. As long as the three men stayed out of the way and didn't hinder the investigation, then the chief was okay with them staying. It helped that Shane was like a nephew to Hughes, who'd been best man at the younger man's parents' wedding long ago.

Lane glanced at the clock. They had about fifteen more minutes, maybe less, before the call came in to let them know where to deliver the money. It hadn't taken more than three seconds for the mayor to order the bank manager to get the ransom together after finding out his granddaughter was one of the hostages. The police would do everything they could to ensure the money was returned at the end of the day, but with nineteen lives in danger, they couldn't risk trying to trick the suspects with a bag stuffed with newspaper or clothing.

The front door to the station burst open, and the school principal, Marianne Burton, rushed into the police station, waving a piece of paper. The forty-two-year-old woman breathlessly called out, "Chief! I may know how to find them!"

Everyone in the room stopped their conversations and stared at her.

Leaving the wall map he'd been using to coordinate the search, Hughes stepped toward her. "How?"

She took a few deep breaths as the entire room waited. "The town bought . . . the bus from another school district. It has a GPS feature and . . . and a panic alarm system in it, but the damn mayor said we didn't need to activate them. He didn't want to pay the extra money for the monitoring." Clearly, she hadn't seen the man standing in the corner opposite Shane, Tuck, and their employee. Kline, at least, had the decency to look remorseful. "Anyway, here's the name of the company that monitored it for the school district we got it from. They may still be able to track it."

Hughes took the papers from her and then kissed her on the cheek. "You're a genius, Mari! Hopefully, it works."

The chief hurried over to the closest landline, probably to ensure the department name appeared on any caller ID. Within minutes, he had the longitude and latitude of where the bus currently sat on the property of an old, abandoned farm that'd been up for sale for years without any interest. It wasn't far from the road the bus had taken on its way to the Native American Village.

"How do you want to do this, Graham?" the county

sheriff asked, having responded in person along with a bunch of his men.

It wasn't the first time the sheriff or other chiefs in the county had deferred to Hughes regarding a high-risk situation. Back in the day, the man had been in the Army's Special Forces. He'd then served Garden City's police force, as well as their SWAT team, for a few years until he'd taken a bullet interrupting a convenience store robbery one day while off duty. Six months later, after he recovered, he handed in his resignation and took the top cop job that'd been offered to him in Hazard Falls. At fifty-four, he was still in excellent condition and sparred with some of his officers on a regular basis.

The chief checked his watch. "We're too close to when Nicole said they'd call back. I say we wait until they call with the drop location. It'll probably be somewhere other than the farmhouse, meaning at least one suspect will have to leave. We won't be able to stage a rescue that fast. One less person guarding the hostages will reduce the chances of any of them getting hurt when we go in after them. We can hide a few lookouts along the escape routes and wait until the pickup guy is out of the way. Have a team waiting for him at the drop site. Once he's out of sight, we'll do a stealth approach and try to hit the remaining two suspects before they even know we're there."

"We're going with you." Shane stepped forward with Tuck and Hank right beside him. Rage and fear battled for supremacy on all their faces. "Deputize us."

"Absolutely not, Shane," Hughes responded, his voice filled with sympathy and authority. "I know Ari, Paige, Joey, and Nicole are in danger, along with all the others, but that means you can't be objective on this. I trust that every shield in this county will do whatever they possibly can to get every single hostage back unharmed. Let us do what we're trained to do."

Lane knew it took a lot of faith and strength when, after a few moments' hesitation, Shane, Tuck, and Hank backed down.

Chapter Thirty

" I have to go to the bathroom," one of the boys whined from the back of the bus, and Paige silently agreed with him. They'd been inside an old barn for over an hour, and she'd been crossing her legs for the past fifteen minutes, trying not to pee her pants. She hadn't wanted to ask if she could get off the bus and step into one of the stalls to use a corner to relieve herself, but she was going to have to soon.

Nicole had made the second call at gunpoint and given the police chief the location for the money to be dropped. Minutes later, the third creep, named Eddie, who'd been driving the Cadi earlier, left in the vehicle to retrieve the ransom after Ty had repeated several warnings about watching out for an ambush at the drop site. That left just Ty and his buddy, Derek, outside the bus.

Sunlight poured through openings where several boards were missing in the roof and a loft window.

Nicole had said earlier she knew what abandoned farm they were on, but she hadn't been able to think of a clue to give to the police to help them locate the hostages. Her one attempt at giving more information than she was supposed to had resulted in getting her head yanked back by her hair and a gun thrust into her face while her terrified daughter and the others looked on. Now, she sat with Joey on her lap and waited for whatever would happen next. Ari was tucked under one of Paige's arms while Brooke hung on her other one. The little girl was sucking her thumb and would freeze anytime her sister's boyfriend yelled anything or came back on the bus.

The other children were huddled together in the seats throughout the bus. Clem was looking paler and diaphoretic and kept rubbing his sternum. He'd started getting sharp chest pains about ten minutes after they'd arrived at the barn, but the three punks had been unsympathetic. Melanie was doing her best to keep both her husband and the students calm. Paige and Nicole had joined her in taking turns walking to the back of the bus and checking on the children every few minutes. Some were sitting in silence, with dried tear tracks on their cheeks. Others were talking softly to each other, and a few had fallen into a restless sleep after having an adrenaline crash.

Paige and Nicole had done their best to find some sort of weapon they could use, but resources were limited on the bus. Ty and his friends had taken their cell phones and those that any of the kids had had. The only thing the women had on hand was a small pocket knife on Nicole's keychain that their kidnappers had overlooked. And *small* was an understatement. While it was sharp, it wouldn't cause enough damage to someone unless she shoved it in their eye. However, Nicole kept it handy just in case it could buy them some time.

"I have to go to the bathroom too," another student, this time a little girl, cried.

Soon the others would start whining and crying, which might piss off their captors. Paige had to prevent that from happening. Patting both Ari's and Brooke's arms, she stood and reassured them. "I'll be right back."

She moved to the front and slowly descended the steps, her heart pounding in her chest. When she reached the bottom step, she stopped and cleared her throat. "Excuse me."

Derek and Ty brought their guns up from where they'd been standing a few feet away. The latter snarled. "What?"

"W-we need to go to the bathroom, especially the children. If they pee in their pants, it'll smell, and they'll really start crying."

Ty waved his hands around. "Do you see a bathroom in here, you fucking cunt? Go sit down."

She stood her ground. "Please. I'm trying to keep them from getting on your nerves, and that's what will happen if you don't let them go. I can take them into those stalls over there, one or two at a time, and they can pee on the floor. They'll be a lot quieter if they're comfortable."

Seconds passed as he just glared at Paige.

Derek broke the silence. "Let 'em go, Ty. They can't escape, and it'll keep 'em quiet. I don't want to listen to a bunch of brats whining."

There was another moment's hesitation before he strode over to the stalls she'd pointed to, looked in one of them, then came back. "Fine. No more than two at a time. Make it fast, then get the brats back on the bus and tell them to keep their traps shut."

"Thank you." She turned and hurried back up the stairs. "Okay, kids. I'm going to take two of you at a time to go to the bathroom. Try to hang on until I get to you. Ari, Brooke, come with me."

The two girls stood warily and took Paige's outstretched hands. She kept her body between them and the two men as she hurried them over to the old horse stalls. Pointing to two corners, she said, "Go squat and urinate over there. Don't worry, I won't let anyone come in while you're going." She didn't know if either punk was a pedophile and didn't want to find out, but there was no way she'd let either of them watch the children while they were exposed.

It took a few moments for the girls to relax enough to do their business after they'd pulled down their shorts and squatted, but soon they were done, and Paige hurried them back onto the bus. Two by two, she brought the children to the makeshift restroom and then back again. After the first couple of times, Ty and

Derek ignored them. They went back to checking the doors and looking out any opening they could find in the dilapidated barn. On one of the trips, Paige ducked her head into the stall next to the one the children were using and spotted a pitchfork within reach. She quickly moved back when she heard one of the kidnappers approaching, then continued escorting her charges. Once they were all taken care of, Paige would watch the stall's doorway if Nicole and Melanie needed to go, then have one of them stand guard while she relieved herself.

Paige was just about to head back to the bus with the last lone boy when, from the other side of the barn, Ty shouted, "Derek! Someone's out there! It's the fucking cops!"

"Shit! How'd they find us?"

Temporary relief flashed through Paige, but she knew they weren't out of danger yet. Pushing the little boy back into the stall, she reached into the other one and grabbed the pitchfork. When Derek ran from the front of the barn, past what had once been a tack room, his gun was up, looking for a target. Paige didn't hesitate, thrusting the large, pointed tool forward as hard as she could, catching him in the gut. He froze in confusion, then disbelief, before glancing down while stumbling backward. Paige let go of the handle as he fell to the floor, bleeding from his deep wounds.

In shock, Paige took a few steps back, her hand over her wide-open mouth. The little boy moved from the stall to her side, staring at the dying man with bulging eyes.

"You bitch!" Ty had rounded the front of the bus and stopped at the vehicle's door. Rage covered his face as he raised his gun hand.

Paige had nowhere to go. All she knew was she had to protect the boy next to her. Pivoting, she shoved him as far as possible so he'd be out of the line of fire. There was a violent boom, and a brutal force slammed into her, knocking her to the ground. Her breath left her lungs with a whoosh, and pain exploded in her head. The last thing she heard before her world went black was screaming.

SHANE PACED BACK AND FORTH IN THE ICU WAITING room, trying hard not to punch a wall in front of everyone. It'd been four hours since Paige had been airlifted, unconscious, to St. Catherine Hospital in Garden City, the closest facility needed for her head injury. The cops had also gotten a second helicopter to transport Clem for what had turned out to be a heart attack. The man was stable in the CCU with his wife and children by his side.

The kids, Nicole, and Melanie had been driven back into town, where a crowd of relieved and grateful parents greeted them. Once they had Arianna safely in their arms again, Shane and Tuck buckled her into Shane's truck and made a beeline for the hospital, an hour away. Their little girl fell asleep after only ten minutes on the road. Seth was holding down the fort at the ranch where the Triple-R employees anxiously awaited news on Paige.

Hank, Nicole, and their three children had driven to Garden City as well. Nicole said she needed to be there for her new friend after everything they'd gone through, but she couldn't let Joey out of her sight just yet. Hank thought it was best to keep his entire family together until everyone calmed down.

Also in the waiting room were Lane, Lila, Gavin, Betty Lou, and a few of Shane and Tuck's other friends. Tuck's parents were on a plane from Arizona to Kansas, despite their son's insistence that they stay out west. Paige was important to Tuck, Shane, Ari, and Lila. Therefore, she was important to Zach and Emily Jones. Gavin offered to go to the airport and pick them up when they arrived, and Shane thanked him—it was one less thing he had to deal with right now.

He glanced around the room. They weren't the only family waiting for a doctor to tell them how their loved one was doing, but they did have the most people supporting them. Ari had fallen back to sleep on Lila's lap as she spoke softly with Gavin. Lane had his head in his hands, and surprisingly, Lou was sitting next to him, rubbing his back with her hand in moral support. The man blamed himself for Paige's condition, and no amount of reassurance from

Tucker, Shane, and Nicole had eased his perceived guilt.

From what Shane learned, all hell had broken loose when one of the kidnappers spotted the cops advancing on the barn. Unfortunately, it was a risk they had to take because there were very few places to conceal themselves as they approached. Lane and another officer managed to silently climb through a paneless window in an old tack room moments before the alarm was raised. Before either man could get out the door, Paige had stabbed one of the hostage-takers with a fucking pitchfork, of all things. Although he wished she hadn't needed to do it, he was damn proud of her. The bastard died on the barn floor before medical help could arrive.

But after she'd eliminated the one guy, the other had appeared and pointed his gun at Paige. Not thinking of herself, she'd tried to protect the young boy standing next to her. Unable to shoot because of the kids and adults on the bus directly behind the threat, Lane had done the only other thing he could think of. He'd tackled Paige to the ground. When the gun went off, the bullet lodged into an upright beam right behind where Paige had been standing. Unfortunately, as Lane landed on top of her, she'd hit her head hard against the floor and been knocked out. In the meantime, one of the cops, who'd come in through a backdoor they kicked in, had shot and killed the suspect before he could fire his weapon a second time.

The third kidnapper was arrested at the money

drop-off point. According to him, the whole plot was Ty Eldredge's idea after he'd overheard Brooke talking about the field trip a few days earlier while Brenna had been babysitting her. The three men had staked out the school, and once they were certain of the bus's route to its destination, they'd taken a dirt road shortcut and came out ahead of it. After that, it was just a matter of positioning their car, waiting in the ditch, and hoping the bus driver would stop to check on the "disabled" vehicle.

None of the children had been harmed, but many of them would probably need to talk about what happened with counselors. The school was already arranging to have some come in and speak with them as a group to see if any needed one-on-one counseling.

Hopefully, when Paige woke up, Lane would come to realize he'd saved her life, even though he'd hurt her in the process. Shane didn't blame him and didn't want his friend to blame himself, either.

When Paige woke up . . . He had to keep thinking that way. Under no circumstances was he going to think "if" instead of "when." They'd just found her. She was supposed to spend many long years loving and being loved by Shane, Tuck, and Ari. They couldn't lose her.

On his next pass across the room, a woman in a white lab coat walked in. "Paige Merritt's family?"

"Here." Shane rushed over. "How is she?"

"I'm Doctor Dobrynski from Neurology. Are you her husband?"

"Fiancé," he replied since he and Tuck would put a

ring on her finger soon. They'd been talking about it this morning after she'd driven Arianna to school for the field trip. "This is all the family she has—her parents are gone. Is she awake?"

The doctor shook her head, but at least she didn't look grim about it. "As you know, she took a hard hit to the side of her head. It's an injury we often see with football players. We did a CT scan, and there's some moderate swelling and minor bruising on the right side of her brain. The left side is okay. Currently, there's no evidence of any clots, so we don't need to operate, but we'll see how the next few hours go. She's still unconscious but breathing on her own, and we're monitoring her closely."

"When will she wake up?" Shane's mind was going in fifty directions at once, trying to absorb everything he'd just been told.

"I'm sorry, I can't answer that. It's an injury I've seen in people who never lost consciousness and in others who were in comas for several weeks."

"But she *will* wake up, right?" Tuck asked desperately.

The doctor hedged, clearly looking for the right words of comfort which didn't offer false hope that Paige waking up was a surety. "We'll have to wait and see. I wish I could give you a better answer than that, but I can't." She scanned the faces of those standing before her and smiled at Arianna, who was in Lila's arms, resting her head on her aunt's shoulder.

"Someone looks like she needs a good night's sleep. There's nothing we can do but wait right now, so why don't you all go home and get some rest? I promise we'll call you if there's any change."

"Thanks, Doctor," Shane replied. "Is it all right if some of us stay? Can we see her?"

"Yes, certainly. I'll let the nurses know. They'll be able to let two people in at the top of the hour for only a few minutes, but I'm sorry, the little girl can't go in."

"I understand. Thank you." When the physician left the room, Shane turned to the group. "Y'all can head home. I'll call if there's any news."

As the others began to collect their things, Nicole stepped forward, glancing between Tuck and Shane. "If you both want to stay, we can take Arianna home with us. The girls will probably sleep better together tonight."

Tuck cleared his throat. "Um . . . thanks, but I'm going to take Ari home. I think she should sleep in her own bed tonight."

Shane's eyes narrowed. Those had been the most words Tuck had strung together in hours. He'd barely said a word to anyone since they'd gotten into the truck to drive into the city, and even then, it'd only been to answer a direct question with the shortest possible response.

"Then I can take her back to your place and stay with her," Lila volunteered. "You stay here with Shane."

"Thanks, sis, but I'll take her home."

Putting a hand on his husband's arm to get his attention, Shane tilted his head toward the door. "Let's talk outside for a minute."

He could see it was the last thing his husband wanted to do, but fuck that. Shane strode out the door once Tuck nodded his acquiescence. But when they reached the hallway, a few people were standing around. A quick check of the other doors revealed one was a linen room. Grabbing Tuck's arm, Shane dragged him inside the small space and shut the door behind them.

"What, Shane?"

He shoved Tuck against a tall linen cart and got right up into his face. "Don't do it. Don't you dare fucking do it. You're shutting down. I've seen it before, and I won't let you do it again, damn it."

"What the hell are you talking about?"

"Are you serious?" Shane asked incredulously. "You have to fucking ask? You shut down when Sarah died, Tuck. Hell, you started shutting down before she died. And it was okay. I could deal with it. We both dealt with her dying in different ways. I came to terms with it before you did, and that's okay." He grasped the back of Tuck's neck and touched their foreheads together. "It's okay. But now . . . I can't do it alone this time, babe. I can't be strong for everyone on my own. I need you out there. In private, you can break down, you can ask me to fuck you into oblivion, hell, you can even use me as a punching bag. But out there, with Paige, with everyone else, I need your help. I'm not strong enough this time. We could have lost both Paige and Ari today. I'm barely holding on by a thread here. I want to go ballistic and beat the hell out of those two dead punks and the one that's sitting in jail. I don't want to think about a world without Paige in it. I can't. If we lose her . . ."

Tears rolled down his cheeks as he choked on the words he couldn't say. Tuck cupped his jaw and kissed him hard. It was then Shane realized he wasn't the only one crying. Tongues danced as each man tried to soothe and draw strength from the other. Their five o'clock shadows rasped together.

A noise in the hall had them pulling apart but not letting go. Tuck's thumbs brushed away Shane's tears. "I'm so sorry. I didn't realize I was pulling away from you. You're right, we can't lose her."

"We won't. We'll both be here when she wakes up—and she *will* wake up. Let Nicole take Ari home with her and stay with me. Please. Ari will be fine there, and if she needs to talk to us, Nicole can get us on the phone. Tomorrow, I think it's important she goes to school to meet with the counselors and be with her friends. One of us will drive back and take her. You can do it if you want, then bring back a change of clothes for me. We'll take turns going back and forth. You know Lila, Seth, and Nic will help in any way they can. But we need to do this together."

"We will." He brushed his lips against Shane's once

more. "I promise we will. And when Paige wakes up, we'll take her home and put a ring on her damn finger and spend the rest of our very long lives with her."

Shane wanted that more than anything and was thrilled Tuck was back on the same page.

Chapter Thirty-One

Tucker sat next to Paige's bed as the monitors beeped steadily. He held her hand in his and caressed her wrist. It was Saturday afternoon, and she'd been unconscious for about forty hours so far. Another CT scan yesterday afternoon showed the swelling of her brain had decreased a bit. The neurologist had said it was a positive sign, but she still had no idea if and when Paige would wake up. However, Tuck was determined to take it as a move in the right direction. The doctor approved her being transferred to the step-down unit that morning since all her vitals had remained stable. While they were still keeping a close eye on her with the telemetry monitors, she was now in a regular room instead of a small cubicle, so Shane and Tuck could stay with her all day if they wanted instead of a few minutes at the top of each hour.

He glanced at the clock. Shane would be back soon. Tuck had offered to stay while he went home to check on a few things. They booked a hotel room across the street from the hospital yesterday after spending the first night in the ICU waiting room, which had left them both with cricks in their backs and a severe lack of sleep. If they were going to be here for Paige, they needed their rest too. The staff knew how to contact them if there was any change, and the two men could be back there in a heartbeat if needed.

Tuck thanked God they had an amazing bunch of employees. Between the office staff and ranch hands, Triple-R was being well taken care of in the absence of its owners. His parents had also arrived and were staying in the guest bedroom at the house, doing what they could to help. Tuck's mom loved cooking and had appointed herself the head chef until further notice. His dad helped Seth with whatever needed to be done in and around the house. Lila and Gavin had joined them for dinner last night, and when Tuck got a call from his parents this morning, checking on Paige, they said they approved of the man their daughter was dating. He was glad to hear it. Lila deserved to be happy as much as anyone else in this world. He just hoped he could introduce Paige to his folks soon. He prayed Sarah was watching over them and would somehow find a way to help Paige return to them.

Yesterday, Tuck arrived home in time to take Ari to school. True to their word, the school board arranged for counselors to meet with the children. Their parents were warned the kids might not show PTSD symptoms for days, weeks, or months and were given a list of things to look out for. Not one, but two substitute teachers were brought in to temporarily fill in for Melanie Dwyer while Clem recovered from what was, thankfully, a mild heart attack. The subs would be able to keep a closer watch on the first graders to make sure none were struggling in the aftermath of the kidnapping. So far, it appeared Ari was faring well, her only concern being her inability to see and talk to Paige.

Prayers, get-well wishes, flowers, food, and offers to help with whatever needed to be done had been pouring in from all over Hazard Falls. Word spread quickly about how Paige had thrown the little boy out of the line of fire, and many called her a heroine. Some people who'd turned their noses up at her before, due to either her relationship with Tuck and Shane, the media shit-storm that descended on the town weeks earlier, or the fact her ex-husband had been a criminal, were seeing Paige in a different light. She was now officially one of Hazard Falls's own. This time, when the media had rolled into town, the interviews were filled with accolades for not only Paige but for Nicole, Melanie, and Clem too. Not a bad word was said about them—at least not any that ended up in the news articles. There were still community members who would look at Paige in disdain—that was life in a small town —but the number was now far less than it'd been.

Betty Lou called a little while ago to check on Paige and fill Tuck in on some news. The media had descended on Bridget's house this morning, just before 8:00 a.m., after a reporter had learned of her eighteen-year-old daughter's relationship with one of the now-dead kidnappers. The feeding frenzy now had a new target, and from Lou's chuckling, Tuck had a good idea who'd dropped that side of beef in the shark pool. He highly doubted she would've done it if Brooke's father hadn't insisted his seven-year-old daughter stay with him for the next few weeks, away from the chaos, where she'd be out of the spotlight. He also planned to ensure she received some counseling. Meanwhile, Bridget had, apparently, left town until she figured out a way to regain her status among the snobbish elite of the county, leaving her parents and Brenna to deal with the media. Again, it was clear where the woman's priorities lay.

Paige's arm twitched, as it had done occasionally for a few hours now, and Tuck leaned forward. "Hey, beautiful. I'm still sitting here waiting for you to wake up. Shane should be back soon, and I know he'd love to walk in here and see those gorgeous eyes of yours. You have no idea how much we love you. We were all set to tell you the other night. I never thought I'd fall in love with another woman ever again. I thought it would just be Shane and me raising Ari, and I was okay with that. But then you came to us and showed me . . . showed both of us what we were missing. You filled the holes in our hearts that we never expected to be filled. We love you, baby. I love you. And I need you to come back to us so I know you heard me say the words."

Paige did not respond, but a hand squeezed Tuck's shoulder. He glanced up to see Shane. "No change?"

Tuck shook his head. "She's still making involuntary movements like they said she would, but nothing else. Everything okay?"

"Yeah. The bodyguards Quinn hired replaced the hospital's security guards outside the door. He's headed to Hazard to spend some time with Ari. Graham's got two patrol cars at the entrance to the ranch to deal with the media, and the hands are watching for anyone trying to sneak onto the property. I told Nic and Hank to stay in the empty cottage with the kids until everything calms down. Seth and your folks are holding down the fort with no problems other than the house phone ringing incessantly." The media hadn't only gone after Bridget, Brenna, and the kidnapper's families. They'd tried to get interviews with everyone else involved. It was national news that Paige Merritt-Winthrope had gone from being the wife of a convicted Ponzi schemer to a small-town heroine who'd risked her life to protect a child. Shane's cousin had also flown in yesterday for a few days. Quinn felt he needed to be there for Paige and ended up taking over her private security detail after two tabloid reporters managed to gain entry to her room late last night. Both men now sported black eyes, courtesy of Shane and Tucker, and were in police custody for trespassing.

Rounding the bed to the other side, Shane sat in another chair and gently took Paige's left hand. "Hi, sweetheart. I'm back. I heard everything Tuck said, and he was right. We love you so much and need you to come back to us. Ari wants to visit you, but she's not allowed until you're awake. We miss you—your smile, your laughter, making love to you, all of it. Tuck can't wait to introduce you to his folks, and they're anxious to meet you too." He paused, and then his gaze met Tuck's. "Tell her. Don't ask, just tell her."

He knew what Shane meant. His husband had been the one to propose to Sarah, and he was now declaring Tuck should be the one to propose to Paige. Would she hear him?

Bringing her hand to his lips, he gently kissed her knuckles. "Paige, baby, this isn't how I thought we would do this. I figured there'd be a little romancing first, then both of us making sweet love to you together, then asking you to marry us. But things change. I'm not asking, Paige. I'm telling you to come back to us and marry us. We belong together—you, me, Shane, and Ari. You'll be a wonderful mother to our little girl, and maybe someday we can give her a brother or sister. We want to spend the rest of our lives with you, so wake up and say yes, Paige. Please."

The only thing breaking the sudden silence in the room was the beeping of the heart monitor. Tuck's gut clenched, and his head dropped forward. What if she didn't wake up? How would either of them or Ari live through it if Paige left them?

"Paige?"

Tuck lifted his head at the surprise in Shane's voice. "What?"

"Paige, honey, did you just squeeze my hand? Do it again."

Seconds passed. Her hand twitched in Tuck's. No, wait. It wasn't a twitch. Her hand closed around his. His gaze shot to her face, then to where she and Shane were connected. She was squeezing his hand too.

Shane brushed her brow. "Come on, baby. Wake up. Let me see those beautiful blue eyes of yours."

Her eyes remained shut, but her mouth opened. "So ... bossy," she murmured. "Love you too."

As she fell back asleep, relieved smiles spread across both men's faces. Their woman wouldn't leave them, and they'd get that ring on her finger as fast as they could. Paige Wilson had a nice sound to it. Reaching across her torso, Tuck grasped his husband's hand, completing the circle between the trio. He silently thanked the woman who'd once been their wife and would forever be their guardian angel.

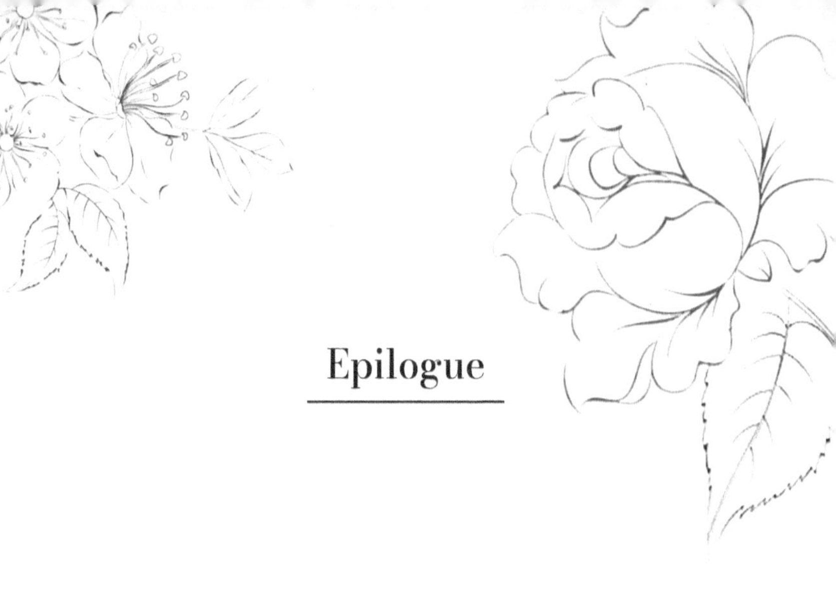

Epilogue

"Here, Mom. There's eighteen of them," Ari announced as she brought a basket of eggs from the hen house into the kitchen. It was one of the jobs she insisted Shane give her for the summer so she could earn her own money to buy the baby a present. The new addition to the family was three days overdue, and Paige wished she'd go into labor soon. Her feet were swollen—at least she thought they were since she couldn't see them—and her back was killing her. She felt like one of the pregnant heifers out in the fields. Ari had hoped her new baby sister would be born on her own birthday last week, but when that hadn't happened, she admitted it was probably better if they didn't have to share their big days.

After she'd been released from the hospital thirteen months ago, Tuck and Shane had proposed to Paige again since she apparently was unconscious the first time they'd done it. Once she'd gotten home, Tuck's parents stayed through the summer months to help her around the house, letting her ease her way back into a routine as she slowly recovered from her ordeal. After going home to Arizona, they returned to Kansas for Thanksgiving and Christmas and just recently again for the birth of their second granddaughter. This morning, following breakfast, they took Paige's SUV to run a few errands.

Tuck and Shane had moved her into their bedroom for good on her first night home, and she'd fallen asleep between the two of them every night since. Of course, that meant she needed to wake one of them every night over the past two months because the baby took up space that her bladder usually did. Her men assured her they didn't mind at all. They were always attentive, but their overprotective natures were evident to everyone during her pregnancy. Paige couldn't remember what it was like to sleep without them. She never thought in her wildest dreams—well, maybe in her *really* wildest dreams—she'd fall in love with two men and be in a full ménage relationship. But it felt right, and nobody would ever make her feel ashamed for loving Shane and Tuck.

Ari had asked if she could call Paige "Mom" as soon as the trio announced their engagement. Paige had been so honored. Even though this baby was growing inside her and Ari hadn't, the eight-year-old girl would always be Paige's daughter.

The night before their wedding last June, when Paige had legally married Tuck and symbolically married Shane, she took the ranch's golf cart and drove to the family cemetery alone. She brought a bouquet of lilies, the same that would be in her bridal spray the next day—they'd been Sarah's favorite—and laid them on the woman's grave.

"I WANTED TO COME AND TALK TO YOU FOR A BIT BEFORE tomorrow. I owe you so much. If it hadn't been for you, Shane and Tuck might never have fallen in love, and they definitely wouldn't have Arianna. That also means I never would have met them. I want you to know that I love them all so much, and I'll take care of them the best I can. But I'm all right with you helping me if that's how things work. I'm convinced you were with us in that barn when I asked you to watch over all of us. I don't know where I got the courage to do what I did, but I honestly think you played a big part in it somehow. You gave me the strength I needed to make sure we all were safe and unharmed in the end. Thank you, Sarah. Thank you for loving Shane and Tuck first and forging the path that led us to this day. I never want any of them, or you, to feel like I pushed you from their memories. You'll always be special—to all of us.

AS SHE FONDLY REMEMBERED THEIR WEDDING DAY, PAIGE wiped down the kitchen counter for the third or fourth time that morning. Tuck's mother told her she was "nesting" and it was normal to want everything perfect while waiting for the baby to come. As she turned back toward the table to clean it again, she paused as another mild cramp stirred in her lower abdomen. She'd been having Braxton Hicks contractions on and off for the past week, so she was used to them.

Grasping the back of a chair, she waited for the cramp to ease. But this time, it didn't let up. Hell, it got worse. Paige leaned over, and suddenly, there was a rush of fluid from between her legs. *Oh shit!*

"*Eew*, Mom. What's that?"

"What's what?" Shane asked Ari as he strode into the kitchen from where he'd been working in his office. One or the other of her men had always been nearby as her due date approached, and for once, she was grateful for their hovering.

"Oh, crap!" He was by her side in an instant. "Contractions?"

"Mm-hmm," Paige managed to reply as the pain eased a little. She tried to remember the Lamaze breathing techniques Nicole had taught her. "First one that feels like the real deal."

"Um . . . okay . . . great." He glanced around as if trying to remember what he was supposed to do next, then took her arm and gently helped her move away from the slick puddle on the floor. "Let's get you to the hospital then. Ari, run and tell Papa we have to go. He's in the barn."

"Yay!" The little girl ran out the screened backdoor,

letting it slam behind her, yelling at the top of her lungs, "Papa! It's time to meet Ashley Sarah! She's coming!"

Continue reading the Hazard Falls series with
Don't Shoot the Messenger.

Preview of Don't Shoot the Messenger

T. Carter settled back on the couch in the living room of the hotel suite he'd been staying in for the past twenty-five days and watched Grant Hadley pace back and forth. Although the CIA spook had been released from the US military hospital in Landstuhl, Germany, yesterday, Hadley was a shell of his former self. Despite being rehydrated and fed healthy food, his clothes hung from his thin frame, and his sallow skin still hadn't returned to normal. That's what happens when you spend over six years in a North Korean prison camp for espionage while the United States government thinks you're dead.

Carter was still trying to wrap his brain around the fact that his buddy was alive and not thousands of feet below the surface in the Sea of Japan. He'd been too far away to rescue the man he'd thought was Hadley after seeing a body, wrapped in a tarp with weights attached, tossed into one of the deepest trenches found in those waters. Even if he'd had SCUBA gear with him, Carter never would have reached the area in time after agents from the Ministry of State Security— MSS—had finally headed their cabin cruiser inland again. He'd been on his own, in a much smaller boat, with only two handguns and a KABAR knife, and wouldn't have stood a chance against five heavily armed and highly trained MSS agents.

Carter worked as an operative for Deimos, a US black ops agency. Currently, he waited for his CIA counterpart to ask the questions he'd been dreading. In fact, he was surprised they hadn't come up during the past three weeks of debriefing and rehabilitation Hadley had gone through.

A few times since the rescue op, Carter had almost slipped and called the other man Evan Walker, which had been his main undercover persona. It was the only reason Hadley could return to the US using his real surname.

Sitting in a chair across the coffee table from Carter, Hadley leaned forward and rested his elbows on his knees. His scraggly beard and mustache had been shaved off, and his thin, dark-brown hair had been trimmed by a barber yesterday after his release from the hospital. He looked far different from the dirty, raggedly clothed, emaciated man Carter and a team of retired Navy SEALs had rescued, but his hazel eyes still appeared sunken. He took two deep breaths, then asked in a coarse voice, "How is she? How did she take it?"

Carter bit his bottom lip for a moment before replying. *She* was Blair Canterfield, the woman Hadley had been engaged to. The woman who'd thought her fiancé had been a Secret Service agent temporarily assigned to the ambassador to South Korea six years ago. The woman the US government had lied to, telling her Hadley had fallen overboard from a yacht he'd been on with his charge during a storm, and his body hadn't been recovered. The woman who had no clue Hadley was, in fact, alive.

"She's doing okay—took it really hard, but . . ." He couldn't finish the sentence, needing the other man to ask each question at his own pace.

There was a heavy pause as Hadley stared at Carter before continuing. "Has she moved on? I mean, has she . . ."

"She moved back to Hazard Falls not long after the memorial service they had for you . . . she's married."

The man nodded as resignation appeared in his eyes. "I'm not surprised—Blair's a beautiful woman, and it's . . . it's been a long time—but I was hoping . . ." He ran a hand down his face. "Who? Someone from Hazard? Do I know him?"

Here it came. The hardest thing Carter had to tell his old friend. "Grant . . . she's married to Drake."

Hadley froze, stunned to silence, as Carter waited for the inevitable words of disbelief followed by an explosion.

Shaking his head, Hadley said, "This is no time for

jokes, jackass." He stood and paced back and forth again. "No . . . no fucking way."

"I'm not joking, man. I'm sorry."

He stopped in front of Carter and put his hands on his hips. "Blair married Drake? She married my fucking brother?" When Carter nodded, Hadley glared and asked, "When? When, damn it!"

The black-ops agent sighed. Shit, he hated to be the one doing this, but he owed it to Hadley. He could've lied, but things would be worse when the man found out the truth later on. Blair had probably been his lifeline over the past six years, the main reason he'd survived the hellhole he'd been in—he wouldn't let her go without knowing all the facts. Carter took a deep breath and let it out. "Six weeks after the funeral."

"The fuck you say!"

With rage-filled eyes, Hadley lunged at Carter, but the Deimos spy was far quicker, leaping up and side-stepping out of the way. Hadley landed partially on the couch, his knees hitting the floor, and he struggled to stand. Once on his feet again, he swung at his target, who easily blocked the fist coming toward his face. Carter spun him around, tucked his hands under Hadley's armpits, and put him in a headlock—not for Carter's own protection, but to keep the broken man from harming himself.

"Get off me! Get the fuck off me, you bastard!"

Bucking, twisting, and kicking, Hadley made every effort to break the hold, but his weakened body was no match against the other man's physically-fit one. He finally gave up, and his knees buckled. Tears rolled down his face, and a sob ripped from his chest as Carter lowered him to the floor, relaxing his grip but not completely letting go. "I'm sorry, Grant. I'm so sorry."

For a few minutes, Carter silently allowed the other man to let it all out—the grief, the rage, the fear he'd never be rescued that'd plagued him for so long, and the relief when he'd realized the rescue was really happening and wasn't a dream. This was the first time Hadley had broken down since Carter and his team had found him in a North Korean mountainside prison camp. He'd been living in a dirty cage, unfit for any animal, covered in scars and cigarette burns in various stages of healing, The US operatives had killed every one of his fourteen captors and had also rescued a French national, two South Koreans, and a member of the UK's MI6. Those men, all in a similar condition to Hadley, had each been returned to their respective countries under a cloak of secrecy. There hadn't been a single mention of the dead North Korean soldiers left in the mountains on any media outlet, which meant it'd been covered up.

Carter had been shocked when his boss had called him with the news that a man who looked eerily like Hadley had been spotted and photographed by an MSS mole who'd passed the information onto his Deimos handler. Upon seeing the images, guilt and remorse had overwhelmed Carter. He hadn't taken things at face value all those years ago. Still, the investigation that'd followed, after seeing the body tossed overboard, hadn't turned up anything to dispute the belief that Hadley had ended up at the bottom of the sea.

Seven or eight minutes passed before Hadley caught his breath and stopped sobbing. Carter let him go and got to his feet as the other man slowly stood and wiped his face with his bare hands. "Tell me . . . tell me the rest. There's more, isn't there?"

Surprisingly, Hadley's mind was still sharp after all he'd been through. Carter nodded. "There is."

Instead of launching into the next bit of intel he had to report, he strode over to the suite's wet bar and poured the expensive Macallan Fine Oak scotch he preferred into two lowball glasses. He handed one to Hadley, who'd slumped into the chair again, then returned to his seat on the couch. Taking a sip, he relished the familiar burn and waited for the other man to stop coughing after knocking back a swig of the amber liquid.

Hadley looked at him. His voice was even raspier than before. "Tell me."

"The reason Blair and Drake got married—she was three and a half months pregnant."

The man's brow furrowed in confusion, but not for long as the true meaning of Carter's words sunk into his brain. "Pregnant? I . . . she was pregnant . . . with my child?"

He nodded. "Apparently, she found out the week after you left on the assignment. She was waiting for you to come home to surprise you. When she told

Drake after the funeral, he stepped in and married her so she'd be on his insurance. She'd already decided to return to Hazard, and he didn't want her to worry about anything. He knew if something happened, and the baby needed medical care, or Blair couldn't work, it would be harder to get him on the insurance policy after the fact, so Drake made sure they were both covered in advance."

Hadley blinked. "Him? I-I have a son?"

"Yeah. Trevor—cute kid. Smart as a whip."

He leaned back in the chair and pondered that for a few moments. "So . . . it was for the insurance only? They weren't . . . together?" He sounded hopeful, as if there was a chance his former life could still be salvaged.

Shit, here comes the next bomb. At least Hadley was unarmed, so he couldn't shoot the messenger, no matter how much he would probably want to. "No, not at first . . . but down the road, I guess they fell for each other. They have two more kids now—a girl and another boy. Regan is three, and Michael just turned two."

His jaw clenched, and his eyes went blank before he drank the rest of his scotch in two gulps. Standing, he dropped the glass on the coffee table with a *clunk* and headed for the door to the hallway and the elevator beyond. Carter stared after him. "Where are you going?"

"Doesn't fucking matter."

The Deimos operative sighed heavily, downed the

remainder of his own drink, and glanced at his watch. He had an hour before he was due to check in with his woman, Jordyn Alvarez, who was currently on an assignment in North Africa after assisting with Grant's rescue. She'd managed to visit him for two days last week, but it felt like a month since then. Although they'd known each other for years, their boyfriend/girlfriend and Dominant/submissive relationships were relatively new.

Getting to his feet, he followed Hadley. The guy may not want company, but since he didn't have any ID or a dime in his pocket, it was Carter's duty to at least tail him and ensure he stayed out of trouble. Yeah, that was probably going to be easier said than done.

Other Books by Samantha Cole

***Denotes titles/series that are only available on select digital sites. Paperbacks and audiobooks are available on most book sites.

THE TRIDENT SECURITY SERIES

Leather & Lace

His Angel

Waiting For Him

Not Negotiable: A Novella

Topping The Alpha

Watching From the Shadows

Whiskey Tribute: A Novella

Tickle His Fancy

No Way in Hell: A Steel Corp/Trident Security Crossover (co-authored with J.B. Havens)

Absolving His Sins

Option Number Three: A Novella

Salvaging His Soul

Trident Security Field Manual

Torn In Half: A Novella

Burning For Him

***HEELS, RHYMES, & NURSERY CRIMES SERIES

(WITH **13** OTHER AUTHORS)

Jack Be Nimble: A Trident Security-Related Short Story

*****THE DEIMOS SERIES**

Handling Haven: Special Forces: Operation Alpha

Cheating the Devil: Special Forces: Operation Alpha

THE TRIDENT SECURITY OMEGA TEAM SERIES

Mountain of Evil

A Dead Man's Pulse

Forty Days & One Knight

THE DOMS OF THE COVENANT SERIES

Double Down & Dirty

Entertaining Distraction

Knot a Chance

Finding His Forever

Reclaiming His Soulmate

THE BLACKHAWK SECURITY SERIES

Tuff Enough

Blood Bound

MASTER KEY SERIES

Master Key Resort

Master Cordell

HAZARD FALLS SERIES

Don't Fight It

Don't Shoot the Messenger

THE MALONE BROTHERS SERIES

Her Secret

Her Sleuth

LARGO RIDGE SERIES

Cold Feet

***ANTELOPE ROCK SERIES

(CO-AUTHORED WITH J.B. HAVENS)

Wannabe in Wyoming

Wistful in Wyoming

AWARD-WINNING STANDALONE BOOKS

Where the Broken Bloom

Scattered Moments in Time: A Collection of Short Stories & More

***THE BID ON LOVE SERIES

(WITH 7 OTHER AUTHORS!)

Going, Going, Gone: Book 2

***THE COLLECTIVE: SEASON TWO

(WITH 7 OTHER AUTHORS!)

Angst: Book 7

SPECIAL COLLECTIONS

Trident Security Series: Volume I

Trident Security Series: Volume II

Trident Security Series: Volume III

Trident Security Series: Volume IV

Trident Security Series: Volume V

Trident Security Series: Volume VI

About Samantha Cole

USA Today Bestselling Author and Award-Winning Author Samantha Cole is a retired policewoman and former paramedic. Using her life experiences and training, she strives to find the perfect mix of suspense and romance for her readers to enjoy.

Awards:

Wannabe in Wyoming (co-authored by J.B. Havens) won the bronze medal in the 2021 Readers' Favorite Awards in the General Romance category.

Scattered Moments in Time, won the gold medal in the 2020 Readers' Favorite Awards in the Fiction Anthology category.

The Road to Solace (formerly *The Friar*), won the silver medal in the 2017 Readers' Favorite Awards in the Contemporary Romance category.

Samantha has over thirty-five books published throughout several different series as well as a few standalone novels. A full list can be found on her website.

Sexy Six-Pack's Sirens Group on Facebook
Website: www.samanthacoleauthor.com
Newsletter: www.samanthacoleauthor.com/newsletter-signup

facebook.com/SamanthaColeAuthor
instagram.com/samanthacoleauthor
bookbub.com/profile/samantha-a-cole
goodreads.com/SamanthaCole
amazon.com/Samantha-A-Cole/e/B00X53K3X8

www.ingramcontent.com/pod-product-compliance
Lightning Source LLC
Chambersburg PA
CBHW032338310726
48973CB00007B/1758